Augusta Campbell Watson

Off Lynnport Light

A Novel

Augusta Campbell Watson

Off Lynnport Light
A Novel

ISBN/EAN: 9783337001100

Printed in Europe, USA, Canada, Australia, Japan

Cover: Foto ©Andreas Hilbeck / pixelio.de

More available books at **www.hansebooks.com**

OFF LYNNPORT LIGHT

A NOVEL

BY

AUGUSTA CAMPBELL WATSON

AUTHOR OF "THE OLD HARBOR TOWN,"
"DOROTHY THE PURITAN," ETC.

NEW YORK

E. P. DUTTON & COMPANY

31 WEST TWENTY-THIRD STREET

1895

CONTENTS.

OFF LYNNPORT LIGHT.

CHAPTER I.

THE OLD MANOR-HOUSE.

THE century grows old, bowed to earth with the accumulated incidents of its hundred years: One looks backward and speculates upon the events and varied-colored life that ushered in its infancy. The contemplation of that far-off time of courtly dame, of gay gallant, opens the portals of long silent and forgotten places. The shadowy host, asleep these many years, rise and pass before our watching eyes. We hear the rustle of silks and laces and the clank of swords. We see figures bow in the slow rhythm of the stately minuet to the plaintive chords of the spinet. We smell the perfume of sandalwood and musk rising heavily upon the atmosphere.

Have we slept through the passing years? Has the busy strife and toil of the century been a dream, a fading picture? Are these long-dead spirits the reality, the present a dream?

It seems as if it must be so. Rising slowly from the misty, intangible vapors of time, we evolve a stately colonial home, and the tall, slim figure of our heroine, Ruth Lorrimer, leaning in the doorway. She is clad in the scant skirts of a decade ago; her hair is piled high upon her shapely head, around a towering comb; the lace mitts are drawn high upon her white arms, a silken bag hangs by her side, and the small feet are incased in slippers with the laces crossing and recrossing above the high-arched in- step. The girlish figure is leaning listlessly against the doorway, and in one hand she holds a letter. Her blue eyes are looking across the smooth-shaven lawn to the sea, which is shining like a field of pol- ished diamonds beneath the brilliant rays of the warm June sun.

Ruth Lorrimer was very fair, sweet, and young, her face dimpled, and arch in expression. A cer- tain dignity pervaded her presence—a legacy from a long line of gentle ancestors, whose rather forbid- ding likenesses frown from the walls in the long, high-domed drawing-room of her home.

She stood looking dreamily over the grounds, an

unfathomable glow in her soft eyes, appearing in her youthful grace the finishing touch to the setting of the picture—the life in the canvas.

For this fine old country-seat was a picture, with its stately columns, its great wide hall, its oaken staircase that the villagers boasted was wide enough for a coach and four to ascend and not touch the paneled walls, its high-vaulted bedchambers, and its wide-mouthed fireplaces surrounded by scriptural tiles. This imposing mansion, shaded by towering elms, was the show-place of the little New England sea-coast village of Lynnport.

The Lorrimers were the great people, the fine family, the aristocracy. Had not old Gerald Weston, the first denizen of the mansion, emigrated with the early settlers, fleeing from an enraged sovereign for free speech against the tyranny of those in high places? Had he not built himself a fine abode in the colonies? And in time from across the sea came various articles to embellish the great house. Carved chairs, settles, rugs, and silverware, great canopied bedsteads, a chaise for postilions at the rear, costly articles of apparel in silk, velvet, and embroidery. On the mantel in the state drawing-room stood solid silver candelabra, so heavy they were seldom moved except when necessary to clean them.

Ruth, however, was not thinking of this as she leaned against the open doorway. Contact with luxury had made her familiar all her life with the accessories of her position; she accepted everything without speculation as to the possibility of having been the particularly favored one of fortune. It was very still about the house. It was early in the summer afternoon, and the sun was shining with a steady brilliancy. The old manor stood on the outskirts of a tiny fishing-village, and the hoarse shouts of fishermen came faintly and at intervals to the ears of the dreaming girl. A happy smile played about her red lips, bringing into relief two coquettish dimples. She took up the letter again and gazed long and lovingly at the clear, bold handwriting.

"Jack," Ruth whispered, softly, "Jack." She drew the letter across her lips and kissed it; then with a blush hid it in the bosom of her short-waisted gown.

"Ruth, Ruth, child, what are you doing—idling, idling, as usual?"

The voice of some new-comer rang out short, crisp,

staccato-like in tones, each word rising louder and shriller.

Ruth composed her laughing face into a resigned expression and turned her head impatiently.

Click, click came a pair of high heels, and a tall figure stepped with quick, nervous tread over the polished surface of the hall and stood by the girl's side in the doorway. At first glance the woman who approached seemed almost gigantic in stature; in reality, though nature had endowed her with great height, fully a foot had been added by a tremendous head-dress that rose in almost appalling prominence above a thin, long-featured face—a face full of nervous activity and erratic power. Her dress was made in the conventional mode of that time, and the material displayed a large flowered pattern of unusual design, in accordance with a peculiar taste of her own.

" Ruth, you are a lazy girl," she said, shaking her long forefinger. " Ah me! at your age I was all fire and life; dreaming was not known in my young days." She paused and looked suspiciously toward her companion, who stood eying her with a laugh in her blue eyes.

" What did you hide in your dress as I came up?

I saw you from the staircase; there is no use trying to hide anything from Aunt Jane. Come now, child, confess.''

'' Suppose I should tell you it was a love-letter?'' said Ruth.

'' Love-letter, indeed!   What foolishness is this? Let me tell you, Ruth Lorrimer, if you are senseless enough to believe in love and love-letters you are even more of an addle-pate than I thought. You will find out what a man's constancy amounts to soon enough—*not that!*''   She snapped her fingers, and shook her head till the towering head-dress reeled like a ship at sea.

'' I am not going to profit by another's experience, Aunt Jane,'' said Ruth, sharply. '' I want my own. You are hard and cold. Why should I not be like other girls, and have a lover? It is always the same old story—no man is true and constant; every woman is deceived.''

'' They are all alike, child, all alike. It isn't their own goodness, honesty, and faithfulness that lead them in the eyes of the world at times in the right direction; it's because some women are too sharp for them.''   She glanced triumphantly at her niece as she concluded : '' Too sharp, thank Heaven! ''

Ruth had not heard her. She turned away, with her hand over her heart, close to where the letter lay. She knew of one who was true and faithful, if all the rest of the world were false.

Ruth Lorrimer was an orphan almost from infancy, her young mother having died after a short married life. Her father, surviving but a few years his great and overwhelming sorrow, had bequeathed his little daughter to his mother and her sister, his Aunt Jane. So the child came to dwell in the old homestead, to be its light and life; to fill the lonely hearts of the aging women; to make the great rooms reëcho with childish glee; and to grow into womanhood, a sweet-faced, fair-haired girl, laughter-loving and buoyant with health—the health given by a free, active, country life. Her soft cheek was fanned by breezes from the sea, till she seemed imbued with the same restless life that surged and swelled in hurrying waves along the shore.

The little town of Lynnport lay upon a steep hillside, its few grass-grown streets straggling in most erratic fashion up the stony ascent, till, finally reaching the summit, they converged into the highway. This upper road ran toward the north and was the thoroughfare upon which the stage-coach, the lumbering vehicle of the early part of the century, rattled by—the link that kept the scattered towns in contact with one another.

On this highway above the town was situated an old inn, a long, rambling building, with outside chimneys of pressed yellow brick imported from England, and from which the cheerful smoke was often seen, giving evidence of the good things being prepared below in the open-mouthed cavern of the huge fireplace. The town was inhabited principally by a hardy, roistering company of seafaring men, whose brawny arms, weather-beaten faces, and stentorian voices proclaimed them toilers of the sea; men whose constant contact with danger made them fearless, and yet whose nearness to the presence of the great God of storms gave them the simple faith of a child. Sailing-vessels went forth yearly from Lynnport in those old days; but they were few in number, the generality of the fishermen going on short cruises for cod, herring, or mackerel, the fish thus caught being sent by sea to distant cities on the coast and thence inland.

On a narrow street facing the water were congregated grog-houses for the sailors, adjoining the junkshops, whose strangely assorted articles lay in heaps on the dusty shelves and still more dusty floor. In the warm grog-shops the men congregated on cold winter nights, and talked, as they hobnobbed over their steaming toddy, of their latest haul of fish or the last bit of gossip in the town. They shook their heads solemnly as the shrill wind whistled and rattled at the wooden shutters, dying with a moan along the narrow street, and wondered whether the last crew out had rounded the cape.

If not—they would look into the blazing fire, take up their pipes again, and smoke without a word. Doubtless they saw in the rising smoke cruel rocks of the dangerous hidden reefs off the cape, their ragged edges, like sharks' teeth, gleaming beneath the shallow waters.

" It's a hard life, mates," sometimes an old sailor would volunteer; " it's a hard life."

No one would answer. They only smoked the faster and listened to the snapping of the fierce winter's gale; till the landlord, worthy Peter Simpson, would look in curiously, then quietly retire to confide to his wife that " the men were a-thinkin' o' the sea, and you couldn't get a word out o' them. There they sit like so many owls, a-blinkin' and a-lookin' into the fire. None o' your seafarin' life for me, wife; it never did come nat'ral to me. I tell you it's a hard row." To which platitudes his wife would sniff contemptuously and snap out sharply, "You ain't no great one anyhow, Peter Simpson. I'm a sailor's daughter, and you know I'm the only one of the eight girls that has married a landlubber." Then she would go in and replenish the men's glasses, stir up the fire, and volunteer the information that she "thought the wind was a-changin', and would blow the crew out to sea and off the cape." The men would glance dubiously toward her, get up and put their chairs against the wall, draw their woolen mufflers around their throats, and go out into the night. Mrs. Simpson would pause a moment after closing the door upon them, and look into the fire.

"Heaven help 'em! it's a hard life," she would sigh.

Lynnport was a typical New England fishing-town. Salt breezes blew through its crooked streets, and on every side the smell of fish and seaweed assailed the nostrils. Whaling-vessels started yearly for long cruises to the north, and at all times the harbor was filled with the boats of the fishing-fleet, rolling and pitching restlessly. Ah! but those were sad days

when the stately whalers started on their three years'
cruise—sad for the "sweethearts and wives": three
years—a long enough time for the great events of
a life to occur.   Many a tear-dimmed eye watched
the white sails of the fleet till lost to sight over the
bar.

Once in a while a stately vessel would come into
harbor from the Indies and China, loaded with spices,
fruits, and East India sweets.   She would discharge
a small cargo, then go to Boston; and the Captain,
with a jolly laugh, would shake hands with the men
on the wharf, for he was a prime favorite throughout Lynnport.

The Lorrimer place stood upon quite an elevation,
and its grounds sloped to the shore.   At the back of
the house lay fine farming lands, and a quaint garden sheltered from the high winds by Norway pines
and the spreading branches of the spruce, through
whose dark boughs the breezes murmured and sang,
in a minor tone, to the great song of the ocean
beyond.

It was a beautiful old garden, a blaze of glorious
color in the summer-time, with the gorgeous tints of
roses, Dianthus, four-o'clocks, peonies, and the tall
spiral cones of foxglove and larkspur rising sentinel-

like, at stated intervals, in the richly hued beds. The garden had entrance-gates of rough-hewn cedar-boughs, over which trailed climbing vines. There were also benches beneath the fruit-trees which filled part of the inclosure. Near the sun-dial stood a small summer-house of cedar. In the center of the garden, on a level piece of grassy sward, was the well and well-sweep, its long, swinging arm holding the bucket tied by a chain. Along the curb of the well, fostered into life by the constant dripping moisture, sprang tiny, dainty ferns, lichens, and moss. Through openings in the trees one caught glimpses, toward the north, of the fishing-village, not a mile away, huddled up against its protecting hill-side; to the south, a grand wide view of old ocean; and far away, like a gray streak against the sky, an outline of the dangerous cape. This sequestered spot was the favorite place for old Mrs. Lorrimer to take her exercise.

There in the early morning and toward evening the stately figure might be seen walking sedately up and down the box-bordered path. Her thin, blue-veined hands were covered by long lace mitts, and her soft silk skirts made no rustle as she walked. Old Mrs. Lorrimer was indeed a grand dame, gentle, courtly, dignified, her high-bred, patrician face, surrounded by its halo of snow-white hair, impressing one instantly with the value of gentle ancestry. Not that she informed strangers that she was a Lorrimer—one of the Lorrimers of Lynnport—and a daughter of General Weston; but she lived her position. Upon a mimic stage, all unconscious to herself, she posed, the reigning star. -Perhaps—who can tell?—this superiority of thought, long continued, became second nature, and far down in the recesses of the sweet, placid old lady's being the inevitable social barrier had been raised a notch higher, and she felt herself better than her fellows. Thus we meet her for the first time in her beloved garden this pleasant June evening. Ruth was by her side, and they were walking silently along the paths, Mrs. Lorrimer holding some flowers in her hand, and the fast-decreasing sunlight falling across her face. Jane was seated in the summer-house by the sun-dial, holding on her lap a fat, pampered spaniel, who was condescendingly nibbling at a bit of cake she was offering him. In Ruth's hand was the letter, which she had crumpled and crushed between her small fingers.

"Grandmother," she said, in a low voice, "I have

wanted to speak to you all day. I—I—have a letter. Old John Halleck brought it from the wharf this morning. His—his—ship has come in from the Indies. They have discharged the Lynnport cargo, and—and—now he is going to Boston. He will be back in three or four days."

This had been told in rather a hurried and impetuous fashion. Ruth's eyes were lowered—she was scraping her feet along the graveled roadway—and her cheeks were flushed. Mrs. Lorrimer turned swiftly in the path and faced her granddaughter.

"What letter, child?" she said. "I do not understand you. Whose ship?"

"Why, grandmother"—the girl's blue eyes opened widely—"I thought you knew. Why, Captain Jack Hathaway's ship, of course."

In speaking his name Ruth blushed again and glanced downward.

Mrs. Lorrimer did not reply immediately, but shivered and drew her fine lace shawl about her shoulders. Then, placing a hand against her side, she gave a little cry and stepped backward in the path.

The cry brought Jane flying from the summerhouse, much to the consternation of the fat spaniel, who was deposited rather unceremoniously upon his back on the floor, where he remained in mute protest and indignation, with his legs in the air.

Jane hastened to her sister, and putting her arms around her drew her head upon her shoulder, scowling fiercely in the meanwhile at her niece.

"What is it, dearie?" she said, tenderly.

"Oh, nothing, Jane, nothing. I am getting old. Perhaps I am weaker than I thought. It is nothing, I say. Go back to Tetsy. Just see the poor dear; he is on his back yet."

"Tetsy can take care of himself," said Jane, "and turn himself over when he gets ready. I insist upon knowing what Ruth has said to you."

The high head-dress trembled ominously, and the angular shoulders twitched angrily.

"I only said Jack Hathaway's ship was back from the Indies, and he was coming here to see us in a few days," Ruth volunteered, timidly.

Jane Weston pushed her sister from her. "Well, I must say, Mary Lorrimer, you are a weak woman. If I had known that was all I wouldn't have left Tetsy and nearly broken his back in the bargain. For goodness' sake, if he isn't on his back yet! Just like his intelligence: he knows that if he waits long enough I'll carry him."

Jane Weston walked away impatiently, and Mrs. Lorrimer put a little lace handkerchief to her eyes, taken from the embroidered bag at her side, and shed a few tears.

"Oh, tell me, tell me, grandmother, have I offended you? I would not for anything. You know that I would not."

"No, no, child; forget it. I was thinking of other days—that is all. I think it must have been the odor of these roses that made me feel faint. I remember so well when I was a little girl and father first planted them in the garden. A little girl! What am I saying?" She paused and her lips trembled. "I was quite as old as you are, and you are eighteen, my pet. Ah yes! that was what I was thinking of —when I was eighteen, like you; and—and—there was some one else I was thinking of—some one—" here the old lady placed her handkerchief again to her eyes. "Ruth, child," she concluded, earnestly, after a pause, "I do not care for this sea-captain. Why does he wish to come to the manor?"

Ruth did not speak, but drew aside from her grandmother and turned her face away. At that instant they were joined rather impetuously by Jane and the now complacent Tetsy, who lay in her arms.

"Come, come, Mary," she said, hurriedly, "let us go indoors. The dampness is falling; I shall be stiff with the rheumatism. A garden at night is all very well for moonstruck lovers, but not for sensible folks. Tetsy has been coughing for the last fifteen minutes."

Mrs. Lorrimer turned to her sister eagerly. "This—this sea-captain," she said; "tell Ruth we do not know him. She is too young for suitors. Speak to her, Jane."

"Who spoke of suitors, Mary? Here is a young man in port for a few days, who is calling upon some old friends; at least Ruth, if not exactly a friend, has met him. Then he sails away for three years. Have you no discernment, sister?" Her sharp voice rang out angrily as she opened the garden gate with a loud click of the latch. "I see no use of discussing this matter further," she concluded, testily. "Let us go to the house."

CHAPTER II.

VILLAGE LIFE.

ONE would imagine, in a small, remote New England town more than half a century ago, that the social barriers which were built so readily and quickly in places of size and importance would have been of very flimsy texture, if existing at all. Such, however, was not the case at Lynnport. No prominent center ever prided itself more upon its great families, its claim for social distinction, than did those simple folks of that tiny town—defining the gradations with jealous care, placing all interlopers outside the sacred borders. Had they not the Lorrimers, the Hinsdales, and the Burtons, who had descended from gentle stock? What was the outside world to those worthy people? Had they not a world of their own? In their eyes did they not hold a miniature court of stately elegance and decorum in the Lynnport tea-parties, the gatherings at the rectory, and in their stately visits at stated times upon one another? Had not one of their number written learned books, another held a high position under the government? Did not the whole village thrill with honest pride when this latter personage left for his seat of office? Ah! Lynnport was the place in which to live, the residents would aver, with a proud shake of the head—Lynnport was the place.

After all, is not that placid contentment with one's lot the better part? If one's horizon is narrow it no doubt hedges in happiness and hides the darker possibilities of a wider sphere.

On one of the straggling streets stood a number of fine old houses—great square mansions with imposing fronts, painted white, with small-paned windows and gambreled roofs. In a few the narrow dormer reared its protruding head as though the better to gaze over the fishermen's homes at the foot of the hill to the sea beyond. These houses stood not far back from the street, and before them, in almost all cases, tall, ungraceful poplar-trees threw their slanting shadows. In the small gardens between the houses and the street lilac-bushes flourished, also hardy roses and shrubs. In front of the large mansions small, contracted porches loomed under low, flat roofs, and on the heavy doors bright knockers, polished to the highest degree, glistened and sparkled. The daily cleaning of these knockers was the cause of some envy among the housekeepers of Lynnport, and was often the subject of much discussion at the high teas: whether soap, Bath brick, or grease was the best cleanser, all generally deciding with serious aspect that "just good hard rubbing is better than those newfangled things they are using nowadays."

The Lynnporters felt a deep pity for the poor people who could not live in their town, where the advantages were so great; feeling sympathy for the whole world outside its wonderful borders. Indeed, there is no manner of doubt that they fully appreciated their blessings and privileges, and did full justice to the same, not concealing at times, to a casual stranger, pride in the knowledge of possessing a superior position in the world.

One of the great amusements during the long winter evenings was whist; not the giggling, carelessly played whist of the young people of to-day, but a long, hotly contested, serious game, which made them unconscious of the surf booming on the beach, the rattling of the casements, or the loud ticking of the clock on the stairway. On they played, their faces close together, the blended light of candle and fire casting a glow upon their earnest countenances. Sometimes the fire would burn low, little drafts would circle and eddy along the polished floor, and the candle would glimmer close to its socket, casting weird and grotesque shadows upon the high ceiling. Still they played, with knitted brows and pursed-up lips, till suddenly the clock called out nine strokes.

"God bless us, nine o'clock!" Dr. Goodyear, the most inveterate whist-player in Lynnport, would boom out in his deep bass voice. "Nine o'clock— time all good Christians were in bed. The toddy, Mistress Hinsdale, and then good-night. Not too stiff, my dear madam; not too stiff, mind. I was scandalized to see the next morning, in the snow, the most erratic steps I had made the night before, after your last whist-party, Mistress Hinsdale."

It was a day or so after Ruth had received her letter from the gallant Captain that she, Aunt Jane, Mrs. Lorrimer, and Tetsy were bidden to a high tea at Mrs. Matthew Burton's. Tetsy was not desired by any means; in fact, to almost all Lynnport he was

considered an ill-conditioned, badly brought-up little animal; but to offend Tetsy was to offend Aunt
Jane. So on the afternoon of the day appointed, in
best apparel, the four wended their way along the
lovely country road toward the town; for Tetsy was
in fine attire also, a linen blanket edged with narrow
lace resting upon his plump back.

Ruth Lorrimer was a vision of sweetness and
coolness in her quaint gown of blue India silk,
broad lace collar upon her bare neck, mitts drawn
up to her elbows, and a large, flapping straw hat
tied under her chin in a great blue bow. Her
flower-like face looked out from these blue surroundings like a rosy cloud in the sky at sunset.

Mrs. Lorrimer walked slowly, her delicate white
hand resting on her granddaughter's arm. She was
never loquacious, and this afternoon did not speak
a word; only listened to Ruth's prattle as she talked
rapidly.

For some undefined reason Ruth did not speak of
Captain Hathaway. Perhaps it was on account of
some feeling of distrust evinced in Mrs. Lorrimer's
manner when she spoke of him—an added coldness,
a scarcely perceptible repugnance to the sound of
his name. Ruth kept her thoughts and her dreams

to herself, brooding over them with tender yet wistful retrospection.

Old Mrs. Lorrimer loved her granddaughter. Her affection was deep and sincere; and what she most desired was Ruth's happiness. Ever since the death of her only son, who left his daughter to her care, Mrs. Lorrimer had endeavored to do her duty, that duty impelled by unchanging affection. She gazed with gentle, faded eyes upon the sweet face by her side, thinking that never had there been so fair and winsome a girl as Ruth.

Ruth's laughing voice was often interrupted by exclamations from Jane, who stalked in the rear, stern and majestic in carriage, the fat Tetsy waddling by her side; exclamations against tea-parties, dusty roads, and briers, with little yelps of despair from Tetsy interspersing her remarks, as he stepped on some thorny vine that protruded into the road, or in his curiosity sniffed some flower wherein lay concealed a hungry honey-bee.

"Jane, you should leave Tetsy at home," said Mrs. Lorrimer; "he is troublesome."

"Humph!" sniffed Jane, twitching her scant skirts angrily at this implied disapprobation of her pet. "Where I go Tetsy goes. If they don't want Tetsy they don't want me." Not another word did she speak till the ladies reached the narrow street that ran along the water-side, and on which stood the principal shops of the town, when she declared with dignity that as Tetsy's feet were dusty she would go into Mrs. Simpson's side door and have her brush them, and then would carry him the rest of the distance. Mrs. Lorrimer sighed patiently, and Ruth laughed. At that instant the three ladies were startled at hearing a loud sonorous voice hailing them from the opposite side of the street.

" Good afternoon, ladies, good afternoon; hearty health to you. My respects, Mrs. Lorrimer. How fares it, little Ruth? Miss Jane, your servant; and how is my adored Tetsy?"

These words were spoken in loud, trumpet-like tones, and Dr. Goodyear came rushing across the road toward the ladies.

" Good afternoon, Dr. Goodyear," said Mrs. Lorrimer, with a little old-fashioned courtesy. Jane gave him a stiff, chilling bow.

Dr. Goodyear was a short, stout man, with a red face, shrewd, twinkling eyes, and bushy gray beard. He was the village doctor, a large-hearted, liberal man, perhaps a little erratic in some ways. The ladies thought this was because he was a bachelor and neglected. There was a funny unreadable twinkle in the doctor's eyes as he looked at Jane's forbidding countenance, which instantly changed to one of deepest concern as he caught her watching him.

"Has Tetsy been ill, Miss Jane?"

"No, he is quite well. But you must really pardon us, doctor; we are due at Mrs. Burton's for tea, and I am afraid we are late."

"I thought you were about to enter Mrs. Simpson's."

"Oh no, you are mistaken. Come, Tetsy. Good afternoon, doctor. Come, Tetsy, don't you hear me?"

Jane marched off, pushing Mrs. Lorrimer and Ruth peremptorily before her, leaving the doctor silently convulsed.

"Jane Weston is a rare woman; there's not another like her in Lynnport—a rare woman," he chuckled. Then he stood watching them slowly ascending the steep, stony street, Jane stopping now and then to remonstrate with Tetsy.

A high tea at Lynnport was quite a formidable affair, and was conducted with state and ceremony, the gentry of the town fully recognizing its social significance.   Its quiet decorum savored of much dignity and elegance.

When the ladies from the manor arrived at Mrs. Burton's, after passing through the row of lilac-bushes bordering the walk, they found the front door hospitably ajar, and heard the low hum of voices issuing from the large drawing-room that ran along the entire north side of the house.   Some moments later the trio, on entering the room, were greeted pleasantly by the hostess, and found to their chagrin that they were the last comers.   There were some twenty ladies present, scattered about the long apartment.   All were talking in low, well-modulated voices, and all were dressed in scant skirts, scarfs on their necks, lace mitts covering their hands, and wore the hair dressed high, with great combs rising above the smooth coils.   Tetsy was duly admired and commented upon, some every-day matters discussed, when the hostess gave the signal to repair to the dining-room.   The ladies silently and with great dignity, varied by numerous little courtesies and simpers, took their places about the table, that was covered with a fine assortment of substantial edibles, in addition to rich jellies, preserves, many kinds of cake, and small glass dishes of East India sweets and candied ginger. The tea was hot and of the best quality, and under its benign influence conversation gradually asserted itself.

"Have you heard," said Mrs. Burton, "that they had mutiny on board Captain Hathaway's ship when at sea? I heard it this morning. They say the Captain wishes it kept quiet, but la! you might as well tell the sea to stop breaking on the rocks as to tell the Lynnport gossips to be quiet."

Mrs. Lorrimer lowered her eyes at these words, and Aunt Jane's hand came down so heavily on Tetsy, who lay in her lap, that he gave an ominous growl which startled the entire company.

"He is dreaming," said Jane, "and always breathes heavily when asleep."

Ruth leaned forward eagerly, her lovely face flushed and eyes shining.

"Tell us, Mrs. Burton," she said, "what did you hear about the mutiny?"

"Old Hal Porter from the Point told me when he came here this morning, with some fish just caught off Hallet's Reef. He said it happened on the high seas, and that Captain Hathaway was the bravest man that ever sailed a ship. Some of the men had been rebellious and complained of the food and work.   There had been a storm and they were rather short for sleep.   The Captain had suspected their dissatisfaction, but did not apprehend any serious danger.   It seems, however, some of the other men had been influenced, and when the Captain came on deck one morning to give orders to reef the sails, only one third of the crew responded. He commanded their obedience, but they refused it.   One man shouted that they were going to put the Captain in irons and run the ship themselves. Now you know Captain Hathaway is young and—"

The ladies had laid down their knives and forks, and were listening intently, with their heads craned forward.

"Yes, yes," said Ruth; "what then? oh! what then?   Please hasten, Mrs. Burton."

"Old Hal said—and he got it straight from one of the crew, so I think it is true—that the Captain just stepped up to the leader, took out his pistol, and said, 'The first man who refuses to obey me I shall shoot.   I am master on my ship.   Reef the sails,' he commanded."   Mrs. Burton held the teapot out before her as if it were a weapon, and her voice rose with excitement.

"Go on, Mrs. Burton; hasten.   You make me

nervous," called the voice of a little old maid from the foot of the table. "You really do—I am all of a shiver."

"Would you believe it," cried Mrs. Burton, still brandishing the teapot, "that wretched leader had a big knife in his hand, but when he looked in the Captain's eye he just dropped it on the deck and slunk away. The men lowered their heads, and the Captain said, 'Boys, reef the sails, and extra grog for supper.' Then the men cried, 'Hurrah for Captain Jack!' He only punished the leader, who was put in irons till he reached port, and was then passed over to the authorities."

A strange thing happened at the conclusion of this exciting narrative. Mrs. Lorrimer, who had been listening with her eyes cast down, now raising them, caught sight of Ruth's beaming face, and dropped the spoon so heavily upon her saucer that it broke the fragile porcelain into many pieces. Tetsy, awakened suddenly from his happy dreams, sat up straight on his mistress's lap and gave vent to a series of long, dismal howls.

"It is of no consequence, Mrs. Lorrimer; do not distress yourself," said Mrs. Burton, kindly, as Mrs. Lorrimer, whose eyes had filled with tears, endeavored to ask pardon for her awkwardness. Jane glanced at her sister sharply for a moment, then shook Tetsy a little roughly, causing that surprised bit of importance to look up with a threatening aspect.

Two or three ladies cried in chorus, " I must say Captain Jack Hathaway is a brave man; and, Mrs. Burton, isn't he handsome?" One lady said, " I never saw so bold and bright an eye in any man's head; and such a figure! He is a fine mate for any girl in Lynnport. Well, well, if I were young I am sure I should give him many a shy glance."

" I'll warrant you would," said Mrs. Burton. " But mercy, Ruth, what are you blushing for? Why, look at the child; her face is like a peony."

Thus brought into unpleasant prominence, Ruth's cheeks flamed to a brilliant carmine, and she threw the curls back from her face nervously.

" I am warm," she said.

" It is warm for this time of year," said Jane Weston, in her short, crisp voice; " and I must say, ladies, that Captain Hathaway's good looks are not the deepest subject of conversation to be found in the calendar." She shook her high head-dress impatiently, and glanced angrily toward Ruth's blushing countenance, from which the color was now slowly receding, leaving it quite pale except the scarlet of her pouting lips.

No one made any answer. Silence reigned for an instant, nothing being heard but the rattle of knives and forks and the gentle bubbling of hot water over the spirit-lamp, when suddenly Tetsy, spying the tender leg of a chicken resting upon a platter on the other side of the table, sat erect, his long ears twitching in a most unusual manner. Jane looked down upon him surprised, not comprehending this unusual emotion evinced by the generally phlegmatic Tetsy; but before she had time to inquire into the vagaries of his mind he darted from her lap and made a precipitate rush for the chicken-bone. Straight across country he went, not stopping for ditch or stile, but, like a plucky hunter, overcoming all obstacles with a leap and a run. Dashing by jelly-molds, cake-trays, and batches of hot muffins, he seized the coveted prize, and, with a most comical expression of triumph on his fat face, sat down in the chicken-platter, and with the bone in his mouth looked around upon the scandalized company.

Jane did not speak: she was too much overcome for that. She covered her face with her hands and bowed her proud head in humiliation for the disgrace of her pet.

Fortunately the tea-party was nearly over. Mrs. Burton arose, and, with a slightly increased coldness in her pleasant voice, said:

"Ladies, we will adjourn to the drawing-room. Mrs. Lorrimer, let me escort you. Jane, we must leave Tetsy to your tender mercies."

Left alone with Tetsy, Jane watched him anxiously. She dared not interfere while he was enjoying such a repast, so he sat serenely in the china platter, munching and crunching his bone. Once Jane endeavored—feebly, it is true—to remonstrate with him; but a guttural tone and a defiant gleam in his eye warned her to keep her distance. She waited patiently, and when he was ready marched severely into the drawing-room.

"I hope you have punished that dog, Jane," said Mrs. Lorrimer. "Did you whip him? He deserved it."

"I did not whip him," said Jane.

"Did not! How did you punish him then?"

"I—I—reasoned with him," said Jane.

The Burton's high tea broke up. The ladies walked home through the sweet-scented country

road in the fading glow of the summer evening.
The changing colors of the sunset were reflected
on their faces, and the soft sea-breeze blew across
them. Mrs. Lorrimer leaned upon her granddaughter's shoulder and looked eagerly into the sweet
face. Ruth did not appear to be aware of the earnest glance. She was looking across the hills and
sea to the setting sun. Her eyes were dreamy with
a diffused love-light—the light born of a young girl's
dreams. Perhaps unconsciously she was influenced
by the sights and sounds about her, the serene beauty
of nature, and the loveliness of the twilight. Ah!
those vague, intangible dreams of youth; those airy
phantoms without substance, like will-o'-the-wisps,
throwing gleams of light, then leaving us in darkness.

"What are you thinking of, Ruth?" said her
grandmother, softly, as they were turning in at the
iron gates that led to the manor.

"I was thinking of Captain Hathaway and his
bravery in the mutiny. O grandmother, how noble
he is! No other captain could have done as well;
and think, if that dreadful man had killed him!"
She stood still and looked toward Mrs. Lorrimer
with terror on her face.

Mrs. Lorrimer did not reply, but turned her head aside, a slight and hardly perceptible tremor upon her lips; and in silence the three ladies walked up the elm-shaded avenue to the house. Mrs. Lorrimer stood for a moment on the piazza. She was tired, and rested an instant, leaning upon the vine-wreathed pillar. Ruth went indoors, and Jane stood waiting by her sister's side.

"Jane—Jane—" said Mrs. Lorrimer, "this has been a hard, weary evening. Can you not see how things are tending? Ruth is already interested in this young man. I cannot endure it, Jane; I cannot."

"I cannot help you, Mary," said Jane, not unkindly. "We must let things drift. There is a long step between interest and marriage. Don't, for mercy's sake, 'cross bridges before you come to them.'"

CHAPTER III.

JACK HATHAWAY.

RUTH was expecting Captain Hathaway, who
had said he would be in Lynnport to-day, and she
knew he would come. The stage-coach from Boston would pass the inn between three and four in
the afternoon; shortly after that he would be at the
homestead. She flew like a bird about the house,
and, like a bird, sang snatches of sweet, old-fashioned
melodies which, heard now at dusk in some country house of a past decade (the aged singer's tired,
quavering voice rising and falling in dull monotony),
bring back to our minds old memories long stifled,
if unforgotten. Perhaps it was of these things, these
memories of the past, that Mrs. Lorrimer was thinking as she sat on the wide, sunny piazza, in a high-
backed, carved chair, with eyes closed and her delicate, blue-veined hands clasped idly in her lap. At
times she would glance at Ruth, who passed in and
out of the opened door with bunches of roses and

lilacs in her hands, and long, trailing branches of the golden Aaron's-rod. Ruth's cheeks were as pink as the roses she carried, and the glitter of the yellow blossoms was reflected among the light-brown strands of her hair.

"Child, how restless you are!" said Mrs. Lorrimer, when the click of Ruth's little slippered feet sounded many times upon the oaken staircase. "Come, dear—the vases are all filled in the drawing-room. Come and sit by me; I wish to talk with you."

Ruth sat down upon the step at her grandmother's feet, and laid her head against the old lady's knee.

"Well, grandmother," she said, after a pause, lifting her sparkling face, "what have you to tell me? Are you going to scold?"

"Oh no, I could not do that, my dear," she said, as she laid her hand on Ruth's head. Ruth felt its tremulous motion, and thought, "Grandmother is not strong. Why should her hand tremble so?"

"Why are you so happy to-day, Ruth? Is it because Captain Hathaway said he was coming to see us?" Then, suddenly withdrawing her hand from the girl's head, she continued, sharply, "What has he said to you, Ruth? Tell me—tell me every word. Keep nothing from me—I must know."

"He has said nothing; has only been kind and friendly—that is all. You know I have not seen him in a long while—you surely remember how long he has been at sea? Sometimes he would send me messages through his sister Kate's letters—just little ordinary messages. I have nothing more to tell, except that he wrote me this note the other day, saying he would call at the homestead on his return from Boston."

"He will be here to-day?" asked Mrs. Lorrimer, quickly.

"Yes," said Ruth, softly, "he will be here to-day." A glow overspread her face. She turned away her head and looked expectantly down the shaded avenue. She was suddenly recalled from building her intangible air-castle—that was slowly raising its ghostlike structure with its frail supports —by the abrupt motion of her grandmother's rising hurriedly from her chair.

Ruth turned quickly, and saw the old lady sway slightly and put out her hand to support herself by the back of her chair.

"Are you ill?" said Ruth, excitedly, rising from the step.

"No, no, child, I am not ill." Mrs. Lorrimer

repulsed the girl, pushed her away; then, turning almost fiercely upon her, said, " I do not like this Captain Jack Hathaway. I am sorry he is coming here. I do not wish his visits encouraged."

The glow died out of Ruth's face; her figure seemed to shrink into itself; she dropped the roses, and her hands hung limp by her side. She could not understand this vehemence, this almost malicious vindictiveness in her sweet and gentle grandmother; this strange and unaccountable dislike against a young man whom she hardly knew. It was inexplicable. Suddenly a possible solution of the mystery dawned upon her. Mrs. Lorrimer had not been strong for years; was, in fact, a semi-invalid; and what more natural than that her mind had been weakened by the effect of bodily disease? She would humor her, poor dear. No doubt she had taken one of those peculiar dislikes, which is so natural to a sick mind, against the very person whom in health she would have liked and trusted. Thus reasoning, Ruth arose, and, putting her arm around the old lady, guided her footsteps into the house, into the cool, shaded drawing-room, and placed her in the window that overlooked Lynnport harbor.

Mrs. Lorrimer clung helplessly to her grand-daughter. "What was I saying, Ruth? Did I startle you?" She looked piteously into the tender blue eyes watching her anxiously.

"No, dear. It was about Captain Hathaway."

"Oh yes. He—he—must not come here. You will obey me. He must not come here. He—he—cannot be friends with the Lorrimer family; at least it were better not. Oh dear! oh dear! what have I said? What will Jane say?"

"I cannot forbid him the house," said Ruth, gently.

"No, no, of course not; but you must not be too cordial."

Ruth did not reply. She was drawing the soft lace shawl about the thin, stooping shoulders, and her head was averted. At that instant Jane Weston entered the room. She took in the situation at a glance: Ruth's troubled, pale face, and Mrs. Lorrimer's evident agitation, which had left her in a state of exhaustion.

"Well, well, here's a pretty howdy-do," she said, in her sharp voice. "If you are my sister, Mary Lorrimer, I must say I am ashamed of you. Have you been raking up those Hathaway skeletons again?" Ruth started at these words and bent forward eagerly. Her aunt did not notice her. "For Heaven's sake, let their old bones rest! I am sure I for one don't want them flung in my face."

"Jane, Jane, do not speak so," said Mrs. Lorrimer, piteously. "You forget it does not seem so long ago to me. I am old, Jane; I am nearing my rest. The past becomes more vivid. It seems as though it were but yesterday when—when—I hear that name. I—" She held out her hands, which trembled like withered leaves. "Do not reproach me, Jane; do not; I cannot bear it. Have I not suffered?" She bowed her head on her breast.

Jane turned to Ruth, who, with wide-wondering eyes, was listening to these strange words.

"Ruth, go into the garden. I will stay with your grandmother. If Captain Hathaway comes by the harbor I will send him to you; if he comes by the road you will see him pass the garden gate and can call him. Your grandmother is not well enough to see visitors to-day."

Ruth turned slowly, and was walking toward the door when Mrs. Lorrimer rose from her chair and, looking entreatingly at her sister, said:

"Jane, do not let her go. You can see him when he comes, and—and—tell him we do not desire his presence at the homestead. Say I—do not desire it—I, Mrs. Lorrimer."

"I shall do no such thing, Mary Lorrimer. Do you suppose I want to be the laughing-stock of Lynnport? Tell a young man that he cannot call at a house! What reason have I? Why, Dr. Goodyear would be up here in no time, tapping my head to find if I had a grain of sense left in it. Ruth, go to the garden."

Ruth left the room and walked down the graveled path to the garden.

"You could explain," said Mrs. Lorrimer, after the sound of Ruth's footsteps died away.

"Explain what?" Jane said, shortly. "Your humiliation?"

Mrs. Lorrimer gave a sharp cry and placed her hand to her side; then crouched lower in the chair and stared stonily before her.

"Yes," she said, hoarsely, "you are right; my humiliation—no, I cannot explain."

"Mary, Mary, forgive me. I did not mean to be cruel. You can see I cannot tell half and not all. Forgive me, sister."

"Yes, yes, I see." Her head fell forward; then, raising her eyes, she looked up into the blue clouds as they floated by the window. "We will leave it in God's hands," she whispered. "He knows best. He will guide the child's footsteps." She clasped her hands and said, "May it be Thy will, Almighty One, to keep our dear one safe!"

Jane Weston laid her hand on her sister's shoulder. "Mary," she said—her sharp voice spoke in softer tones—"Mary, can you not forget? You are growing old; you are nearing the better world. Does not the light from that clear up the darkness of this?"

"No, no, Jane. I am like an Indian; I cannot forgive or forget."

Jane Weston sighed. "Did I not suffer also?" she said, in a tense tone.

"Yes; yet your suffering was not like mine. It was not my heart alone, but my wounded pride, my birthright from a line of noble ancestors, dragged in the dust of shame. It is that thought, Jane, that stings, burns, and bores into my soul."

Jane took her sister's hand. She did not speak, only held it tightly clasped in hers, as she glanced over the shimmering waters of the harbor.

Ruth walked slowly toward the garden, hardly comprehending why so great a change had fallen upon the beauty of the day, the sun not appearing to shine as brightly, nor the sky to look as clear, as an hour ago. What could Aunt Jane have meant when she spoke of the Hathaway skeleton? Surely Captain Jack had done no harm? Why, he was scarcely thirty years of age, and twelve years of that time he had been at sea, with only short intervals on shore. What could she have meant? Perhaps it was some idle tale heard from a village gossip. Still it was not like Aunt Jane to believe old women's stories. She passed her hand across her hair, brushing the stray curly strands back from her forehead. There was a troubled look in her blue eyes as she unfastened the garden gate, lifting the wooden latch and letting it fall absently into its groove.

The wooden gate was built of cedar—straight boughs, with part of the bark remaining—and was the entrance to an arbor over which hung heavy vines. After walking through the arbor one came suddenly into the heart of the garden. From earliest childhood all things lovely in nature had appealed to Ruth's sensitive, poetical organization, and Mrs.

Lorrimer had encouraged this artistic temperament, allowing the child to have her way in all things pertaining to the planning of her garden. Sheltered by tall, majestic rows of pines, with here and there an elm throwing its drooping branches over the dark, somber foliage beneath, lay about two acres of ground blooming in brightness and color.

Ruth walked through rose-arbors and by many beds of flowers growing in clumps of varied colors: dianthus, marigolds, phlox, love-in-the-mist, tall yellow lilies and roses, large red roses and little white ones—every spot where Ruth could plant them; for she said, " Can one have too much sweetness in this world ? "

Ruth walked slowly toward the well, and laid her hand on the long sweep of cedar-wood which held the bucket by the iron chain. She had made the well picturesque by planting ferns and lichens on its curb. Their water-craving nature, fully satisfied by the constant moisture, had blossomed into almost tropical growth, their large fronds encircling the well like a green wreath. She was thinking of her Aunt Jane's strange words and of Captain Hathaway. She knew it was nearly four o'clock, for the shadows of the tall pines fell in longer lines across the flower-beds, and the breeze that always came up toward evening from the sea was lifting the ferns upon the well-curb and letting them fall idly again.

It was time for the Captain. She took the little note from the bosom of her dress and read it over for the twentieth time. "He can walk from the inn in a short while," she thought. "It is only a little over a mile. He will soon be here." Her checks became flushed, and her small hands trembled slightly as she put the note back. From where she stood she could see, through the branches of the trees, the highway that was at the rear of the homestead grounds, and which terminated upon the sea-shore a quarter of a mile beyond. Some instinct told her the Captain would come that way; for she knew the wind was off-shore, and he would have to beat down the harbor if he sailed; while if he rowed the heat of the sun would make it a tiresome trip. No, she was sure he would come by the highway.

She watched nervously the opening through the trees. Presently the handsome Captain passed along the road with a quick, firm step, and entered the entrance-gates that stood at the head of the avenue.

When he reached the south side of the garden she called to him. He turned quickly and looked inquiringly over the hedge in her direction.

Ruth left the well and hurried to lift the latch of the cedar gate. She looked very rosy when she bade him enter and rest in the shade before going to the house. Her grandmother could not see him to-day—she was ill; but presently they would go to the house and see Aunt Jane. Would he not come and take a seat on the rustic bench near the sun-dial? It was always so pleasant there under the shade of the pear-tree.

Captain Jack did not desire a second invitation. He clasped the hand she held out to him, and said, in a loud, hearty voice:

"Miss Lorrimer, I'm in luck. What a beautiful spot this is! After a long sea-voyage it is like a glimpse of Paradise. You must have some secret power over the flowers to make them flourish like this."

Captain John Hathaway, or rather Jack Hathaway, as he was generally called in Lynnport, was a remarkably handsome man, tall, muscular, and straight, and had a dark, Spanish-hued face, with the strange contrast of blue eyes. His chin was smooth-shaven and his mouth was strong, with lines denoting will and endurance.

He seemed to carry with him the breath of the sea, and was a born sailor, not a made one. From earliest boyhood he had lived more or less upon the water. He was stifled in the inland; the hills seemed to close about him like walls to bury him. Perhaps in his veins flowed a strain inherited from some viking of the northlands, some Norseman conqueror of storm and gale.

His father had died when Captain Jack was about twenty years of age, leaving him a small fortune, part of which was invested in the merchantman he commanded and owned, and which plied between Boston and China.

His mother died when he and his twin sister Kate were eight years old—the sister whom he loved, revered, and pitied. Kate Hathaway was born deformed, and had struggled through life fighting a great and patient fight with weakness and suffering, her little pinched face and deep-set eyes telling only too well the sad story. When the Captain went to sea he installed her in a pretty dormer-windowed cottage on the hill above the town, and there, with an attendant, Mrs. Sarah Munn, a widow from a small hamlet beyond Lynnport, she lived her life. Poor little Kate! the joy and happiness of whose existence was her handsome brother; her occupations, little parish duties and rigid struggles to hide her sufferings. She would say to Mrs. Munn:

"Why should two suffer when it is only necessary for one? If I can hide my pain from Jack and you and my friends in Lynnport, it is clearly my duty to do so."

Mrs. Munn, at such remarks, would wipe her eyes on her coarse gingham apron, and hurry from the room to the kitchen, where she would inform the pots and pans, in a fierce whisper, that, "for her part, the ways of Providence was the curioust ways she'd ever hearn on; and if it warn't that there was another world comin', where the loose ends o' this one would be straightened out, she, for her part, would rather die, and die for good, and get red of it all." After which rather irreverent outburst she would remorsefully put on her glasses, take her Bible from the shelf above the fireplace, and with sundry loud sighs and groans read a chapter.

The Hathaways of past generations had been well known and respected in Lynnport. They had lived there many years. In fact, the Hathaway farm-house on the turnpike road to Boston had been built for nearly a century, but was now in the hands of strangers.

Not much was known of Jack's father in later years, he, with his wife, having lived the lives of recluses on a small island in the harbor, seldom coming to the town. Upon the death of his wife he left his lonely island home, taking a house on the outskirts of Lynnport, where he passed a hermit's existence, shunning all intercourse with his neighbors—a silent, morose creature who was feared and disliked. In this atmosphere of gloom and depression, with their taciturn, lonely parent, the little twins struggled from childhood to youth.

When old Mr. Hathaway died it was found that there was considerable property, which he had divided equally between his children.

Jack could now realize the dream of his life, which was to own his ship and be her captain. He left Lynnport one fine morning, standing upon the deck of the "Bonny Kate," the youngest captain that ever sailed from the harbor.

He had met Ruth at his sister's during the intervals of his long sea-voyages. Sunday afternoons Kate Hathaway taught a small class of children

and read them Bible stories. Mrs. Lorrimer and
Jane gave their consent to the child Ruth's joining
them. At these classes the young Captain first
met the little one, whom he teased and petted; and
when Ruth was about sixteen he was startled by the
loveliness that was slowly expanding as the years
went by.

There is an unswerving fate shaping all destinies.
Mrs. Lorrimer had seen no danger in the child bringing a stray bit of comfort to the crippled girl; had
not seen the cloud in the sky, nor heard the rumble
of the storm afar off, nor appreciated the dawning of
an interest that in future years would expand into
stronger growth. The little one went to her les-
sons, and at long intervals saw Captain Jack when
he came home for a short furlough. In the meantime the years passed like stealthy shadows; Ruth
became a woman, and the old people dozed on at
the manor, all unconscious that the hand of fate was
shaping her life.

The Captain had thought of Ruth many times during the long nights at sea; so many times, in fact,
that he had written her, when port was reached, that
he would call at the homestead. Now that he was
here, holding her hand and looking into her face, he

understood why, during those starlight nights in the tropics, when the ship passed through long, undulating lines of moonlight, he had seen neither stars nor moonlight, but instead his sister's cottage, with Ruth sitting by the fireside that October afternoon before the ship had sailed. How young and girlish she looked, and how sadly she had spoken when she said: "We shall miss you so much, Captain Jack. You will not be gone three years this time, will you?"

He had only stayed two years. Now he was in her garden, she by his side, looking up at him with shy, beaming eyes. Ruth appeared to him even more lovely than the visions he had of her at sea. He felt the sweetness of her presence, the stillness and beauty of the garden tending to enhance that sweetness. To him she was like a white lily standing among other flowers of a more transient growth. The Captain was not a poetical man; he only felt this in some vague, intangible way. He could not have put into words his feelings if he had so wished. Instead he talked of commonplace matters—his voyage, his sister's health, the Lynnport news, and said he was glad they were well at the homestead, and remarked how much she had grown.

Ruth sat very quiet and listened, the blush creeping up into her face and the long-lashed lids drooping. Sometimes she ventured a remark in a low voice. She had forgotten about the Hathaway skeletons; the rattle of their old bones was stilled; the closed door of the closet was securely locked upon them. Why should she think of them? Was she not happy—very, very happy?

The shadows of the pines fell across the garden —long and slender lines of gloom, that lay upon the grass, then crept slowly upon the dial. Still they talked on. What was time to them as they read together the first pages of the sweet old love-story, those first pages so full of promise, the last chapters blessedly hidden in a flood of hope?

CHAPTER IV.

MRS. LORRIMER'S SUSPICIONS.

JANE WESTON stood silently by her sister's side for some moments after Ruth left them, then said, gently:

"Mary, let me take you upstairs to your room. I will see this young man. You can trust me; I will be discreet."

The old lady struggled feebly to her feet. Leaning on Jane's arm, she slowly crossed the room and ascended the staircase. When part way up, on the wide landing where the tall clock stood, with two high-backed, carved chairs beside it, she wearily seated herself, and looked wistfully from the oval window, which commanded a wide view of the sea and the lighthouse.

"Jane," she said, "I am surely more feeble than I was last summer. I never had to rest on the landing before."

"It is nothing, Mary; don't fret. This young man's visit has upset you."

"Ah well! perhaps so."

It happened that when Captain Hathaway and Ruth, some half an hour later, came slowly toward the house from the direction of the garden, Aunt Jane, grim and dignified, and Tetsy, fat and complacent, were awaiting them on the piazza.

"Captain Hathaway," said Ruth, blushing, "my aunt, Miss Weston."

Miss Weston bowed stiffly, her body erect like a ramrod, and her head merely bending a trifle forward. She gave the Captain a sharp glance from her shrewd eyes, then indicated by a motion of the hand that he was to seat himself in one of the chairs on the piazza. He did as she desired. Then an awkward pause ensued, which was broken in a most unexpected manner.

Tetsy had been asleep, or presumably so, on a soft pillow placed upon a chair near by. When the Captain became seated our four-footed friend lifted himself erect, gave the visitor a keen glance, shook himself slightly, and slowly and laboriously descended from his bed. He crossed the floor, paused directly before the Captain, and, lifting himself upon his hind feet, placed one fore paw upon the Captain's arm, and offered him the other to shake —offered it in a good-natured, cordial fashion, not limp and nerveless.

Aunt Jane was amazed at this mark of attention conferred by her favorite. He was generally so chary of caresses, and unduly suspicious of strangers, that she had begun to put a high value upon his powers of discernment and intuition. Not content with a mere hand-shake, he jumped into the Captain's lap and sat looking reproachfully at his mistress, as though reproving her for a lack of hospitality.

" He's a fine dog," said the Captain, patting his soft, silken coat.

" Yes," said Jane, shortly.

" He seldom shakes hands with strangers," said Ruth ; " you are favored."

" Ah!" said Jack, " the old fellow likes me; that is a good sign. Do you know, Miss Weston, I would rather have a good honest dog for a friend than half the people one meets. Why, the ' Bonny Kate' could not put out to sea without my Rover; he's the most precious freight aboard. I always say, ' Boys, if there is a wreck, remember Rover's to go in the first life-boat.'   'Aye, aye,' they say, with a will, every man of them."

"Yes?" said Jane, stiffly.

Captain Hathaway looked at her in surprise, then across at Ruth's pained, embarrassed face.   Something was wrong evidently.   After some further desultory conversation he arose with a sensation of chill and disappointment creeping over him.   Had he offended, unconsciously wounded, this stern-visaged old aunt?   He was hurt and puzzled.   "I must get back to Lynnport," he said.

Jane did not speak.   She arose also, but did not hold out her hand.

Ruth's generally sweet face was clouded, and her small hands twitched nervously.

"Good afternoon," said the Captain, his hat in his hand, the sun shining full on his bronzed, handsome face.   "The homestead is a beautiful spot. May I come again, Miss Weston?"   There was a little wistfulness in his voice.   Jane was not proof against it, and did what she ever afterward deeply regretted—she smiled slightly, and said:

"If you wish, Captain Hathaway."   She would have given much to recall the words after they had been uttered.   It was too late; they had been forced from her involuntarily. Fate had interposed, and the fine blue eyes of the Captain lit up with pleasure.

"Thank you, Miss Weston," he said; "thank you. I shall come again."

Ruth walked with him down the avenue that led to the highroad, Tetsy following slowly, basely deserting his mistress, who watched them till a bend in the shaded path hid them from view. Then she stood very still a moment, and looked strangely before her, with an expression of having seen an apparition.

"How very like he is," she said; "how very like! Heaven help me! have I made a mistake?"

When the Captain and Ruth reached the iron entrance-gates they paused. He stooped and picked some grasses and a few daisies that had sprung up close to the gates. The country road was very quiet; no vehicles were passing; a rise in the road hid the nearest house from view. In the distance they could see the roofs of the village, rising one above the other on the terraced hillside, while through the trees on their right they caught a glimpse of the ocean and heard its soft lap on the rocks.

Jack leaned over Ruth and held out the daisies.

"Your aunt was not cordial in her welcome," he said; "perhaps she does not like seafaring men. I know some have a prejudice that way." He looked thoughtful a moment, then added, brightly, "Perhaps I imagined it. What could she have against me? At any rate, she has permitted me to call again."

"She can have nothing against you," said Ruth, in a low voice, with her head averted.

"Miss Lorrimer, Ruth—let me call you Ruth, as I did when you were a little girl." He took her hand and laid the bunch of flowers in it. Her hand closed over them, and she looked down shyly. "You bid me welcome, Ruth, do you not? Can I not come again to the homestead?"

A tremor shook the girl from head to foot, and her breath came shortly.

"They—they"— she paused—"seem not to like your coming. I know not why, but I—" She stopped.

"Yes, yes," said the Captain, "let us leave them out of the question. This is a subject for you and me to settle."

"I—I—want you to come," she said, softly.

The Captain caught her hand fiercely. "Then I shall come. Not all the aunts or grandmothers in the world can keep me away, so long, Ruth, as you bid me come."

He did not seem to know how tightly he was holding her hand. It was red from the marks of his fingers when he released it. She said nothing and held her hand behind her.

"They may be—be—rude to you," said Ruth, reddening. "Not grandmother—grandmother could not be rude to any one; but Aunt Jane—she—"

"She will not be rude to me," said Captain Hathaway. "I think I understand Jane Weston. At any rate, one must expect a few breakers on every voyage."

Ruth placed the bunch of daisies in the belt of her gown, and drew the lace cape more closely over her shoulders, but did not reply.

The Captain seemed to be thinking; suddenly he said, abruptly:

"Ruth, I must go to Boston to-morrow, and shall probably be gone until July. It is about the cargo. When I return I shall have the rest of the summer to myself. I shall not sail until September. Can you write to me while I am in Boston?"

"No, no," she said.   "I dare not; I could not deceive grandmother."

His face darkened for an instant, and he tapped his foot impatiently on the ground.

"I do not understand this talk of deception," he said.   "Why should you deceive any one?   Tell them; they cannot object."

"They would, they would," she said.   "Do not ask me; I cannot explain.   I know nothing, but I fear much.   At times a great dread comes over me —no, I dare not write."

"Well, then, I shall write you and send my letters to my sister.   You can get them there."

"No, no, that would be the same.   I could not do that."

"Great Neptune!   Ruth, explain matters.   What am I to do?"

"I don't know," she said, helplessly, the tears standing thickly on her long, curling lashes.

"Well, then, let it be so," he said, impatiently. "We will not write.   In July, if I am a living man, I am coming to the homestead to have matters cleared up.   In the meantime, Ruth, give a few thoughts to the sailor lad, won't you?"

"Yes," she said, softly.

"Now tell me," he said, laughingly, "how many times do you suppose you will think of me?"

"I think—I shall think a good many times."

"Well, how many?" he urged, coaxingly.

"I could not count them," she said, in a whisper.

He heard her and laughed. He stepped lightly through the opened gateway, then came back again and lifted her face to his and looked sharply into her clear eyes.

"I trust you," he said, earnestly. He seemed satisfied. At that instant they heard the crunch of wagon-wheels on the other side of the rise of ground, and presently Dr. Goodyear, in his old-fashioned, two-wheeled gig, came in sight.

The doctor looked inquiringly at the couple standing so close together by the gate—a scrutinizing glance through his steel-bowed spectacles—then, leaning over the side of the carriage, he cried, in a gruff voice:

"Do you know the dew is beginning to fall, and there is a big fog-bank off the ledge? Reef your sails, Captain Hathaway, and get into the wind. Steer for smooth waters, my boy; steer for smooth waters. It's stormy off the manor-house rocks."

"Aye, aye," said Jack. With a bow and a wave

of the hand he passed on, wondering, as he walked
rapidly, what significance lay in the doctor's speech
—some hidden meaning, he was sure.

"I was coming to see your grandmother, Ruth,"
said the doctor.   "How is she to-day?"

"Not so well," said Ruth.

The doctor was guiding his horse up the avenue
of elms, and Ruth was walking by the side of the
gig.   Tetsy was seated by the doctor's side on the
seat, whither he had insisted upon being placed; his
fat body rolled backward and forward with every
jolt of the vehicle.

"What do you think of the Captain, little girl?"
presently said the doctor, giving her a sharp glance.

Ruth's sensitive, telltale face spoke for itself.
"Oh, I think I like him very much, doctor," she
said.   "He—he—is so handsome, and—and—so
brave and strong.   Do you not think so?"

"Humph!—yes, I suppose he is all that.   But
these sea-dogs are a roving lot, here to-day, gone
to-morrow, shifting as the sands of the sea.   I tell
you, now, they are not the men to put your faith
in, or to—well, we will say, just for a simile, to
marry.   Think of a woman, now, that never sees
her husband, say, for anywhere from three to seven

years—what kind of a home can she have?   If she
goes to sea with him what kind of a life is that, I'd
like to know?"

"Yes, but, doctor, many women marry sailors
and are happy."

"I'd like to know the happy ones.   Those I see
always look strained and wild, as though they were
seeing wrecks at sea and drowning men.   You go
into the cottages on the shore stormy winter nights
when the fleet is out, if you want to see the happy
sailors' wives."

"If I cared for any one very much," said Ruth,
firmly, "I would rather see him once in seven.years
—yes, ten years, if it had to be so—than to see any
one I did not like oftener, even if he adored me all
the time."

"Why, child, I was not talking about you.   How
you apply cases to yourself!   Of course you must
stay with Mrs. Lorrimer.   Your duty is to her.   If
you marry, he must be a landsman, remember, and
a good son to the old lady.   She's done everything
for you, Ruth; remember that.   She loves you better than life itself.   She's had sorrow, my little girl
—more than falls often to the lot of mortals."

Ruth turned away her head.   The doctor touched

his old horse sharply with the whip, waking him from his nap so abruptly that Tetsy was deposited rather unceremoniously in the bottom of the carriage, from which the doctor extricated him as speedily as possible, as he caught a glimpse of a high head-dress outlined against one of the windows of the house.

It was Sunday afternoon when Mrs. Lorrimer came downstairs again. Dr. Goodyear had cautioned Miss Weston that she must be kept very quiet. Her heart was weak; they must hide annoying things from her.

Ruth had heard him give this parting injunction as he stood on the landing of the stairs. There was a grave look in his eyes. Her heart seemed to throb more quickly for an instant. Could it be that her grandmother was really ill?

When the doctor reached the outer door she joined him, and, laying her hand on his sleeve, said, in a whisper:

"Is grandmother very ill?"

"Not to say very ill," said the doctor, kindly; "only old—and weak."

Ruth looked earnestly into his face.

"What caused this last attack? Was she troubled by anything, doctor?"

"Troubled?   Nonsense, child; what could trouble her?"

"I don't know; only I thought perhaps—"

"Well, what?" said the doctor, sharply.

"I thought it had something to do with Captain Hathaway's visit.   She was taken worse that afternoon."

The doctor was drawing on his gloves, and,.turning to her, said:

"Well, well, don't fret, child.   Be a good granddaughter to the old lady, and—and—don't give a thought to that handsome rover of the sea."

When Mrs. Lorrimer came down that Sunday afternoon and took her seat in the north drawing-room, she seemed to have suddenly aged.   Though the exquisite patrician air of the gentlewoman was yet apparent, it was like the last bright flame flickering before the fire burns low; like the dainty porcelain that has an invisible weak place in its surface, and which the slightest touch would shatter into a thousand fragments.   Her shoulders stooped, and the beautiful white hands were never still; they fluttered tremulously and crossed and recrossed as they lay in her lap.   The contour of her perfect features was outlined with unusual sharpness as her head rested against the back of her chair. She sat very quietly for some time, her eyes wandering through the open window over the familiar country; then she turned her gaze, and looked up and down the long room at the portraits of her ancestors which lined the walls. Stern-visaged, many of them, as they appeared to return her intent gaze; gold-laced, powdered-wigged, proud in their day and generation. Westons and Lorrimers, there their portraits hung —all that was left to tell of the fine old New England family; " and," thought Mrs. Lorrimer, " they are all dead. None left of the good old stock but Jane and little Ruth and me. And I—I—shall soon be asleep. .I am very weary; it will be better so."

There she sat that Sunday afternoon in the old house, thinking, thinking, ever thinking—the solace of the aged when all other effort is too great.

Presently Jane and Ruth came from· service in the village church. They stepped softly across the threshold, and when they saw Mrs. Lorrimer's position thought her asleep. Her head was resting against the back of her chair; the rays of the sun, that was going down beyond the hills that lined the harbor, rested in yellow lines upon her hair. She smiled when she heard their steps.

"I was not asleep," she said; "I was watching the sunset. It seemed quite as good to me as going to church. I read God's power and goodness in the beauty of the clouds. I have seen so many sunsets in my life, and yet to-night it seemed more wonderful than any."

Ruth kissed her grandmother, but did not speak.

"Sing something for me, Ruth—one of the old hymns. Never mind the spinet. Come and sit close to me and put your hand in mine. We will sing together." Jane went softly from the room.

They sang together, in Mrs. Lorrimer's feeble treble and Ruth's sweet, clear voice, some of the Puritan hymns—those strains that first rang out in the resonant tones of the early settlers in the wilderness.

When the hymns were finished, and the shadows were filling the long room, making the bewigged ancestors look gloomy and taciturn as they peered from their frames in the gloom, Mrs. Lorrimer laid her hand on Ruth's head and drew her closely to her.

"My dear child," she said, solemnly, "something tells me that I am growing more feeble each day, and that perhaps my time here is not very long."

"Oh no, no," said Ruth, holding Mrs. Lorrimer's hand tightly.

"It must be so, Ruth; I am an old woman. What I want, dear, is that you will promise to stay with the old grandmother while I live. It must not be idle words, but a solemn promise. I know that if you give me your word you will keep it."

"But where could I go, grandmother?" said Ruth. "This is the only home I have."

A strange feeling of depression crept over the girl as she waited her grandmother's reply. The shadows in the long room grew blacker, and the faces of the portraits took on a menacing and threatening aspect. One white-faced lady in frill and pompadour appeared pointing her long slender finger in a warning attitude.

"I know you have no other home at present. One cannot tell, however, what the future may hold; what gallant young lover may woo and win my little maid."

"And you would not want me to go to him?" queried Ruth.

"No," said Mrs. Lorrimer—her voice sounded quite strong and clear—"I would not want you to go to him. You must give me your promise you—"

"Mary," said Jane Weston, from the threshold of the door. The two turned their heads quickly. Jane's tall, angular figure towered in the doorway. "For goodness' sake, what are you sitting in the dark for? Why, it is as black as Egypt. I never could understand this mooning in the dark. For my part, give me a good candelabra, with straight wicks, and no shrouds or thieves in the flame."

While speaking she crossed the room, and, carefully guarding against unpleasant contact with the furniture, hastily lit the candles on the mantel.

Ruth arose with an air of great relief. What terrible load had been removed! What cold fingers had released their clasp upon her heart! How her knees shook! Suppose she had given this promise, she would have kept it, for she had inherited strong conscientious scruples from her Puritan ancestors. A promise given was a most sacred thing; nothing but death would have broken it. What a fearful thought—waiting for death to release one! Ruth rose and crossed the room to step out upon the piazza and watch the lights come out one by one in the village—a favorite occupation of hers at nightfall. As she stood there in the intense quiet she could hear the subdued hum of voices through the opened windows of the drawing-room, and once she thought she distinguished a stifled sob. She listened, her head inclined forward, and heard her aunt say, in a half-whisper, with a sharp intonation:

"It was unfair to the child, Mary. Thank God I was here in time to prevent her making that promise! Do you realize what you are doing? Binding a child almost on the very threshold of her life by a promise which you know, once given, she would keep at any cost."

"I shall not live long. I did it for the best, Jane. I love her; it was for her good."

"Nonsense! it was to gratify your desire for revenge. No, I shall not spare you. I am your best friend, Mary Lorrimer, and you know it. I shall not stand by and see you false to your own kind heart and your common sense."

"Hush! she will hear you," whispered Mrs. Lorrimer.

Ruth did not listen further, but walked over the lawn toward the water. Surely some secret lurked in the past annals of the old house—some secret that affected her—and—and Captain Hathaway. What could it be? The mystery was known to

Aunt Jane, her grandmother, and Dr. Goodyear—
of that she felt assured.

She racked her mind to see if she could remember
any strange events connected with her childhood.
No, all seemed clear and commonplace; she could
think of nothing. No, it concerned Captain Hathaway—of that she was convinced. What could it
be?

Ruth made a resolution, as she stood there in the
darkness of the starless summer night, that nothing
but crime, or his own wish to renounce her, would
make her false to her lover. That Captain Hathaway loved her she never doubted for an instant.
That he was good, honest, and true she firmly believed.

CHAPTER V.

THE LOVERS.

JUNE passed by; the 1st of July had come. Mrs. Lorrimer still remained feeble. She did not again allude to the subject so earnestly discussed with Ruth that Sunday afternoon; in fact, appeared rather to avoid any allusion to Captain Hathaway or his possible return to Lynnport. This silence, which Ruth divined was intentional, hurt her. She, on her part, became reserved and shy, avoiding the mention of his name. The very reticence she felt impelled to preserve only tended to enhance her interest in him, and her thoughts, turned inward, kept constantly revolving on the selfsame topic. What was the secret? would it be weighty enough to separate them? she asked herself many times. She became silent and preoccupied, her mind filled with dire forebodings of the possible result of a separation between herself and her lover.

Aunt Jane appeared altered. Her rasping, high-pitched voice took on more tender tones. A sort of unspoken sympathy was in her voice when she addressed her niece.

Once Ruth thought she detected tears in her aunt's eyes when she noticed her watching her furtively, though perhaps she might have been mistaken, as Jane declared, with asperity, that "this everlasting glare from the sea made her eyes water."

It was the 5th of July. Ruth had been restless all day. The heat had been great, and she had been too languid to work among her flowers. Toward afternoon, as the sun began to take its downward course, leaving one side of the highway in shadow, she started abruptly, saying she would go to the village and stop at old Miss Treadles's for some more cotton to finish knitting her antimacassar.

"Child, it is too hot," said Mrs. Lorrimer, feebly, from her chair on the piazza.

"Do, for goodness' sake, Ruth, quiet yourself," exclaimed Aunt Jane. "I never saw any one like you. Anchor yourself somewhere, as Dr. Good-year says."

"I am going to the village," said Ruth, decidedly, her small mouth set and defiant.

The ladies making no reply, with a crisp little good-by she walked rapidly down the avenue, and was soon out of sight.

It was hot on the highway, and very dusty. The yellow loam rose in flying clouds about her feet, the air appeared vibrating in sultry waves, and her face grew flushed and heated under the wide straw hat. She hurried on. Instead of stopping, however, at Miss Treadles's for the cotton (a little shop near the waterside), she climbed the steep street that ran along the ridge of the hill. Pausing before a low white cottage that lay back some distance from the upper street, she laid her hand upon a wooden gate that inclosed a diminutive garden. She hesitated, thinking intently. Should she go in or should she return home? Her hand was still resting on the gate, and she drew her foot back and forth irresolutely over the graveled path. The street was very quiet; no one seemed astir in the front of the houses that at intervals lined the thoroughfare. According to the custom of the villagers they were all resting during the hot hours of the day in the back of the houses, the shutters being closely drawn in front.

Ruth had almost decided to give up her intention of entering the little white cottage when, suddenly raising her eyes, she beheld far off on the horizon a ship scudding onward before the breeze. She concentrated her gaze upon the on-coming ship, which was growing larger and whiter every instant, its sails unfurled to catch every bit of air stirring. The sunlight was gleaming on the canvas, making it look like a vast shield of gold, and the white spray rose high as the bows cut sharply through the blue water.

Ruth stood with dilated eyes and parted lips. "It is—it is—the 'Bonny Kate,'" she said,. softly ; and, going quickly up the narrow, box-bordered path of the little garden, she lifted the brass knocker on the door, letting it fall loudly. A grumbling voice was heard from the back part of the house. Presently a heavy step crossed the interior hallway, and the door was quickly opened. In the doorway stood Mrs. Sarah Munn, in a short calico gown and a long apron that hung below the hem of her skirt. On her head she had a wide-brimmed straw hat such as the farmers wore in the field. The perspiration was rolling down her face, and her hands were covered with red stains.

"Well, for the land's sake, Miss Ruth!" she exclaimed. "Don't tell me you have gone and walked all the way from the homestead this bilin' afternoon

—a good mile. Come right in, do. Come into the settin'-room and I'll call Miss Kate. I think she's expectin' the Captain some this afternoon; he's about due. I'll tell you, but don't say anything: I made her a cup of strong tea and got her to lie down; and what with that and the heat she fell asleep. If it hadn't 'a' been for that I'd never been able to make the currants jell in the world. Why, she'd 'a' had me climbin' the stairs every blessed minit to the garret chamber, to see if the 'Bonny Kate' was in sight."

All the time Mrs. Munn was speaking she was ushering in her visitor, pushing a chair forward, opening shutters, and bustling about like a large and very noisy fly.

"I think I saw the Captain's ship east of the ledge just now," said Ruth, trying to speak indifferently.

"For the land's sake! you don't say so!" said Mrs. Munn, craning her head out of the window. "Why, to be sure, it is, and they're a-comin' on flyin'. Miss Kate will be happy, poor dear. Why, he'll be here in less than an hour. I'm nigh distracted, for he'll want a good supper." Mrs. Munn suddenly sprang up. "Would you mind helpin'

Miss Kate to dress? What with them heathenish currants, and the supper to get, I've got my hands full. And now, speakin' of currants "—she rested her hands on her hips and eyed Ruth earnestly— " they're the most unreliable fruits in creation to preserve. If they're a little too ripe they won't jell; if they're not quite ripe enough they won't jell. They're just like some o' these contrary folks as thinks the Lord always makes the days too hot or too cold—never just right—and needs them to help Him set the creation right."

" I never thought of currants in that way," laughed Ruth. It was such a girlish, ringing laugh that Mrs. Munn started.

At this moment a sweet voice called from an upper room:

'" Mrs. Munn, I see the ' Bonny Kate ' coming. I want you."

" I'm a-comin', Miss Kate, I'm a-comin'; and here's Miss Ruth—she'll help you. There's a lot of work in the kitchen. You know the Captain likes a masterful lot of cookin'."

Mrs. Munn was calling up the staircase. Ruth had hurried on before her. As the pleasant greetings were heard coming from the room above, Mrs.

Munn listened with a pleased smile on her shrewd face, then retreated to the kitchen.

"I declare," she said, as she attacked the refractory jelly with renewed vigor, "I never see a sweeter creature than Miss Ruth.   Not that she has only a pretty face—she's got something besides that. She's a good girl, and I wish the Captain would cast a glance that way.   But for the land's sake! I always used to say to the departed Munn, a man's like a mole: he's a-burrowin' and a-workin' and a-makin' the dirt fly, and all the time he don't know where he's goin', and that his greatest blessin' may be right under his nose.   I can't say as Munn agreed with me, but I always would contend that point."

As this soliloquy ended the jelly boiled over, and with a "Drat that jelly!" Mrs. Munn removed the bubbling preserve-kettle to the back of the stove.

Kate Hathaway was a hunchback. Her head lay low between her shoulders, and the poor little dwarfish figure was no larger than a ten-year-old child's.   Her face was very beautiful—beautiful with the spiritual light that glowed like a never-ending gleam in her dark, deep-set eyes.   Around her sweet, sensitive mouth were deep lines, made by patient silence under suffering.

Kate's life was passed very near the border-land; so near that the peace of that world shed its gentle luster over this. Perhaps when she was alone, and the pain left her poor racked body, shadowy hands lifted the thin veil, and she saw beyond and felt in some undefined manner the reason for our sorrows here. When friends would ask her, at such times, of what she was thinking, she would say:

"I was dreaming; I was not thinking. And very happy dreams they were, and very real ones."

Kate could walk about the house, but she could not climb the steep, hilly streets of Lynnport; so they had a carriage made for her, and she was quite a familiar figure upon the streets in fine weather, the ever-faithful and loquacious Mrs. Munn pushing the vehicle, jealously guarding this task from any other hand.

Kate was very fond of Ruth. Sometimes she had thought she would like to have her for a sister. She had always observed that the ladies of the homestead, for some unaccountable reason, kept aloof, and of late had thought Ruth altered. In her simple nature and narrow life she could not fathom any reason for the reticence of the great ladies of the town. That they thought themselves

above her she never dreamed. She was a Hathaway; she was of good blood. No, it must be because she was so ugly, so repulsive; and poor Kate
wept in secret many tears. She always made Mrs.
Munn hurry up some side street with her carriage
if she saw the manor-house ladies approaching.

When she greeted Ruth in her bright little sitting-
room that afternoon she watched her closely. Kate
was a good reader of character, and her powers of
intuition, probably fostered by loneliness, were marvelous.

Ruth helped her dress and listened to her exclamations of pleasure at the prospect of having her
brother with her till September. "Till September!
Is it not splendid?" she said. "Three months.
Ah, then, after that—I hate to think of it—I may
not see him for five years. There are to be changes
in the Boston firm, and the course of the 'Bonny
Kate' is to be altered, bringing her to Boston at
longer intervals."

"Five years!" echoed Ruth, with a start. "That
is a long time."

"Yes," said Kate, giving her a sharp glance, "a
long time."

So it happened that when the Captain entered the cottage parlor Ruth stood by the window, in the shadow of the vines that climbed over the trellis outside. At the neck of her white gown she had pinned a bunch of daisies and grasses as like as possible to a bunch of withered ones lying in a sandal-wood box at home.

The Captain crossed the tiny parlor quickly, and, looking down into her face, took her hand, bent his handsome head, and kissed her red lips.

Kate uttered a sharp cry—a cry like a wounded animal. It was the first time in her life that her brother had passed her by. He had not seemed to see the little shrunken form as she sat huddled in a chair, with her long, thin hands held out toward him. Instead, he had passed by without a word or a sign, and had gone straight to Ruth. At the sharpness of her cry he turned, his hand still in Ruth's. Drawing her with him, he went to his sister.

"Kate," he said, "forgive me. It was the only time I forgot you and it shall be the last. I forget everything at sight of Ruth. Have you not guessed, with your discernment? It was the thought of Ruth that brought me home from sea a year earlier."

Kate did not speak instantly.   Her sensitive mouth was trembling; in her large eyes a moisture had gathered.

"It is all right, Jack," she said, in a low voice, "and as it should be.   I am very happy.   Come, little sister.   I have always wanted a sister, and God has given me the one I shall love best."

There was a great deal of happiness concentrated in the cottage parlor that evening, for it was evening before Ruth began to appreciate the passing of the hours and the probable displeasure at her prolonged absence from the homestead.   Mrs. Munn had brought in the tempting tea, and with her shrewd gaze had taken in the situation: Ruth's nearness to the Captain, his arm about her waist, and her dear, adored Miss Kate with a smile on her lips, but tears in her eyes.

Mrs. Munn had changed her dress.   She wore a dark-brown woolen gown and a white apron.   On her head was a clean cap with a bunch of green lutestring ribbons resting on the top, a little to one side, which gave rather a rakish appearance to her sober, plain countenance.   She bustled about the table, keeping up a fire of running comments as she rattled the dishes.   Mrs. Munn was a privileged character. She could say what she liked, but was too proud to ask questions, or to pry, till she had been informed of the startling piece of news that had befallen the family.

The Captain understood her perfectly, and took a quiet amusement in keeping her in a state of nervous expectancy. Presently he said, looking up pleasantly:

"Mrs. Munn, what do you think of my engaging a new mate for the 'Bonny Kate'?"

"Well, sir," she said, refusing to be told in this roundabout manner, "if you need a new mate I should say get one. The wharves of Lynnport are full of idle good-for-nothings wearing out the planks and taking in the sea-breeze because they get that free and don't have to work for it."

"Come now, Mrs. Munn, you understand me; here's the new mate." He laid his hand on Ruth's shoulder. "The best mate a good ship ever carried, God bless her!"

Ruth looked up and laughed.

"But I'm not going to sea, Captain Hathaway."

"Oh yes, you are. The very next voyage I make from Lynnport you must report on deck before we leave the harbor's mouth."

" But—but— "

" We'll settle that later," said the Captain. "Never argue with your superior officer.   I wouldn't want to put the little new mate in irons."

Mrs. Munn had not spoken.   She stood silently watching them, shaking her head solemnly from side to side.   She held some knives and forks in her hand, the grease from them dropping on the carpet. She did not notice that.   Suddenly she said:

" Well, well, I'm sure I wish you happiness and a long life together."   Her words were accompanied by such a deep-drawn sigh that they looked up in surprise.

" What is the matter, Mrs. Munn ? " said the Captain, much amused.   " Not thinking of old Munn, are you ? "

" Yes, that is just what I was thinking of, Captain.   Your words to Miss Ruth are the very words he used to me.   ' You're best mate now, Sarah,' he says, and—and—ah well, he's dead and gone, and I'm hopin' they ain't too hard on him where he's gone ; but he was a crusty man.   And I never was first mate from the start ; I was never promoted above the cook's scullion.   I always says, and I will contend, that marriage is a tight noose around the neck, and the more one struggles the tighter it grows."

"But every one is not like old Mr. Munn," said Ruth.

"Ah well, Miss Ruth, there's many a one like Munn. The trouble with us is that we must try for ourselves; and the Lord have mercy on us!" She put her apron to her eyes with the hand that still held the knives and forks. "Don't mind me," she sniffled: "I always cry at weddin's and smile at funerals. The minister has spoken to me more times than once about it. He says it's onseemly, but I says to him, 'That's the way life seems to me, and it seems the proper thing to do.'"

"We're going to show you a model couple," said the Captain. "Cheer up, Mrs. Munn; don't cry over us."

"Well, well, I'm sure I wish you all luck," she replied. "As for cryin', it always did come easier to me than laughin'."

The sunset lingered long that warm July evening. At last, when it went down behind the hills, a great red ball, it left a brilliant twilight, making one think of the tropics and far eastern lands. A yellow gleam lingered in the sky till dark.

Jack and Ruth wandered slowly along the country road in the twilight. They talked softly, in whispers. In some vague manner the beauty and stillness of the hour made their happiness more complete—no jarring discord to break the peace. They were living only in the present. Why should they trouble themselves about the future? Were they not together? Did they not love each other? Had not a great Power above, unseen by them, sent this love into their hearts? So they wandered on through the pleasant country road, past fields of clover nearly ready for the sickle, past corn just springing up in long, regular lines of green. A light dew was on the wild-flowers and creepers that straggled over the stone walls that lined the road, their perfume filling the air with a sweet, spicy fragrance.

Before reaching the homestead gates they paused a moment, and leaned upon a stone wall that separated an uncultivated pasture-lot from the sea. The twilight had almost deepened into night, and the beautiful evening star appeared, reigning alone in the clear sky. Jack looked up at the star.

"See, Ruth," he said. "How often, when at sea, I have watched the evening star and thought of you! I cannot tell how it is; . never thought I should care so much for any one. As a boy I had a strange bringing-up. My father was a cold, silent man, rarely speaking to us; and when he did, it was always to blame us. I grew morose; I was lonely. But for Kate I should have run away to sea before I was twelve years old." He paused and drew his breath hard. "Now all is changed," he continued. "I know how I can feel and love. Ruth, it is all centered in you. If anything should happen to part us it would crush the very life and heart out of me."

Ruth trembled and drew closer to him.

"Are you cold?" he said.

"Yes; the wind is coming in from the sea. Nothing can part us, Jack," she whispered; "nothing shall part us, unless—unless—you renounce me."

"Renounce you?" he said, quickly. "Nothing, Ruth, shall ever make me do that. Why should I renounce the greatest happiness that has ever come to me?"

The pasture-lot near which they were standing was entirely devoid of trees. In the clear light that lay over its bare surface a person crossing it could be distinctly seen by any one in the road.

Suddenly a tall figure stepped abruptly from the overhanging boughs of the trees that grew near the north side of the homestead, and came quickly toward them. As the figure approached they saw it was Jane Weston. They stood still and waited for her to come up to them. She had hurried over the rough field, hastening her steps, almost running, as she drew nearer, and her breath was short when she addressed them.

"Ruth, Ruth," she cried, "where have you been? Your grandmother is ill fretting about you. I have been to the gate at least twenty times. Do you know you left the house before four o'clock this afternoon?"

"Let me explain," said Captain Hathaway, stepping forward. "I returned from Boston this afternoon. Ruth was at my sister's." Jane started when he said "Ruth." "We urged her to stay and drink tea with us. I brought her home." He paused a moment, then, lifting Ruth's cold little hand that hung by her side, said, "Miss Weston, Ruth has promised to marry me."

Jane did not speak. She swayed forward slightly and clutched at the stone wall.

"To marry you?" she said, slowly. "Surely

that cannot be. You scarcely know each other;
she was but a child when you went away. No, no,
there must be some mistake."

"We have known each other long enough to
love each other, Aunt Jane. I have given him my
promise."

Ruth spoke firmly. She drew closer to Jack's
side. Jack did not speak; he was watching Jane's
face closely. In the uncertain light it looked gray
and drawn.

"Captain Hathaway," said Jane, slowly, "I do
not know what to say. Perhaps you may have
noticed that my manner has not been cordial to you
heretofore. I had reasons for my conduct—good
reasons. I wish to speak plainly. I am a straightforward woman, and I find it always the better
course to pursue."

Jack bowed, but did not reply.

Miss Weston hesitated; she appeared to be thinking intently. It was very still; no vehicles were
passing. Nothing was heard except the soft lapping of the surf at the foot of the pasture-lot and
the whirring hum of the summer insects. Suddenly
she said:

"Captain Hathaway, my sister, Mrs. Lorrimer,

and I have grave reasons why you should not come to the homestead. I cannot explain these reasons; they must be our secret. It would be cruel to tell you. In the most pointed manner we made you feel you were not welcome; still you persisted. We cannot blame ourselves—we did our best. As for marrying Ruth, that is utterly impossible. It cannot be; Mrs. Lorrimer would never consent. Dearly as she loves the child she would see her dead first."

In the gleam that fell from the now star-lighted sky Ruth saw Captain Hathaway clench and unclench his strong brown hands, and the cords swell in ridges upon his forehead. He was a strong-willed man, not used to opposition.

"Then, Miss Weston, I understand that I am to give up Ruth on a paltry, insignificant explanation —some old woman's nonsensical gossip. No, I shall not obey your wishes. An explanation is due Ruth and me, without which I shall continue in my course."

"It is no gossip," said Jane, solemnly; "it is truth—sad, sad truth. It is hard for you, but it must be; there is no other way."

"It shall not be," he said, fiercely. "I will not give her up. She is mine; she has given herself to me. No power less than God's above shall part us."

Jane started as if struck at his vehemence. She had not bargained upon the power of his affection. She bowed her head as though in tribute to his strength and courage. He was a brave man; she admired him for that.

"I can say no more," she said, sadly. "Come, Ruth, let us go home. Say good-night; it is growing late."

"Good-night, Jack," said Ruth, putting both arms about his neck and kissing him. "It will come right. Remember, I shall always be true; nothing shall change me."

He watched them gloomily as they crossed the field and were soon lost in the darkness of the trees of the avenue. "What bugbears are these old women conjuring up?" he muttered. "I see it all; they don't wish Ruth to go to sea. The selfishness of age is wonderful. They have had their day, now they wish Ruth to be sacrificed for their comfort; to grow old wearing her life away dreaming in the manor, waiting on them, reading to them. Bah! she's worth a better life than that. The end of it will be I'll have to run away with her."

CHAPTER VI.

DR. GOODYEAR'S OFFER REJECTED.

THE morning following the conversation in which Jane Weston had given her ultimatum in regard to Ruth's betrothal, Captain Hathaway made his way to the residence of Dr. Goodyear. It was early. No one was astir in the aristocratic portion of the town, though down below the hill, near the water-side, could be heard the shrill voices of the fisher-men's wives, as they bustled in and out of their houses, busy at the morning's work. The fleet of fishing-vessels, broad, strong-ribbed boats, with their square-trimmed sails, was bobbing about in the harbor. The lusty shouts of "Heave ahoy, hey, my boys!" interspersed with bits of stronger language and snatches of song, rang out loudly and at intervals on the still morning air.

Captain Hathaway looked grave and preoccupied. He had not slept well, and his brilliant blue eyes had lost some of their habitual sparkle. He switched with a stick he carried in his hand the heads of the inoffensive daisies that grew along the walk. At times he stopped and bit his lip impatiently, and gazed in a meditative manner over the town below, toward the "Bonny Kate," where she rode gracefully on the tide, the sunlight shining on her glistening sides.

"Dr. Goodyear knows this absurd secret, whatever it is," he thought, "and I'll have it out of him. He's known the family since his boyhood, and knows all about them. If there's anything to tell he's the man to tell it."

Dr. Goodyear was an early riser. When the Captain lifted the latch of the garden gate the doctor was at work at his favorite occupation, that of pruning and tending his roses. The doctor's rose-garden was the pride and pleasure of his life, and in fact it was the pride of Lynnport. A more beautiful spot could not be found on the New England coast than the doctor's rose-garden in the last two weeks of June and the first two of July. Roses— roses everywhere; white, yellow, red, and pink. And the doctor, looking not unlike a very much overblown cabbage-rose himself, might be seen standing during many of his spare hours among his lovely favorites.

The doctor had put on a long apron, and wore on his head a large-brimmed hat. He was standing on a chair, endeavoring to tack a refractory rose-vine to a trellis.

"Good morning, Captain," he shouted. "On deck early, hey?"

"Yes," said the Captain, in a rather depressed tone.

The doctor started at the sound of his voice, and, turning with his mouth full of tacks and a hammer uplifted, glanced at him sharply.

"What's up, Captain? Want medical advice? Going to take a reef in your sails, hey?"

"No," said Jack, moodily. "Get down from that chair, doctor. I wish to discuss a serious matter with you; at least it is serious to me. I want your close attention."

Dr. Goodyear stepped down from the chair, threw off his apron, and stepping up to the Captain laid his hand kindly on his arm.

"Well, what is it, my boy?"

"It's about Ruth. I have asked her to marry me. She has consented; but the old people, for some ridiculous reason, have given me my discharge-papers—shipped me off without a word of explanation, except some bosh about a secret they couldn't tell. You know all about the manor folks; I want you to tell me what you know."

The doctor looked grave; his jolly red face took on a serious aspect, and he gazed down sadly.

"Well, Jack, according to their views they are acting right. I do not agree with them, but it is not my business to interfere. I know this secret to which they allude, though I am not at liberty to speak of it. I have never spoken of it to any one since the sad occurrence many years ago. My advice to you would be, give up Ruth Lorrimer, turn the bows of the 'Bonny Kate' toward sea, and in five years' time, when you return to Lynnport, the wound will have healed. I'm a medical man; I know all about wounds; trust me."

"I shall not give her up," cried Jack, vehemently. "By Heaven, I'll marry her if I have to run away with her."

"Hush!" said Dr. Goodyear. "Don't say that; it would kill the old lady. Let me tell you, Captain, her heart is a weak one; one hard blow and—well, she'd be out of it all."

Jack did not heed these words. His eyes flashed with anger.

"Am I to give up the greatest happiness that has ever come into my life—give it up for some paltry whim? I tell you, doctor, I'm not the man to do that. I will know this accursed secret. If Ruth is smirched by its telling I'll marry her the sooner, and love and protect her." There were tears in the Captain's eyes, and his voice trembled as he ceased speaking.

"There is nothing against Ruth; set your mind at rest on that point."

"What is it, then? Tell me. Can you not see what this suspense is costing me?"

"I cannot tell you, Jack. God knows, I am sorry. You are a brave fellow, and I like you. Fate is against you, my boy. I cannot help you."

Jack went back to his sister's. After some moments of irresolution his plans were made. He would see Mrs. Lorrimer—force his presence upon her—and compel her to speak; then declare he would marry Ruth with or without her grandmother's consent. He would not go to the homestead till afternoon, needing some hours to steady his nerves for the interview.

About eleven o'clock of the same day, Jane Weston, with Tetsy at her heels, entered Dr. Goodyear's rose-garden. The doctor was not at home—out seeing patients, she was informed by his housekeeper. She waited impatiently in the summer-house in the garden, with Tetsy dozing at her feet, Poor Jane! she had scarcely slept all night. Her long, thin face wore a mournful expression; even the proud and towering head-dress took part in the general crestfallen appearance. Tetsy for once was forgotten. Two or three times she accidentally kicked him as she moved her feet restlessly; but his menacing grumble quickly brought her to her senses, and she carefully moved her chair back.

At twelve o'clock sharp the doctor came home. Upon seeing his visitor in the arbor he rushed precipitately toward her, with hands outstretched and his face beaming.

"Well, Miss Weston," he said, "this is a pleasure and an honor—a great honor. Do you know, it is thirty years since you have been inside my garden gates—thirty years?"

"Is it so long?" she said, sharply. "Well, what is the use of reminding me of it? I am not so fond of being told I am growing old."

"Oh no, no—certainly not. I did not mean that. You take one up so quickly, Miss Weston."

"You say strange things, Dr. Goodyear. I came here to-day to ask you to tell Captain Hathaway why he cannot marry Ruth." The doctor gazed at her in open-mouthed amazement, then closed his mouth grimly and puckered up his forehead. "You know the whole story," she continued. "There is no use of being particular about the details; tell him all."

"But—but—Miss Weston," stammered the doctor, "I—I—"

"There is no but about it," interrupted Jane. "You must tell it. I cannot go over the miserable affair, and Mary is too weak; it would kill her even to see him. There is no other alternative. You are the man to do it, and I have decided you shall." She gave him a commanding glance.

The doctor gazed at her earnestly for a moment, a crafty gleam in his eyes, then straightened up his stout figure, put one hand in his vest-pocket, and walked in a slow, dignified manner up and down the rose-bordered path before the arbor. Occasionally he balanced himself on his toes and pursed up his mouth in a thoughtful manner. Presently he paused before Jane, who was watching him uneasily, this dignity and decision of character being at variance with his hitherto abject obedience, almost amounting to slavishness, in his dealings with her.

"Jane Weston," he said, clearing his voice in a most impressive manner, "I have asked you to marry me twenty-nine times—once every year for twenty-nine years. Now of your own accord you have come to me, just as I was about thinking of asking you for the thirtieth time. If you will marry me I will do what you wish: I will blast this young man's hopes, get hated by him in the bargain, ruin poor Ruth's happiness, and feel myself the biggest brute on earth.   What do you say, Jane?"

Jane had risen with her most majestic air; and Tetsy had also risen, and was watching the doctor's fat legs with a sinister gleam in his eyes and a suspicious twitching of his jaws.

"I say this, Dr. Goodyear: that you have taken advantage of me, trying to force a promise on such terms, when we are in dire straits.   I am surprised and pained.   For the thirtieth time I say no."

"Very well, Miss Jane, very well, have it your own way; only don't say I am not patient and long-suffering.   I'll never give up trying this side of Jordan; and, if you don't yield, the good book tells us that there is plenty of time to work on the other side of the river."

"You are growing profane, Dr. Goodyear. The good book says there shall be no marriage nor giving in marriage there. I shall not listen to you."

Upon reaching the gate she turned.

"So you will not do this for me?" she said, sadly. "I do not ask many favors of you."

"I will do it on those terms—none other," said the doctor, firmly.

She twitched her shoulders angrily and passed through the gate, the doctor holding it open as she passed through. At the same instant a most blood-curdling howl was heard from Tetsy, whom, whether by accident or design, the doctor had shut-in the gate.

The doctor looked extremely innocent and sympathetic when Jane lifted her pet; but giving him a severe, reprimanding glance, she marched off like a grenadier down the hill. After she had disappeared, the doctor stood for a long time among his roses, pruning here and clipping there. Finally he gathered a handful of blown leaves for the potpourri in the parlor.

"Jane Weston is a fine woman," he said to himself. "Much as I would like to have her, and as long as I have waited, it would have come pretty hard to break up Ruth's happiness, poor girl. Yet I would have done it if Jane had said the word. Not she, though; she's stuck it out all these years. I suppose now we're pretty old hulls to be sailing into the sea of matrimony. By Heaven! I can't help it." He brought his hand down heavily upon the back of a rustic garden seat. "Jane Weston always was, and always will be, the only woman in the world for me."

The doctor stayed home the rest of the day, and from his den at the top of the house, which contained a telescope pointed always seaward, detected Captain Hathaway, toward afternoon, going along the highway that skirted the sea, in the direction of the Lorrimer place. He was going at a swinging pace, and the doctor conjectured, as he watched him till he disappeared from sight, that a crisis was approaching. Going to the top of the stairs he called loudly to the old, partially deaf housekeeper: "Tell John to put the mare in the traces and have the gig ready at a moment's notice." Then he went back to the window and looked out ear-

nestly, not removing his gaze often from the highway.

Dr. Goodyear was an earnest, thoughtful man in
spite of his outward exuberance of spirits. He was
a man possessed of keen insight into human nature,
and was blessed, or burdened, as some might inter-
pret it, with a very tender heart. Though his experience had not been great in some respects, having rarely traveled beyond the confines of Lynnport,
still he had sufficient field for study in the little
town, tragedies and comedies being played before
his eyes many times through the passing years.
He had been one of the actors that figured years
before in the sad story that had taken place at the
homestead. He was thinking of it now, as he
watched the highroad, wondering what the end
would be. As for himself, time had cut down the
sharp edges and thrown a mellow light over the
dark places. He knew the ladies did not think as
he did; yet in dwelling on the past they only increased its dreary importance.

To drag Ruth's happy girlhood into their griefs
was wrong and selfish. Why not let her have her
happiness and be silent? What good could it do
them to shatter her idol and show her the dark,

tempestuous side of life?   The story was forgotten in Lynnport; in fact, it had never rightly been understood there, the details, jealously guarded, never reaching the ears of the gossips.   It had happened so many years ago that most of the persons connected with it were dead.   The doctor pondered and waited in his den, looking out moodily from his dormer-window.

Captain Hathaway had given much thought to his intended resolution.   His nerves were steady and he was in complete control of himself as he walked up the avenue of elms to the old manor-house.

Miss Weston was not at home—she had not returned from Lynnport, the maid said at the door. Mrs. Lorrimer was at home and in the north drawing-room.   The girl hesitated.   "She is not well, and I do not think she will see you."

"She will see me," the Captain said, decidedly, removing his hat.

The girl stepped aside, a little frightened at his tone, and he crossed the wide hall.   The door of the drawing-room was ajar, the windows overlooking the sea were open, and he felt the breeze on his face as he entered the room.

Seated in a high-backed chair, her head resting wearily against its cushions, was Mrs. Lorrimer. She was either dozing or thinking intently; her eyes were closed and the exquisite lines of her face were in repose, while the soft white puffs of hair threw a shadow upon her brow. A white embroidered shawl was draped about her shoulders and fastened at the neck by a pin of brilliants. Over her hands fell folds of delicate lace, and the rich silk gown, falling gracefully about her, verily suggested a grand dame of a past age.

Captain Hathaway hesitated in the doorway and watched her covertly an instant. He knew she had not heard him. He was only a plain seafaring man after all, and a barrier appeared to loom up between him and her. She was of the old decade, he of the new. He recognized the exquisite refinement, the gentle dignity, and it impressed him. He turned his gaze upon the long line of pompous ancestors on the wall, with their simpering ladies, much be-wigged and beruffled, beside them, then at the great fireplace with its Dutch scriptural tiles. Set in the cornices of the mantel he saw two portraits that made him start, they appeared so lifelike. Evidently, judging from the places of honor they occupied in the room, they represented the parents of the present owners.   He could trace a likeness in the handsome patrician face of the pictured officer in his continental uniform, the haughty poise of his head, and the proud curve of the mobile mouth, to the old lady in the chair by the window.   Yes, there was the same pride, the same will.   He stepped forward and stood by her side.

Mrs. Lorrimer turned quickly, and with eyes slowly dilating looked at him.   Her face grew white, her slender hands clutched the arms of her chair, and an unearthly glow lit up her features.

" Jack," she said, hoarsely, " Jack, have you come back from the grave to make all right again ? "   She rose partly in her chair and swayed slightly toward him, her lips parted and her hands dropped by her side.

Captain Hathaway was dumbfounded.   He caught her in his arms, placed her gently back in the chair, and stood watching her solicitously.

" Mrs. Lorrimer," he said, presently, " I startled you ; forgive me.   I am Captain Hathaway, captain of the ' Bonny Kate,' that plies between Boston and China.   You have heard Ruth speak of me."

Mrs. Lorrimer's startled features slowly relaxed ;

then, taking on a stony rigidity, she straightened
herself, and, looking the young man unflinchingly in
the face, said:

"How did you enter my house?   I have given
orders you were not to be admitted."

"I felt my right, Mrs. Lorrimer.   I love your
granddaughter and she has promised to marry me.
Miss Weston has told me you would never consent.
I deemed it but common justice that you should
give me an explanation.   My past life is clear; you
can read it.   I can take care of a wife; the 'Bonny
Kate' pays well.   I have spoken plainly.   I am a
plain seaman, Mrs. Lorrimer, and we sailors are
blunt spokesmen."

Mrs. Lorrimer did not speak for some moments;
her face had grown ghastly and her heart was beating rapidly.   Presently she said:

"I would rather bury Ruth than give her to you.
I will never consent to your marriage with her—
never, never!"   She almost screamed, so shrill had
her voice grown.   "My reasons are grave ones.   If
Ruth understood them she would agree with me."

"You will not explain the reasons for your opposition, then?" said the Captain.   He was still standing erect and firm, looking every whit as proud and

handsome as the picture of the continental officer in the mantel cornice.

"No," said Mrs. Lorrimer, "I will not.   The reasons do not prove a lawful barrier.   You might overstep them in your headstrong desire to marry Ruth.   They are strong enough in my eyes, and it is my will that you shall renounce her."

"I will not renounce her," he said, quietly.   "I shall marry her.   You have no right to step between us; your reasons are nothing to me.   Unless I receive dismissal from her own lips she shall be my wife before the summer is over."

Mrs. Lorrimer had now risen; her costly brocade was streaming over the polished floor.   She stood tall and straight, one jeweled hand held out before her; with her forefinger she pointed directly toward Captain Hathaway.

"If you marry her," she said, "I shall never forgive her.   The day she is your wife I shall know her no more."

The quiet decision of her voice impressed Captain Hathaway.   He knew she meant every word she uttered; it was no idle threat.

"So be it," he said.   "If God so ordains it that her own cast her out she shall find a protector for all time in me." His voice was solemn. He stepped toward the door, hat in hand. When on the threshold he looked back. A line of yellow sunlight had fallen over Mrs. Lorrimer's face, and touched the brilliants at her throat. It served, however, only to bring the ghastliness of her features into plainer relief. She was watching her visitor intently with her bright dark eyes, her hand still held out before her.

"Take her, then, Captain Hathaway," she said, "and take an injured woman's curse with her."

"No, no, Mrs. Lorrimer, do not say that," he exclaimed. "Take back those words." He looked wistfully toward her.

"I shall say no more," she replied; "I have finished."

He left her standing in the glow of yellow sunlight, her tall, erect figure looking as stately and defiant as the pictured company upon the wall. When Captain Hathaway gave her a last glance as he still hesitated upon the threshold, impelled by some motive he looked above her head, where the eyes of the continental officer seemed to be watching the two antagonists, measuring their strength as they faced each other. Was it fancy, or the result of

vibrating waves of air in the long, drafty apartment?
The placid features of the picture seemed to lengthen
out, grow grim and stern, and a malicious gleam appeared to settle in the eyes, while above the heart
a dull-red glow like blood flickered a moment, then
passed away.   Jack knew it was only the reflection
from a red-glass vase the sunlight had touched
upon the table; yet a coldness crept over him, a
trembling of the limbs seized him.   Sailors are
naturally superstitious.

When he passed from the subdued gloom of the
drawing-room and stood without, in the warm,
bright sunlight on the piazza, he felt chilled, and
wiped the drops of cold perspiration from his forehead.   As he left the gates at the entrance of the
place he passed Jane Weston, who did not address
him, but gave him an alarmed glance and hastened
on.   When she reached the house she hurried to
Mrs. Lorrimer and found her lying white and still
upon the floor of the drawing-room, beneath the
picture of the officer in the cornice.   She leaned
over her and raised her in her arms.

" Mary, Mary," she called; and her cries alarmed
the household.   Later, when Dr. Goodyear came
rushing in his antique gig down the highway, and

hurried to the homestead, Mrs. Lorrimer was lying in her own room, Ruth and Jane weeping over her. She had spoken once, but her speech was so broken and incoherent that they did not understand her. Then she had relapsed into unconsciousness. Dr. Goodyear said little. He was very grave.

"It is a heart-seizure, Miss Weston," he said, as he was getting into his gig. "Remember, I warned you. Watch her."

Jane spoke impetuously and angrily:

"I have watched her, goodness knows. That wretched young man was here again, and forced himself upon her—just walked by the maid and went into the drawing-room. If you had done what I asked you this morning this would not have happened; he would not have come here again."

"If you had done what I asked *you* this morning I would be a happy man this very minute."

"What utter folly! Haven't I told you for thirty years that the Widow Grims, on the old post-road, would make you a good wife, and a suitable one too? You are a most obstinate man."

"And haven't I told you for thirty years that Dr. Ezekiel Goodyear, of Lynnport, would make you a good husband, and a suitable one too?"

"Good afternoon, doctor," she snapped, shortly. "Shall I give Mary the drops every twenty minutes?"

Jane gathered up her scant skirts and walked sedately up the steps of the piazza. The doctor looked after her a moment with an amused smile, then, taking the reins in his hands, went at a brisk trot down the avenue.

CHAPTER VII.

THE CAPTAIN INTERVIEWS MRS. MUNN.

WHEN Captain Hathaway reached the principal
street of the town he was in a condition of exhaustion from the effects of his rapid walk and the scene
of excitement through which he had passed. His
dark hair was wet with moisture and clung to his
forehead, his bronzed cheeks were pale, and his tall
figure drooped forward listlessly. Passing slowly
along the village street in her wheeled chair sat
Kate, propelled by her faithful companion, who was
jealously looking out that no stone obtruded its
discomforting presence between the wheels and the
pavement. The Captain saw them from a distance,
and surmised, from the constant bobbing forward
of Mrs. Munn's head, and her backward glances at
the passers-by, that she was making comments upon
the neighbors while she pushed her charge along.
The Captain slackened his pace as he joined them,

and, taking the handle of the chair from Mrs. Munn's grasp, said he would wheel Kate up the steep hills. It was growing late, and it was time she returned to the cottage.

Kate could not see his face as he stood at the back of her chair. Mrs. Munn did, however; nothing escaped her keen glance. She knew something had happened; it must be about Miss Ruth. She would bide her time; they would tell her before long. She walked stoically after them, her grim face set, her firm tread coming down heavy and loud upon the walk. When they entered the cottage parlor Jack came and stood by his sister, and looking down upon her said:

"Kate, things are going hard with Ruth and me. The old people have refused their consent, and they mean it; it is not idle talk. Our hopes are crushed, confound their obstinacy!" He seated himself impatiently and rapped nervously on the arms of his chair.

"But why?" said Kate, anxiously. "What are their reasons?"

At this point of the conversation Mrs. Munn rose to leave the room. The Captain called her back.

"Don't go, Mrs. Munn," he said. "You are a

good friend; perhaps you can give me some advice."

Mrs. Munn sat down in a stiff-backed chair. Folding her hands in her lap, she drew her face down to the regulation mournful expression which she considered the occasion required.

"You asked me Mrs. Lorrimer's reasons, Kate. It seems they are so serious that she would rather Ruth were dead than give her to me. Further she will not say. I cannot give her up, Kate; you must know that. She has promised to marry me. What nonsensical yarn can those two old women have conjured?"

"You must not be rash, Jack; perhaps Mrs. Lorrimer will relent."

"No," said Jack, decidedly, "she never will; I am fully convinced of that. Kate, you should have seen the old lady. She frightened me, she looked so pale and fierce."

At these words a contemptuous sniff from Mrs. Munn caused him to look in her direction. She was sitting bolt upright, her angular figure had struck an angry and defiant attitude, and one large, gaitered foot was tapping the floor with systematic treads.

"Those ladies at the homestead are a proud lot,"

she said. " They think you are not good enough,
Captain, for Miss Ruth. Mrs. Lorrimer has had the
courage to fly in the face of Providence. Did she
say she would rather see that pretty creature dead
than married to you? The Lord will lay his hand
hard on her some day, Captain Hathaway—hard
and long."

The Captain stared at her gloomily. " That
won't help us now, Mrs. Munn," he said, sadly.

" No. Let me tell you," she cried, excitedly,
" what happened to Mirandy Evans—she that married Si Evans, that kept the light on the ledge.
Well, she had a son—a good fellow he was, too—
and he was a-goin' to marry as nice a girl as ever lived ;
her home was over to the east of Lynnport, back
of the hollow. For some reason Mirandy was dead
set against the match.. Well, from the very start
she acted offish and cold to the girl, and talked
against her and her folks. Well, the girl was kinder
proud, and she give Si up. She said she wa'n't
goin' into a family that didn't want her." Here
Mrs. Munn paused and looked reflectively out of
the window ; then continued : " Why, it must be
some sixteen years ago it happened ; it seems like
yesterday. Well, as I was a-sayin', when Si found

out she wouldn't have him he went to his mother, and he just stood in front of her (I heard it from a friend who was there), and he says, ' Mother, I'm a-goin' to sea, and I'm never comin' back unless I comes as a corpse, as has no will of its own.'   Mirandy didn't believe him at first, but he went away, and, true enough, he never came back.   Ten years ago come next Thanksgivin' I was at the light. Mirandy was sittin' by the window; she was always a-sittin' there since Si went away, a-watchin' and a-watchin', but she never spoke of him.   I always thought Mirandy kinder daft after her trouble with Si."   Captain Hathaway was listening interestedly; Kate was leaning forward in her chair, her eyes bent earnestly upon Mrs. Munn.   " It was awful rough and stormy that Thanksgivin'; the wind blew, and the surf was fearful high.   Mirandy she sat there, and she never spoke; and my heart did pity her husband, old Si.   Well, all of a sudden she stood up, and she just screamed out, ' Si has come back, Si has come back.'   And sure enough, next mornin' they found his body on the ledge, washed up by the tide.   His ship had foundered outside, and the bodies kept a-washin' up for some days.   We never knew whether Mirandy saw him from the window or not; she never told us.   But she was a poor daft creature till she died, two years ago."

No one spoke for a moment, then Mrs. Munn said:

"You asked for my advice, Captain.   I say, marry Miss Ruth.   The old ladies are proud and high-stomached.   Take heed from Mirandy; she meddled with the Lord's own plans and He punished her."

"I will marry her, Mrs. Munn, if she will consent," said the Captain, solemnly.

Kate did not speak; she sat very still.   She was in one of her day-dreams.   Perhaps in her dream she saw a vision, for, looking up suddenly, she beckoned to her brother.

"Come here, Jack," she said, sadly; "come close beside me;" then, taking his hand, held it tightly in hers.   "If—if—" she said, slowly, "anything should happen to part you and Ruth, would you take it very hard, dear?"   She looked tenderly into his face.

"It would kill me, Kate," he said, vehemently. "I should do as Si did—I should go away forever." Jack's head was bowed and a tremor ran through his strong frame.

"Oh no, no!" said Kate, "not that—forever!"

Here Mrs. Munn interposed; she never could see Kate in tears.

"Now, Captain, don't take on so," she said, briskly. "You know there is another side to everything in this world. Goodness knows, I hope Miss Ruth won't go back on you; but even if she should you won't die, Captain, you won't die. Why, Ebenezer Whitcomb, over at the corners, lost his sweetheart about two years ago. I was there when she died. She was a gentle, good creature, and he went on awful. I never see anything like it. Why, he tore up all his clothes; said he would never want anything any more—what was clothes to him? And he cried so loud you could hear him at the cross-roads, half a mile away. The day of the burial, why, his brothers just held him up, he was so tot-terin'; and he kept a-hollerin,' ' Bury me too. Throw the dirt on me too.' And if it hadn't been for the scandal I'd 'a' thrown a hull handful at him. Well, the end of it all was, he married in six months, a good sharp woman that'll take all the foolishness out of him. No, no, Captain, men never die for a girl; a good case of fever is much more likely."

The Captain did not seem to hear her.   He crossed the room, sat down by the window, looked out through the vines that crept over the trellis, and thought of Ruth.   Yes, he would do as Si did: he would never return to Lynnport if anything parted him from Ruth.   It would harden him —that he knew.   Yet why should he lose her?   He would not think of that.   No, he would drive that horrid thought from him.   How sweet and fair she was! how brave and true!   He could trust her; she would leave all for him.   They would go away together; she would follow the sea with him; and, some day, when he had made his fortune, they would come back to Lynnport.   He would build a great house like the homestead, give up his roving life, and be a model landowner.

The following day was Sunday, and Captain Hathaway wended his way to the village church. The little wooden edifice stood on a high knoll that overlooked the greater portion of the town.   In order to reach the church the townspeople had built steps in the steep incline, in preference to lowering the foundation.   For, as they said in their town-meeting, "Our ancestors set the church upon a hill to serve both as a fort against their enemies, the Indians, and as a beacon to the sailors; so we will not molest it."

Ruth was in church that Sunday morning, and alone. She sat in the square Lorrimer pew, her head not reaching the top of its spacious back. A very forlorn little worshiper she was, troubled and perplexed about many things.

The old Puritan minister droned away through a long, doleful sermon. It seemed to her as though the firstly, secondly, thirdly, fourthly, and "to conclude" would never come to an end and she be free to converse with Jack. She had caught a glimpse of his tall figure as he entered the church. Finally the congregation was dismissed. Ruth tripped down the aisle and out into the sunshine. She looked very dainty and sweet that Sabbath morning, with scant skirts just reaching her slim ankles, and little slippered feet peeping out below dainty lace ruffles, her large, plume-bedecked hat casting a softening shade over the pretty face, her white-silk mitts drawn well up over her arms, and an embroidered bag hanging by her side, containing her handkerchief, smelling-salts, and a simple repast of caraway-seeds.

Captain Hathaway joined her instantly, and drew her away from the thoroughfare, crowded with worshipers, to a quiet side street that led down to the water's edge.   At sight of his face she grew pale and looked troubled.   He hurried her on with an impetuous ardor that frightened her.   Though Ruth knew nothing of what had passed in the interview between Jack and her grandmother, she conjectured it was that interview which had caused the serious seizure, and from which she was slowly recovering.

When they reached a retired spot, sheltered from the gaze of any passers-by, near an overhanging ledge upon which grew scrub-bushes and stunted cedars, the Captain held Ruth closely to his side and looked so earnestly into her face that she became alarmed.

" Jack," she said, " what is it?   Tell me.   Something has happened ; tell me."

" Mrs. Lorrimer has forbidden me to see you ; has commanded me to give you up.   Ruth, you would not give me up, dear? "   His voice trembled and broke.   He held her head against his shoulder, and his blue eyes were looking wistfully into hers.

"No, never," she said. "I will not give you up. I am your promised wife; I will be true to you."

Ruth released herself from his clasp, and stepping nearer to the waterside stood silent a moment, looking over the harbor. The bay was dotted with ships of the fishing-fleet that were anchored over the Sabbath day. Beyond them, rolling gently on the tide, loomed up the black hull and tall masts of the " Bonny Kate." It had rained the night before, and the great sails of the strong brig were spread in the morning breeze to dry. She watched the quiet scene through blinding tears, then came back to Jack's side.

"I have thought it all over, Jack," she said. "I will marry you, but we must wait. I cannot come to you without grandmother's consent."

"She will never give it," he exclaimed, fiercely. "I will not wait for that. I will not wait until the dead, by their silence, give consent to what in life they opposed. No, you must come to me now, Ruth—now while she lives."

"I cannot," she said, sadly. "I would never be happy with you, Jack, if I thought I had broken the heart of the best friend I ever had."

"You must come to me, Ruth." Then, more

quickly : " In September I shall sail for China, to be gone five years. The ' Bonny Kate ' goes to Boston in August to load her cargo. After that we must make our plans. She will lie at the wharf till we sail."

" September!" she said, sadly ; "only two months off, and you will be gone five years."

" I shall be gone forever if I do not take you with me. Do you know what you are doing, Ruth? You care for me—you have told me so—and I—I am too plain of speech to say how much I love you. You must feel it, you must know it, and yet you ask me to go away for five years, only to hear from you at long intervals of months, perhaps years. You cannot mean it. No, we must get married this summer. Before the vessel sails we can take the stage-coach to Boston, embark there, leaving a letter explaining all to Mrs. Lorrimer, and shake the dust of Lynnport off our feet. I swear, Ruth, I'll make you happy. You were intended for a sailor's wife, and you shall have the cosiest nest that was ever made on board a fast clipper." He laughed, and pushed his cap back from his crisp, wavy hair.

" Do not ask me to decide now ; I must think it

over carefully," she said. "We have two months before us."

"Yes, but I cannot see you. I am forbidden to call at the homestead, and you will be watched closely."

"No, my grandmother will never do that. She will trust to my honor; she would not believe me capable of deceiving her. Even now, when I shall be late home from church, she will not think I am with you. It is very hard for me, Jack." Ruth turned impetuously toward him, her pretty face flushed, her eyes full of tears. "I shall not give you up. Some way must be found to right matters. If, when September comes, grandmother is still opposed to our marriage, I will—yes, I will go away with you."

He caught her to him and kissed her passionately.

"Then," he said, "I care for nothing else. What does it matter, after all? We have to live our lives; no one can live them for us. This secret, whatever it may be, can go to their graves with them. It must not darken our prospects."

"Ah! this secret," she murmured; "what can it be? I shudder when I think of it."

At this instant they were disturbed by a crackling in the bushes that grew upon the ledge above them.   Looking upward they saw the jolly red face of Dr. Goodyear through an opening in the pines peering down upon them.

"Well, well, well!" he ejaculated.   "Tut, tut, tut! This will never do—never in the world.   Come up here this instant, you two foolish creatures.   I have been looking for you everywhere."

Jack and Ruth laughed; then Jack helped her up the steep incline, where presently they stood by the doctor's side upon the ledge.   The old man looked at them suspiciously.

"Now, Ruth," he said, "this must not happen again.   It is fully an hour and a half since church was over.   I have already been to the homestead and back.   They are in a nice state of excitement about you—at least your Aunt Jane is.   She has told Mrs. Lorrimer, under my directions (I said I would take the lie on my shoulders), that you had gone home with Mrs. Burton.   I went so far as to say I'd seen you enter Mrs. Burton's gate.   What do you mean by making an old man lie like that— on Sunday morning, too?"

"O doctor, I am so sorry," said Ruth.   "If you

will only drive me home in the gig I will never do it again."

"Well," said the doctor, gruffly, "how about the Captain? What does he promise?"

"I promise nothing," said Jack, haughtily. "I am beholden to no man."

The doctor gave him a keen glance. "So it is to be warfare?" he said.

"Yes, but open warfare. If I can win I shall. I have told them so. I have given them warning. Obstacles are nothing to me. I know my own mind; I am captain of my own ship."

"Go ahead, my boy, go ahead. May a good breeze and fair tide go with you and take you into a safe harbor. Don't say, though, if anything happens, the old doctor didn't give a bit of advice."

"I want no one's advice; I can steer my own course."

The doctor shook his head dubiously.

Ruth was taken to the homestead by the doctor. Jack went back to his sister's cottage.

That evening, after Kate had been made ready for the night, in her pretty room that overlooked the village and the sea, Jack made his way to the kitchen, where he knew he should find Mrs. Munn.

The kitchen was a pleasant room, large and airy. It had a southern exposure that overlooked the vegetable-garden, whose practical growth flourished green and inviting amid a profuse mass of brilliant, hardy annuals. On the walls of the kitchen the tins gleamed in the light of the candles that stood on the shelf, and the open fireplace still held a few dying embers that sputtered feebly underneath the great pot that hung upon the iron crane.

Mrs. Munn was in her Sunday attire of black. She sported a marvelous cap of huge dimensions, surmounted by masses of lavender ribbon. At her throat was a pin made from a lock of the lamented Munn's hair. She was sitting by the table reading her Bible. She looked up when the Captain entered, and laid one hand on its open page.

The Captain leaned against the shelf above the fireplace and gazed moodily into its open, cavernous mouth.

Mrs. Munn did not speak. She watched him silently, with a covert admiration, thinking he was the handsomest man she ever saw.

After some moments he said, abruptly: " Mrs. Munn, can you remember many years back in your life? I don't mean to ask how old you are," he concluded, hastily—"nothing of the kind; only to see if you can recall an incident about which I am puzzled."

Mrs. Munn bridled slightly. She was sensitive about her age, and considered prying on that point an impertinence.

"Yes, I can remember a good number of years back. I always had a good memory."

"Do you remember, or did you ever hear of anything strange happening at the Lorrimer place? It must have been a great many years ago."

Mrs. Munn closed her Bible and gazed reflectively down upon the shining boards of the kitchen floor.

"Well, now you speak of it," she said, "it appears to me I heard somethin' did happen there once. I never heard it from mother, though; she never gossiped, and she was as afraid of a gossip as of a rattlesnake. She used to say to me, 'Now, Sarah, when they begin talking, fly, for those is the warnin' rattles—'"

"What do you remember in connection with this story of the Lorrimers?" interrupted the Captain, impatiently.

"Well, I heard somethin' once from old Nancy

Martin. She had the longest, sharpest tongue in all Lynnport; she just cut right and left with it, like a two-edged sword. She said the Lorrimers and Westons were quality and thought themselves awful big, but if everything was known about them they couldn't hold their heads up in Lynnport again. Then she said old Henry Weston came home from the war because somethin' had happened at the homestead, and it killed him. He did die fearful sudden, I know, and nobody ever knew just what he died of. There was some kind of talk at the time, but it got hushed up."

" Is that all you know? "

" Yes, that's all I ever heard. You see I was young at the time; and la sakes! old Nancy's been dead for years and years. They say she died from cold, taken by being pumped on at the village pump on account of her scandalous stories. She was eighty-six. I guess it wasn't the pump; it was old age." .

" I am sorry you know nothing further," said the Captain, in a disappointed tone. " I had hoped you would remember. At any rate, Mrs. Munn, story or no story, I am going to marry Ruth. We are going to run away together if nothing better offers."

"Well, I declare!" said Mrs. Munn, looking up eagerly. There was quite a spice of romance in her grim, shrewd composition, and she enjoyed intensely being taken into the Captain's confidence. "She's a sweet creature, Captain, Miss Ruth is, and it's all like a story out of a book."

"You must not speak of this, Mrs. Munn. I tell you because I like and trust you."

"I'd be a martyr at the stake before I'd tell a word," she said. Then, with a little sniffle, she gazed around the kitchen, to the rafters hung with herbs and strings of peppers, then back to the Captain; and putting her apron to her eyes, she sobbed aloud.

"Don't speak to me, Captain, don't speak to me; just let me have my cry out. You put me so much in mind of Munn: just the way he stood up, so straight and tall—oh dear, oh dear!—when he said, 'Sarah, we'll be as happy as the day is long.'"

As the Captain in his boyhood had seen the lamented Munn, remembering well his corpulent figure and red, swollen visage, and the terrible life he led his faithful wife, he was not duly impressed by Mrs. Munn's last remark. Going up to her kindly, however, he put his hand on her shoulder, and said:

"Don't feel so, Mrs. Munn. This life isn't so very long after all, and you will meet him again."

This speech had a startling effect. Mrs. Munn rose hastily, and taking her Bible in her hand blew out one of the candles.

"No, Captain," she said, decidedly, "I shall never see Munn again; he is not one of the elect. It is ten o'clock and time for bed."

The Captain not moving instantly, she took the other candle and marched toward the door, leaving him to follow, secretly much amused.

CHAPTER VIII.

RUTH DEMANDS AN EXPLANATION.

JULY and August passed; it was the first week in
September. The weather was fine, just a snap of
coolness in the atmosphere toward evening, and a suspicious glow upon the hills, harbinger of the coming of the blue autumn haze. The mackerel had
put in an appearance off the ledge beyond the harbor's mouth, and the fleet made ready daily, at the
first faint glimmer of the dawn, for operations on
the fishing-grounds.

September was a busy month in Lynnport. The
bluefish would run sometimes until late in the
month, and the mackerel would crowd in upon
their tardy departure, giving the men plenty of
work and hard-earned profits.

The "Bonny Kate" left the bay for Boston in
August, and the handsome brig was missed from

her anchorage, where she had delighted the eyes of the fishermen for weeks past.

During all this time Mrs. Lorrimer remained weak and languid, keeping her room part of the day; then, helped tenderly to the piazza by Ruth and Jane, she would sit in the sunshine, looking silently over the water that rolled swiftly out to sea past the foot of the manor-house grounds.

Now that September had come and the days were shortening, settling down early into chilly nights, she sat in the north drawing-room before a wood-fire that burned brightly in the great open fireplace.

She had never mentioned Captain Hathaway's name in these past weeks. As the days followed one another poor Ruth lost all hope of her grandmother's relenting or explaining.

" No," she thought, " she will never consent. She thinks I have given him up; that everything is over, and I have forgotten him—as if I ever could forget. I dare not speak to her; her heart is weak. They have warned me to be careful."

Ruth had seen Jack many times during the past two months. Many long walks they had taken in the woodlands back from the sea; many a lover's chat had they enjoyed, sitting in the protecting shadow of some kindly boulder. They had grown closer together after each meeting. Perhaps the very fact of their being stolen meetings, secrecy and vigilance attending them, made them the more treasured.

Ruth had grown to understand Jack's passionate nature, his strong, indomitable will, and his exceeding tenderness of heart. She valued his love, grateful for her happiness, surrounded as it was with doubts and misgivings.

At times his impetuous avowals frightened and overwhelmed her. Everything must be swept aside; no obstacles must be heeded, no barriers permitted. Ruth drifted down the sweet, stolen currents of her love-story like a little bark, happy in the protecting guidance of a strong hand; wondering, fearing, and loving deeply.

The middle of September came. On the 24th the "Bonny Kate" would put out to sea, and the Captain must take his bride aboard. Ruth, with her cold, trembling hand in her lover's, promised she would give up her home, the interests of her girlhood, the love of those who had been kind to her from babyhood, and go with him out into that new, untried life.

"It is cruel, Jack," she sobbed; "it is cruel."

When she gave this promise they were standing on a rocky ledge that projected far out into the sea. The little town lay back of them. They seemed quite alone in the world. Everything was very still, except the dull booming of the surf in the caverns below them, and the occasional wild cry of a gull or a cormorant as he winged his swooping flight over the water.

"Cruel!" echoed Jack, vehemently. "Would you rather give me up? Are they more to you than I am?"

"No, no," she cried, clinging to him, "you know they are not. Can you not see what you are to me, when I am willing to renounce them for you? O Jack, do not be harsh to me. Am I not going away into a new world all alone with you? I have never been far from home, Jack."

"Ruth," he said, "I will be more than all to you. I will; I swear it. I will make up to you for all you lose. If not, may God visit it upon me!"

He made the plans, she acquiesced in silence.

On the evening of the 23d they proposed taking the stage that started from the post-house at the cross-roads. They would reach Boston the following day, be married, and go on board the vessel an hour or two before she sailed. Ruth need take very little baggage with her, as she would not require a great deal on board ship; what was necessary she could purchase in Boston. They would send a letter back by the stage-driver to Mrs. Lorrimer, and when she received it the brig would be miles out at sea.

The 20th of September came, and with it a great storm—the "line storm," as the sailors called it. It swept the coast with a relentless fury that kept the fishing-boats anchored in their safe harbor. Even there the motion of the sea penetrated, and the little stout vessels strained, pulled, and dragged at their anchors. Their owners, with their brown, weather-beaten faces filled with a pathetic solicitude, watched them anxiously from shore.

Mrs. Munn wheeled Kate down to the beach in the afternoon, after the rain ceased, to watch the tremendous sea that came rolling in, dashing against the bulkheads, then receding with a dull, baffled roar, casting spray far inland.

The rain was over, but the sky was filled with banks of gray, drifting clouds, that hurried on with impetuous velocity, driven before the wind.

Mrs. Munn had a woolen shawl pinned tightly over her head, and her cotton skirts blew fiercely in the gale, displaying a substantial pair of gaitered feet. She was drawing in her breath with the delicious sense of inhaling drafts of salt air, and her gray eyes were bent seaward. She turned abruptly at the sound of a voice near by.

"Well, Sarah Munn, how is your health these days?"

A sun-browned, middle-aged man was addressing her. His gray hair hung thick and bushy about his face, which was seamed and wrinkled by exposure to the weather. He was dressed in a tarpaulin suit, the water glistening on its oily surface, and in one hand he held a string of fish.

"I'm well, Jim Benton. How are you, and your mother and Mehetabel?"

"Middlin', middlin', Mrs. Munn."

At this instant Mrs. Munn glanced out to sea again. Impelled by some unaccountable motive, she looked toward the east. Outlined against the gray sky she saw two figures standing close together on the ledge near the entrance to the bay.

The man's gaze followed hers. He started and drew nearer to his companion, then looked apprehensively toward Kate. She did not seem to be heeding them; her gaze was riveted on a red glow in the west, where the sun was bursting forth like a fire in the sky, the gray clouds rushing before its light.

"It's the Captain and Miss Ruth," volunteered Jim, clutching Mrs. Munn's sleeve. "They're a-courtin'. How does the old people take it, Mrs. Munn?" He peered up into her face with his small, bright eyes.

"I am sure I don't know what you mean, Jim Benton," replied Mrs. Munn, with some asperity, as she dropped her grasp on the handle of Kate's chair and drew aside a few paces.

"I only asked a civil question. There's good reasons why the old lady shouldn't like it. I'd be salted for a herrin' if I'd like it in her place."

Mrs. Munn looked at him sharply.

"Tell what you know, Jim Benton, and be done with it. If there is anything I hate it is this insinuatin'."

"You're a rude, onsociable woman, Mrs. Munn," said Jim, angrily, as he turned aside. "You can whistle for the story."

Mrs. Munn laid her hand on his arm.

"You're as techy as you can be.   Is there any-thing against the Captain, Jim?"

"No, it ain't that," said Jim, partly mollified. "I never heard anything against him. I never knew the rights on it anyhow, only there was an awful thing happened down at the homestead years ago.   You know old General Weston, who served with General Washington most all through the war?   Well, I heerd he cursed every one of the Hathaways, root and branch.   It was all along o' somethin' some o' the old Hathaways done; and the curse has come home to the whole lot o' them except the Captain.   Look at Miss Kate, there, all hunched out o' shape; ain't that a curse?"

"Pshaw!" said Mrs. Munn.   "You're a bigger silly than I took you to be, Jim Benton.   You, a Christian man, to believe in curses!   The hand of God was laid on Miss Kate as an example to us to be grateful for our better lot; anyhow, that's what my Bible says.   Don't you go round spreadin' her-esy and schism like that."

Jim drew back in rather a shamefaced manner.

"I'm an orthodox man, Mrs. Munn.   I ain't a schism-spreader.   It's only been once in a great while I fished on Sunday, and then I was tempted by the fish walkin', as you might say, right up to my house. The house is almost on the dock. There they was, a-shinin' and a-glistenin', and it wa'n't in weak human nature to let 'em go by; but I sang hymns the whole evenin' with the old mother after the fish was cleaned."

Mrs. Munn eyed him disapprovingly.

"I don't believe in that kind of restitution," she said. "I'll warrant you ate the fish before you sang the hymns." Putting her hand upon her refractory skirts, which stood out like a balloon, she continued, seeing that the old man did not reply: "Well, I must be goin'. It's gettin' dark; it's cold for Miss Kate."

Ruth had made arrangements for her flight. The little possessions that she treasured had been packed with an extra change of clothing in a box she purposed carrying when she left the homestead.

It was the morning of the 23d of September. The long storm was over. She rose early, and with tear-dimmed eyes looked over the lovely prospect that she would perhaps never see again.

Ruth appeared to be in a dream, a daze. She hardly knew herself; her senses were benumbed. When they spoke to her she did not comprehend them; her replies were mechanically forced, and without meaning. As the morning sped on a fever seized upon her. She went into her garden, where all was cool and quiet, where she loved every flower, shrub, and tree. She looked sadly upon the flowers in their decay. The September storm had dealt hardly with them: they were crushed to earth, their beauty tarnished. Here and there some bright, defiant blossom glistened in the sunshine, erect, unconscious of the decree of nature and of time.

"It is better so," she said, softly. "It would have been harder to leave them in their beauty. Now they are all going away, even as I am. The snow will soon come and cover up their graves."

She leaned against the well-sweep; her tears dropped upon the mossy curb where she had planted the ferns and lichens.

The day had been gray and dull at intervals, though bright gleams of sunshine flooded the landscape occasionally, harbingers of a clear day to-morrow. One felt the chill of autumn in the air, saw it in the scanty bloom of the garden, and heard it in the moaning sound among the pines.

Ruth drew her mantle closer about her shoulders

and shivered a little in the cold. The gleam of sunshine suddenly vanished, and the girl's preoccupied gaze wandered drearily around the pleasant inclosure. A few leaves, early fallen, rustled at her feet; she picked them up mechanically and held them in her hand. She did not hear the click of the garden gate, or a step upon the grass at her side. She started, feeling a hand laid on her arm. She turned and saw it was Jane, who looked earnestly at her, with kind sympathy in her eyes.

"Come, Ruth," she said, "it is growing cold; come to the house."

All the pent-up fear, sorrow, and anxiety in Ruth's heart broke forth at the tender tone of sympathy, and she turned impetuously.

"O Aunt Jane," she said, brokenly, "I—"

"Yes, dear, I know; his ship sails to-morrow. I feel deeply for you, Ruth." Aunt Jane, usually so undemonstrative, leaned over Ruth and kissed her gently. "It is hard, my little girl," she said; "be brave."

"Oh, you do not know, Aunt Jane; you do not understand." Ruth was speaking impetuously, the words gushing forth in a torrent. "Why should I give him up? He is more to me than all the world.

He is worthy, good, and true, and I feel it is my
right—it is justice—I should know why you wish
to part us.   I have been silent, yet I have not renounced him—no, he is dearer to me than ever."

Jane drew back appalled at the passionate entreaty
in Ruth's voice.   The sweet face was white and
drawn, the soft eyes had grown dark and luminous
with intensity of feeling.   Jane did not speak; she
was looking down irresolutely.

"You must tell me," cried Ruth.   "You treat
me as a child; I am a woman.   I demand the truth;
I will have it; I will have it now; I shall wait no
longer."

Jane realized that the crisis had come.   She had
feared and dreaded this, still she felt the justice of
the girl's appeal.

"Ruth," she said, slowly, "I will tell you—but
not here; come to the house.   It is growing dark,
growing dark," she repeated.   "O my poor little
girl!"

Ruth paused and glanced about the darkening
landscape.   She was trembling, and her hands were
icy cold.   Would this story, when told, be sufficient to part her from Jack?   That was the
thought now uppermost.   Much as she wished to

hear the disclosure, she feared and dreaded it.   If
it should prove an obstacle to their union, life would
be over for her.   Yet had not her grandmother told
Jack it was not a lawful barrier?   No, it would
probably be one of honor, of principle.   She would
be brave, and hear it; then give up all the world
for him, and they would go away to those foreign
countries of which he had told her.   She hesitated
an instant, with her hand on the wooden latch.

"Come, child, come," said Jane.   "What are
you waiting for?"

"I was only waiting," said Ruth, "and thinking."
Suddenly she caught her aunt's arm and held it like
a vise.   "Will it part us, aunt?   Will it part Jack
and me?" she whispered, hoarsely.

"That is for you to judge, Ruth.   I cannot say;
I dare not.   Your grandmother deems it sufficient."

Ruth did not speak after that, but followed her
aunt down the graveled walk to the house.   It was
not dark in the house yet.   It faced the west.   The
windows were lighted by a red glow that had sprung
from the bank of gray clouds that lay heavy and
threatening over the sea.   The wide manor was
bathed in a ruddy light; its windows glistened like
diamonds.

They entered the hall and paused upon the threshold of the drawing-room, where Mrs. Lorrimer was seated before the fire upon the hearth. She appeared to be looking at the picture in the mantel cornice; the leaping firelight mingled with the departing gleam of the sun, making grotesque shadows across its painted surface.

Jane went directly to her, and said, looking earnestly upon her:

"Mary, I have been a good sister to you, have I not?"

"Yes, Jane," said Mrs. Lorrimer, glancing uneasily toward her, surprised at her tone and words, "you have been a good, kind sister."

"I wish you to grant me a favor.   I wish you to be calm and answer me."

"What is it, Jane?" said Mrs. Lorrimer, anxiously moving her jeweled hands.

"It is a simple act of justice.   You, not I, owe Ruth some reparation for taking away her lover. You have cast the sorrows of the past over the brightness of her early girlhood; you have expected her to receive this blow in silence and make no outcry.   She demands an explanation, and I have come to ask you for permission to speak."

"Has she, then, not forgotten him?" said Mrs. Lorrimer, slowly. "Why this explanation at this late date?"

Ruth, at these words, darted across the polished floor and, throwing herself at her grandmother's feet, said:

"No, grandmother, I have not forgotten him; I never *shall* forget him. I must know why you seek to part us. It is my right; I cannot ruin my life without a reason."

Mrs. Lorrimer rose slowly from her cushioned chair. She stood an instant looking into the fire, then, drawing her hand wearily across her brow, she said:

"Well, Jane, perhaps you are right. Tell her. I would have liked to have kept it from her; it seemed to me it was our grief, not hers; but I see now it is the only course. Our little one is a child no longer, and she must learn her birthright of sorrow. Take her away; do not tell her before me. Take her to the old garret, show her the letters, then let the subject be forever buried between us."

Mrs. Lorrimer turned her face away from them as she finished speaking, and Ruth noticed a scarlet glow overspread her features from brow to chin—a deep crimson stain, almost purple in its intensity. She said nothing further, and they went softly from the room, up the winding stairs to the great garret that lay over the entire upper story of the homestead. Its windows were uncurtained, and through them came sufficient daylight to decipher objects. The immense space was filled with discarded articles of household use, and curios gathered through passing years by different owners of the manor; old swords and scabbards hung on the wall, suspended above the heavily carved mahogany cradle that had rocked the Westons and the Lorrimers in infancy; spinning-wheels, looms, reels, churns, old books, tall battered candelabra, and cumbersome sideboards. Strung upon cords across the garret hung garments of antique pattern, with discolored lace and tarnished buttons.

Ruth caught sight of her discarded doll, sightless and battered, lying across a trunk. Could it be, she wondered, that she was the same being who not many years ago had begged on rainy days for a frolic in the garret? She thought, with that strange incongruity of the vagaries of the mind in relation to outward existing events, how she had dressed in those old garments and made believe she was a grand lady.

Jane walked straight across the garret. In her hand she carried a candle set in an old-fashioned brass candlestick. She had a duty to perform, and, like a surgeon who knows his ground and feels the just demands of the sufferer, did not wait to let the wound smart and throb.

Ruth followed. Jane seated herself in an antique chair beside a magnificently carved chest—a chest brought over the sea nearly a century before the telling of this story, a superb piece of art, which when completed had passed from the hand of a skilled workman of Holland to the keeping of the Weston family.

Ruth watched her earnestly. She took from her pocket a key and held it in her hand a moment, then paused and glanced from the garret window over the wide view beyond. Her plain features twitched slightly and her hands trembled. She balanced the key upon her finger an instant.

"Ruth," she said, "it is many years since I have opened this chest; but you must have your rights. Come closer to me, little one; let me hold you near me. I will tell you the story; then we will look into the chest, and you shall have the letters your grandmother spoke of."

Ruth drew closer to her. She was white, with an unusual pallor. The color had left her lips, but she did not speak; she only watched her aunt with an intent gaze, as a prisoner watches the jury upon whose verdict hangs his hopes.

Jane placed the key in the lock, which grated harshly, from accumulated rust and long disuse.

"Come near me, Ruth. Here, sit on this foot-rest; lean your head against me, and I will tell you the story."

CHAPTER IX.

THE LETTERS IN THE GARRET CHEST.

JANE, after some moments of deep thought, sighed deeply and began the story.

"You know, Ruth," she said, "when our grandfather fled from England to escape the cruelties and exactions of an unjust king, he brought with him love and veneration for his mother-country which had been instilled into his being from childhood.

"After settling in America he built this house and married. A most estimable woman my grandmother was, descended from an old Dutch family living on the island of the New Netherlands, as it was then called.

"My grandparents had one child, a son, my father. He, in early life, married. His wife lived six years after their marriage and died at my birth, leaving her two orphan children to the care of her Aunt Jerusha, who became our second mother.

"After my mother's death I believe my father cared little for Lynnport. He traveled much, coming at long intervals to remain only for a few days at the manor.

"As the years passed our grandparents died, and my beautiful sister Mary grew to womanhood. She was five years my senior and as lovely as I was plain. I worshiped her. And one summer, when father came home after a two years' stay in foreign lands, he started in surprise at her loveliness.

"After that he seemed to live for her and her pleasure. Nothing would do but she must be sent to England to be presented at court by Lady Guy · Weston.

"To court she went, and became the toast and belle of all the gay gallants. Many stories came across the sea of her triumphs and the attentions she received from those high in power. Father's letters were filled with accounts of her conquests. She refused many fine offers of marriage, for Mary was a coquette, and used her powers mercilessly.

"After a while father came home. Trouble was brewing in America; he returned to look after his interests. He missed Mary, and the manor seemed deserted and dull after his London life. He sent for her, and she came back to Lynnport." Jane paused, and looked thoughtful a moment, then resumed, with a sigh:

"Ruth, she was a grand, queenly woman. She was twenty-four at this time; I was nineteen. I had never become better-looking—I was always 'plain Miss Jane'—but Mary—ah, if you could have seen her! she was very, very lovely.

"The day of her arrival at Lynnport she met the man who was to win her heart. It is very mysterious how Providence orders these things. After all her triumphs, to have met her destiny in this quiet place!

"The man was John Hathaway, a young sea-captain"—Ruth started—"of plain, respectable parentage. He was what is called a trading sea-captain. His vessel plied between this port and the Indies—Lynnport was more of a commercial center in those days.

"John Hathaway was a black, piratical-looking sort of man, with the fiercest, brightest eyes I ever saw; perhaps handsome in a way. He cast a spell over Mary from the first. I could see her start and flush when he came near—my courted sister flush and tremble like a foolish girl! He did not woo

her as other men had done; he commanded her.
He knew his power.   I used to see him watching
her in a strange manner, and her eyes would fall
before his.

"Father saw nothing of this.   He would have
been displeased; he looked higher for his beautiful
daughter.

"Mary was cautious, and I watched and feared.   I
always distrusted John Hathaway; I think sometimes
I almost hated him.

"Just at this time war broke out.   Father, to
our surprise, joined the American army, and hastened to the forces gathering around General
Washington.

"When he went away I was crushed.   I knew
nothing stood between Mary and Captain Hathaway.   Aunt Jerusha had grown old and deaf; I
had no control over my spoiled, headstrong sister.

"Father had been gone nearly a year, when one
night my fears of long standing became a reality:
Mary told me she would soon become a mother.
I was wild with grief and perplexity; I did not
know which way to turn.   She would tell me nothing further—answered all my tears and prayers with
silence.

" A few weeks after that a little, sickly, wailing infant lay beside her. Ah! that terrible night comes back to me, Ruth. I sent for our old family doctor. Aunt Jerusha was going from one faint to another; I was the only one that was calm. The doctor had met with an accident and could not come, and instead sent his assistant, Dr. Goodyear, who was then a mere stripling, but had a sensible head on his shoulders. We told him nothing, and he asked no questions. When we spoke to Mary—I on my knees by the bedside—she turned her face away from us and said she could not speak—she had promised.

" I always knew Captain Hathaway was the father of the child, and I hated him with a strong, deadly hatred. I was crazed enough that night to have killed him.

" When the child was about a month old, and Mary was better and could go downstairs, I did what has been to me a lifelong regret: I sent for father—an urgent, pressing message to come home for Mary's sake." Here Jane looked sadly from the window. " It was a terrible mistake; all might have been different but for that."

It was quite dark now; the night had fallen, but

the stars had come out, and the moon—a feeble, watery moon—threw a faint light into the shadowy garret. Ruth had drawn closer to her aunt; her heart was beating wildly, and when a mouse scurried across the floor she almost screamed in terror.

"Father came home. I told him all, and took him to Mary and the child. They were alone for some time. Whatever she told him must have reassured him, for when he rejoined us his face, though saddened and pale, showed no trace of other feeling. Father stayed with us a week, then said he must rejoin the army—Washington was hard pressed and needed all his generals. It was the night before his intended departure. It was late in the fall; the days were cold—we had had a snow-storm. It was near Thanksgiving, and we were all seated before a great fire of hickory logs in the hall. Mary was there, with the child upon her knee; and she looked so beautiful that I could have fallen down and worshiped her. She was dressed in white; a scarlet shawl was about her shoulders. It was growing late; we were thinking of retiring, when Captain Hathaway entered the hall. He went straight to Mary, took the child in his arms, and, taking her by the hand, went up to father, who had risen and stood watching him.

"'General Weston, my wife and my child. Forgive me,' he said.

"Captain Hathaway's face was very white; he did not look at father when he spoke.

"Father said nothing. He tried to, but his voice died away; then he placed Mary's hand in her husband's and turned his face aside. I think it nearly killed him. I could not look at Captain Hathaway; I looked away from him and his wicked, black face, and toward the great oriel window in the end of the hall. The branches of the trees fell across this window. First I thought I saw only them, but I was mistaken, for outlined against the glass I saw a woman's face—a wild face, with great staring eyes. I screamed, rushed forward, and opened the door. On the step stood a trembling creature, holding by the hand a little, crying boy about three years old. I dragged her in out of the cold and the snow. I saw she belonged to the fisher-folk, and detected traces of what was once great beauty in the haggard face she raised to mine. She stood silent a moment, then raised her head and looked straight at Captain Hathaway—a hard, defiant look.

"I followed her gaze. The Captain's face was a picture of horror and fear; there was murder in his eye; he would have killed that woman if he had dared. She knew it, but went fearlessly to father, where he stood leaning against the mantel, and said, 'General Weston, I have been wronged; I am Captain John Hathaway's wife, and this is his child.' She held out her left hand. 'There,' she said, 'is my wedding-ring, and here'—she handed him a crumpled piece of paper drawn from the bosom of her ragged gown—'is my marriage certificate.'

" Mary looked on in a dazed way. Father took the paper, held it in his hand a moment, then read it. He glanced at the woman.

"'Is this true?' he said.

"'As true as there is a God above us!' she cried. 'Dr. Hanson, the minister—you know him, sir—he married us. He has come to Lynnport with me to see me righted. He is in the town.'

" I went to Mary, took the baby from her arms, and tried to make her lean against me. She pushed me away, and stood up as tall and straight as a pine. Then father went to Captain Hathaway.

"'Is this true?' he said.

" Captain Hathaway did not speak; he drew back, but his face gave the answer—he was a traitor.

"'You black-hearted, cowardly cur!' said father,

as he drew his sword.　I screamed, and would have rushed forward to part them, but Mary held me so tightly by the gown that, with the baby in my arms, I could not move.

"'Let father kill him,' she said.

"Captain Hathaway saw the uplifted sword and no way of escape; he was hemmed in by the cornice of the mantel.　He drew his pistol from his belt, and with sure aim sent the bullet straight home. Father threw up his arms and fell forward on the rug before the fire.　The blood gushed forth from his side; it gushed forward to Mary's feet; it crept up her white gown in red streaks.　She did not seem to see it, or that her feet were wet with it.　She went to father, lifted his head, and held it close against her heart.

"'Father,' she said, 'father, speak to me.'

"He raised himself once, and looked toward Captain Hathaway, who was watching him with horrified, dilated eyes.

"'Curses on you,' he said—'on you and yours! I curse you with my dying breath—despoiler, murderer, liar!'　And then, O Ruth, dear, he fell on his side, breathed once, and died."

Jane could not speak for some moments.　She

put her arm around the trembling girl, whose teeth chattered as though with cold, and whose throat and mouth were dry and parched.

"Little girl, I have told you nearly all of the dreadful story. We could not prosecute Captain Hathaway, who had killed father in self-defense; neither could we drag Mary's sad story through the courts. He fled from the country, and his poor wife and child were left to my care. They did not survive many years. She was an ignorant fisherman's daughter, but a most unhappy, wronged woman.

"For five years Mary never left the grounds of the homestead, and from the night of father's death never saw her child again. She disowned him, cast him forth, poor little babe! I prayed the merciful God to take him, and he answered me. When he died I begged her to see him; 'Just once,' I pleaded. She would not. So I buried the little nameless creature in a corner of God's-acre, where the kind Lord will surely find him and give him a name for all eternity."

"Did she ever see Captain Hathaway again?"

"Yes, once, after many years. In the meantime Mr. Lorrimer, a most estimable gentleman, who had loved and wooed Mary in England, came to America to renew his suit.   She told him the story, saying she had no love for any man.   He appeared content, however, and they were married.   Your father was their only child.

"Now she has been a widow many years.   It was some time after Mr..Lorrimer's death that she met Captain Hathaway.   I was with her, and we were coming from the village, and had taken the back road through the woods, when suddenly a wild-looking man stepped before us in the path, from the underbrush that grew on the side of the way. We knew him instantly.   He threw himself on his knees before her, and grasped the hem of her gown.

"'Mary,' he said, 'forgive me.   If you could know what my life has been you would forgive me. No one but God knows the remorse I have suffered—the remorse of a murderer.'

"She dragged her skirts away from his hand and hurried on.   When I looked back he was still kneeling in the dust of the road looking wistfully after us, with his gray hair flying about his face.   Why he came back to Lynnport we never knew; but he did.   With him came a young Italian wife.   By her he had two children born to him in his declining years—the twins, Jack and Kate Hathaway.

He lived the life of a recluse, and we never saw him again.

"As time passed, the story which we had endeavored to keep as much as possible from the public was forgotten. Father's death was ascribed to an accident. I doubt if any one in Lynnport except Dr. Goodyear knows the true facts. He has been our friend throughout it all. Shall we open the chest now?"

Jane had risen and lighted the candle which she had taken from the table in the hall. She placed it on a dusty stand near by. It threw a weird light over the gloom of the vast space; the articles that filled the floor rose up .tall and ghostlike in the dim, flickering glow.

"Let me ask a few questions," said Ruth, who hardly recognized her own voice; it sounded hollow, as though it came from a great distance. "Where was grandmother married?"

"She was married by a dissenting preacher at the tavern on the Boston turnpike road. She wore her wedding-ring on a cord about her neck; her certificate she kept hidden. She was a blind, deluded woman from the very first. Captain Hathaway bade her keep their marriage secret, and she did.

The ring and certificate she gave to me.   I buried them with the baby; I closed his little hand over the ring."

Here Jane burst into a passionate fit of weeping. Ruth took the candle from her, which she had taken from the stand, and she laid her head down on the old chest, her frame shaking with irrepressible sobs. Ruth had never seen her stern aunt give way to her feelings before.   She smoothed her gray hair, and said, softly:

"Oh, don't, Aunt Jane."

Presently she looked up with a shamefaced expression.

"I have not talked about it," she said, "for many years.   I feel as though it changed my life; I might have had a home of my own but for that.   I never could trust any one, and I grew soured and bitter. Oh yes, Ruth, Mary's troubles changed everything for me."

"Not bitter," said Ruth, gently.   "You are too good a woman for that."

"Well, it is all over," said Jane, sadly, "and we are both old women."   She unlocked the chest and threw back the lid.   Ruth held the candle, and the two women peered into the inclosure.   Then Jane leaned over and brought forth a package of letters yellow with time.

"These are the letters," she said, "that Captain Hathaway wrote Mary during the year she thought herself his wife.   He was away from Lynnport much of the time.

"This," she said, drawing forth a military coat of buff and blue, "is the coat father wore the night he was killed.   Look!"   She held up the garment to the light.   Across the buff vest was a dull stain.

Ruth gave a little cry of horror.   "Oh, why did you keep that?" she said.

"Mary wished it—said it was a reminder; if ever she forgot she would come up here, take it out, and look at the stain of blood.   But she never forgot or forgave."

Ruth said nothing.   She handed the letters back to Jane.

"You do not wish to read them?"

"No," said Ruth, "I know enough.   The letters are no doubt filled with vows of love and devotion. Knowing his promises ended as they did, why should I wish to read them?"

Jane closed and locked the chest.   Together they went down the stairs to the light and warmth of the hall below.   It was then for the first time that Jane looked closely at Ruth, who was deathly pale; even her lips were blue, and her eyes had a metallic glitter in their usually soft depths.

"It has frightened you," said Jane.   "I am so thankful, Ruth, you did not allow yourself to become too deeply interested in Captain Hathaway; the story would have been so much harder for you to hear.   I do not feel that his father's sins should be visited upon him—far be it from me to judge any man—but you can see how impossible it would be for Mary to consent to a marriage between you."

At these words Ruth turned fiercely upon her aunt.

"The story has made no difference to me.   He is another man; this is another age.   He knows nothing of it, or he would never have come here."

Jane stood aghast at this passionate outburst.

"Do not say this to your grandmother," she said, sternly.

Ruth did not reply.   She went rapidly down the staircase and into the drawing-room, where Mrs. Lorrimer still sat before the fireplace.   The candles had not been lighted, but the fire made a center of glowing color, and Mrs. Lorrimer's face showed quite plainly from out its surroundings of white hair and soft laces.   Ruth went straight to her and put her arms about her neck.

"Dear grandmother," she said, "you have suffered much and been deeply wronged.   I will never leave you while you live; but I shall love Jack all my life.   Sometime, perhaps years hence, if he will wait for me, I shall marry him."

Mrs. Lorrimer leaned over and took the girl's face between her hands.

"You care for him very much, Ruth?" she said.

"Yes," said Ruth, simply.

"Time will make a difference, my child.   He will go away—I am told his ship sails to-morrow—and you will not see him for years.   I am content, Ruth, with your promise.   We will say no more of this sad story; you will soon be my little light-hearted girl again."

At the words "his ship sails to-morrow" an agony smote Ruth.   She was to have gone with him.   To-night she must meet him, tell the story, and—and—bid him good-by.   She clasped her small hands together till the nails sunk into the tender flesh.   He would be waiting for her at the hollow, on the old back road to the village. Everything was ready for their flight.

A terrible temptation assailed her. Why should she not go with him? Life was short; why should she not grasp her happiness? Why should she thrust it aside?

The temptation passed. No, she had given her word, and duty and honor were due her grandmother.

Jack would wait for her, she knew, and sometime come for her. They were both young; the years would not take long to pass away. As for his father's deed, she could not visit that upon him. If she had known it long ago things would have been different; she would have been too deeply prejudiced to have done aught but scorn him. In innocence she had given her love; she had no power to take it back. His father had died a broken, contrite man, haunted by the ghost of the man he had slain. Should Jack suffer for his father's sins? No. It was an awful fate that had led that sin home to her family a second time, but it was too late now; the fiat had gone forth; she had given what she could never recall.

CHAPTER X.

THE PARTING.

IT was ten o'clock that night when Ruth stole softly and stealthily down the back staircase of the manor-house and out into the night. Everything was still about the house. People kept early hours in those days; the maids were in their beds, and the only light that showed in the darkened front of the mansion was in Mrs. Lorrimer's apartment. Ruth knew her grandmother was a poor sleeper. Since her recent illness she had been in the habit of rising and reading, sometimes till the morning hours. The outline of her figure reflected upon the curtain as she walked slowly about her room, and her once tall, stately form looked bent and stooping. Ruth stood an instant and looked up at the window.

"No," she said, "I will never leave her while she lives. Jack must wait."

Then she passed rapidly down the avenue, thence through the gates to the highway.

The place of meeting had been selected in the loneliness of the seldom-used back road, to avoid the chance encounter of any acquaintance, particularly of Dr. Goodyear, who frequently made late calls upon the scattered inhabitants of the town.

Ruth sped over the ground rapidly, her long cloak clasped tightly about her, for it had grown very cold.

The stars twinkled brightly in the frosty air, and the moonlight lay upon the ground in brilliant white patches.   She had only a short distance to walk on the main road, then she turned into the grass-grown lane of the seldom-used thoroughfare.   As she neared the hollow, where the swamp-lilies and sweet-flag grew in great profusion, a well-known figure stepped from some bushes by the roadside, and hurried with outstretched arms to meet her. It was Jack, who clasped the little trembling form in his arms and rained kisses on her face.

"My brave little girl!" he said.   "So you gave them the slip, did you?   Where is your baggage? Couldn't bring it, hey?   Well, never mind; we'll get the things in Boston.   You ought to see your locker on board the brig; it's the cosiest berth on any ship afloat, though not good enough for you, Ruth, not good enough for you."

Ruth released herself from his arms and drew away from him. Her agitation was so great that she thought she should have fallen at his feet. She leaned heavily against the trunk of a tree near by, and placed one hand over her heart. She thought she could hear its rapid beating.

Jack was watching her sharply, with a mystified air.

"Jack," she said, hoarsely—the words seemed wrung from her in a very agony of feeling—"I cannot go with you; I dare not."

"Dare not, will not go with me, Ruth? You cannot break your promise," he said, sharply.

"I *must* break my promise; I made it in ignorance. I have heard the reasons for their opposition to our marriage. I repeat, I dare not go with you; my duty is here."

"You are crazed, Ruth. Do you know you are breaking your solemn word, almost a vow?"

"I know; yet it is better broken than kept. Do not make this harder than it is, Jack. You will think as I do when you hear all. You will say I have done right. I have come here this night to tell you the story I have heard to-day. It has changed our plans; it must change them—it could not be otherwise."

She was working herself into a frenzy as the conviction became forced upon her that even in the face of what she was about to tell he would still be opposed to her decision.

He watched her gloomily, his face set and stern in the glow of the moonlight that fell across it.

Then Ruth, with bowed head and clasped hands, told the sad story of her grandmother's girlhood and his father's treachery and cruelty. Jack did not interrupt her; he hardly appeared to show the interest an ordinary auditor would have felt in such a tragic disclosure. Yet he felt it deeply, felt it acutely; it cut like a knife into his heart. Now much that was mysterious in his boyhood was made clear: his father's silence and moroseness; his sleepless nights, when his cries and groans and prayers reëchoed through the stillness of their cottage upon the island; his young mother's fear of her gloomy husband; and the shunning of his fellow-beings, from whom he fled as from a pestilence.

Yes, it was true; he could not doubt it in the face of such evidence. Ruth's sweet face was turned to him, her cloak thrown back; her white neck gleamed like snow, her hands were clasped, and her voice was low and pleading as she finished her story.

. "Now you see, Jack, why we must part for a while. I could not marry you while grandmother lives; I could not break her heart. She has suffered much. She was proud, dear; it was harder for her. She had been beautiful, and beloved by many noble gentlemen, and might have been a duchess had she wished. She gave it all up for your father, and he —he broke her heart."

Ruth's voice ceased in a nervous, trembling sob.

"I am not my father," said Jack, fiercely. "He was a hound, if he was my father."

"Hush, hush!" she said, "he is dead; and I am sure, and so is Aunt Jane, that he was truly contrite. We must not judge him."

"Yet you judge me by him," he said. "You cast me forth for his sins. You bid me tear out of my heart the love which is all I have to live for, all that is making me a better man. I had a hard boyhood, Ruth; it is in me to become a hard man. Save me from that, Ruth. My God! you cannot give me up!"

At the last sentence his voice rang out in a cry of vehement entreaty. Ruth shivered and trembled from head to foot; in the palms of her hands cold perspiration gathered in drops.

"No," she said; "I love you and always shall; but we must wait—a few years is not a lifetime. After grandmother is at rest I can come to you. It is an awful fate, Jack, that has given us this love. Once given we cannot return it; would that it were possible—it would be so much better for us both. In all nature it seems that I should hate you and you should shun me."

He took a step toward her, stood tall and straight before her. The moon had risen high in the heavens, and was shining full and clear upon them. Around them it was very still; a rustle of leaves on the ground, as now and then one fluttered to the earth, was all that broke the intense quiet. Occasionally the call of a night-heron far off toward the sea rang out discordant and shrill.

"Ruth," Jack said, "I have thought it over while you have been speaking. Something tells me if I wait a few years I shall wait forever—that is, forever as far as this world is concerned. I have decided you must come with me to-night. You are mine,

I am yours; I will not give you up. Let the past go. Why should we wreck our lives by what happened years ago—something you and I should never have known? No, Ruth, we will go away from them forever, and make a new home in some foreign country where nothing can remind us of this wretched story. We will be happy; it shall never be spoken of between us."

"No, no," she said, "I cannot go. God would never prosper us."

"You will not go?" he said, vehemently.

"No, I dare not," she whispered.

"Is that all you have to say? You renounce me?" he cried.

"No, I do not renounce you; I ask you to wait."

"I will not wait. You must go with me now—now, I say."

"I will not go, Jack," she replied, firmly.

He made a move toward her as though he would have carried her by force, then hesitated.

"It is good-by forever, then," he cried. "You have thrown me over for my father's sins, you have made me suffer for him. You have never loved me: you have a cold heart, Ruth; you lied to me when you said you loved me. You gave me your promise, only to break it at your pleasure. You deceived me, took all I had to give, only to fling it worthless into my face again."

"O Jack, for pity's sake, spare me!   I did love you, I do—"

She held out her trembling hands as if to ward off a blow.   He did not heed her.

"We will part, then.   You will never see me in Lynnport again; when I go this time I go forever.   Mark that, Ruth; I will never see you again if you bid me go."   He waited.   "Shall I go?" he said, taking her in his arms and looking down into her face.   "Tell me, Ruth, tell me," he said.

"I cannot go with you," she replied.

He thrust her roughly from him.   She would have fallen had she not grasped the branch of a tree that fell across the roadside.   She was watching him like some hunted animal, her breath coming in gasps.   Could this icy coldness that was creeping over her be the agony of death—this trance that froze the words upon her tongue?

Jack looked once toward her, a long look of despair and anger.

"Good-by, Ruth; you willed it so; it is forever. I shall keep my word; you shall never see my face again." That was all he said, then he turned and went from her. She watched him till the shadows of night hid him from her gaze, then leaned forward and listened till the echo of his footsteps died away. Without a sound she drew her cloak about her and sank down upon the ground in the darkness.

She heard nothing; she had forgotten her surroundings. Time was swallowed up, obliterated, in the intensity of her great sorrow. Only one thing stood prominently before her mind: Jack had gone, and forever. She would never see him again—she knew he had left her never to return, and he would keep his word. Her precious love-story had been shattered and destroyed by her own hand. She had ruined her life, and had no one to blame but herself. Yet could she have done otherwise? Was any other course possible?

She crouched in the chilliness of the frosty night, a little huddled heap of mental misery. The leaves, driven by a rising wind, fell about her and partially covered her. She heeded nothing—neither the chilliness nor the rising wind.

On the sequestered back road where the meeting between the lovers had taken place stood a few farm-houses, situated at considerable distance from one another. In one of them a woman had been taken suddenly ill. Her husband had hurried across lots to the village for Dr. Goodyear. The doctor made his call, and on returning deemed it the wiser course to leave the rough, badly kept shore road and enter the grassy lane, where the mare could keep her feet safely from ruts and mud-holes.

The doctor had been provoked with his patient, who had gotten him up in the middle of the night merely for some ailment which the family could have relieved. He was grumbling aloud as he drove slowly through the grass-grown road. Suddenly the mare reared upon her hind feet, then stood still, her ears twitching nervously.

"Hoity-toity, old lady!" said the doctor, craning his head forward. "At your age, too! Cutting up didoes, hey?"

At this instant a gray heap moved by the side of the road, and the doctor's face was a study.

"For gracious sake!" he said, "what can that be?" Springing from the gig, he went forward. The mare appeared satisfied; she stood still—she knew a firm hand was on the rein. The doctor leaned over the figure in the road, then drew back aghast. "It's Ruth Lorrimer," he said. Without another word he lifted her from the ground, and, putting his arm about her, guided her steps to the carriage. "Come," he said, "I must take you home."

"No, no, not home," she said; "not there—not yet. Take me to Kate, take me to Kate. She will understand; she knew we were going away together. He has gone, and I—I am left alone."

Dr. Goodyear did not reply. He understood it all; her few words were sufficient. He lifted her gently into the gig and turned his horse's head back over the road upon which he had come, fearing a possible recognition upon the highway.

It was growing late; in fact, the morning hours were rapidly approaching. The moon and stars were showing dim; a pale streak of dull gray was visible in the east.

Mrs. Munn had slept poorly. Kate also had been restless. She knew her brother's plans and hopes; her thoughts were too intent upon him and Ruth for repose. Mrs. Munn had stayed with her and snatched "cat naps," as she called them, upon the sofa in her room.

When at daybreak Mrs. Munn distinguished the sound of wheels upon the road, and heard them stop abruptly before the cottage, she sprang from the lounge, and darting to the window looked out between the closed slats of the shutters.

"For the land's sake!" she whispered, "if it ain't Miss Ruth and Dr. Goodyear. What can it mean?" Regardless of her prodigious night-cap and short flannel. wrapper, after glancing at the bed to assure herself that Miss Kate was asleep, she hurried from the room, down the stairs, and out into the gray morning light.

Dr. Goodyear was leading Ruth into the cottage. She walked slowly; and she did not seem to see any one; her eyes were fixed intently. She was looking upon another picture—Jack's hard-set face when he said good-by.

Mrs. Munn was too sensible to ask questions. She took Ruth's hand in hers, and led her into the guest-chamber, which was upon the ground floor of the cottage.

Ruth mechanically obeyed her in all things. Presently she was lying upon the bed in one of Kate's soft silk wrappers. She had not spoken since entering the house. She did not speak now—she only lay there very still and white, her eyes wide open, looking fixedly before her.

Mrs. Munn left her and joined the doctor, who was pacing restlessly backward and forward in the narrow entry-hall. He appeared careworn and tired in the early morning light that was creeping in gray and cold, displaying the outlines the darkness had hidden.

"This is a nice business, Mrs. Munn," he said, sternly. "So the Captain has been urging Ruth to run away from her home?" He glanced sharply at Mrs. Munn.

Mrs. Munn looked shamefaced an instant; even her night-cap seemed to droop disconsolately. Then she faced the doctor defiantly, and said:

"Yes, doctor, the Captain did want her to go with him. Miss Kate and I knew all about it and advised it. We wanted to see them happy."

"You are foolish women. How could she be happy pursuing such a course? Do you know it would have killed Mrs. Lorrimer?"

"She is a proud, haughty body," replied Mrs. Munn, with asperity.

"You don't know what you are talking about," said the doctor. "Wait till you know more before you give an opinion; you have made a great mistake." He paused and looked thoughtful a moment, then continued: "I want you to go to the home-stead, find Miss Weston, and bring her here. Tell her to deceive Mrs. Lorrimer as to her errand. I will go to the stable and put Miss Kate's horse in the gig—the mare is used up. Drive as fast as you can—hasten."

After a few moments of preparation Mrs. Munn was speeding the horse over the highway to the manor-house.

Jane was aroused from sleep by the knocking of Mrs. Munn's strong knuckles upon her bedroom door, she having refused the maid permission to carry any message. Miss Weston arose, and dressed hastily while Mrs. Munn was acquainting her with the details of the unfortunate affair.

"The Captain did it for the best, Miss Weston," she sobbed, hysterically. "He couldn't get Miss Ruth no other way, and we couldn't see no reason why he shouldn't marry her. Don't bear Miss Kate no ill feelin'. Oh dear, oh dear! this is a sad world. Why at the last she didn't go, for the life of me I can't see. The ways of Providence is past findin' out."

"I know why she did not go, Mrs. Munn. Some-time, perhaps, Ruth will tell you. Poor child, she is young to bear the sorrows which by right others should bear for her."

Mrs. Lorrimer was very weak that morning; the allusion to her mournful story the night previous had unnerved her. When Jane went to her she said she would keep her room for a few days. She did not ask for Ruth, and Jane told her she was going to the village to see a sick woman—Dr. Goodyear had sent for her.

When Jane entered the tiny guest-chamber at the cottage she was shocked at the change a few hours had made in Ruth's appearance. She looked old—lines had deepened in her round face and about her mouth, and a look of indifferent apathy had given place to her usually bright, interested expression.

"She has had a shock," whispered the doctor. "Don't ask her questions—wait till she speaks."

Ruth did not speak for three days. At the end of that time she arose and asked for Kate, Mrs. Munn, and Aunt Jane—she had something to tell them; and she told them the whole story.

It was hard for Jane to listen again to the sad recital of her sister's trouble. She bore it bravely, however; only now and then a tear dropped into her lap.

Mrs. Munn was sobbing piteously when Ruth finished. Her apron was over her head, and she was rocking back and forth.

Kate sat still, her beautiful, spiritual face white as death.

"I tell you this, Kate," Ruth said, wearily, "that you can be my judge. Did I do right to wreck Jack's life? He told me I had ruined him. Did I do right? Tell me, Kate, tell me; you who are so near to God must know. It is the thought of this that makes it all the harder for me."

Kate looked earnestly upon the tearful, pleading face, then beckoned to her, and Ruth came and knelt down beside her.

"Dear," she said, "Jack is my brother, the dearest tie I have on earth; yet I think you chose the best and only course. It is a great grief to you both; you must live it down and not let it ruin your life at the outset."

"I care nothing for my life," cried Ruth, recklessly—"only Jack's. Will it make him hard and unhappy? O Kate, will he come back to Lynnport? Not now—not for many years, perhaps—but will he come sometime?"

For some moments Kate Hathaway did not reply.

Her face revealed the mental struggle through which she was passing. She understood her brother better than any one else did, and knew he would never return to Lynnport; knew that probably they would never hear of him again. Yet it was hard to tell Ruth, this poor little sorrow-tossed girl, struggling with her first great grief; but there was nothing else to do.

"Try and forget him, dear," she said; "he will never come back."

Laying her head against Kate's chair, Ruth burst into a torrent of uncontrollable sobs.

Mrs. Munn would have gone to her and lifted her.

Kate said, "No, it is better for her; it is nature's relief."

At the close of the day Ruth returned to the manor-house. When she stood by Jane in the parlor of the cottage, bidding Kate good-by, she said:

"It is all over, Kate—my old life, I mean. I shall never know what it is to be as happy again, or—or—as miserable. We will not speak of it any more."

"No," said Kate, simply.

Mrs. Munn had been a wretched woman for the past three days. Possessing a strong sense of justice, her cruel condemnation of Mrs. Lorrimer had filled her with remorse. She had spent many hours of the night praying that her own hard heart might be softened. "Poor lady," she thought, "poor lady! Munn was bad, goodness knows, but I hadn't that to suffer."

When Jane was about taking her departure with Ruth they paused awhile in the front garden. Mrs. Munn gathered a small bouquet of autumn flowers for Ruth. "The Captain planted them," she whispered. Mrs. Munn's face was flushed; her hands trembled with extreme agitation.

"Miss Weston," she gasped, "I want to ask your pardon. I've said hard things about you and Mrs. Lorrimer; it was before I knew what I know now. I'm a broken-hearted woman about advisin' the Captain and all. I said the Lord would lay his hand heavy on her, and He's laid it heavy on me instead. I'm sorry, Miss Weston, and you won't bear me no ill will, will you, or Miss Kate?" She paused.

"No, Mrs. Munn," said Jane, kindly. "Think no more about it."

"Well, I'm glad; and it's the last time, if I live to be as old as Methuselah or any of the other prophets, I'll ever meddle in a love-affair again—no, sir, not for the wealth of the Indies. Though I did it for the best—I thought they would be happy."

Ruth did not speak as they drove over the old familiar road. She looked toward the sea and wondered where his ship was. Only three days since he went away; it seemed a year, so much had happened. Was she only three days older? Why, she was a woman now; three days ago she was only a little girl.

She watched the golden-rod and the Michaelmas daisies on the roadside, wondering if they grew in the countries where Jack was going; and if they did, when he saw them, would he think of her and Lynnport? "No," she thought, sadly, "he will have hard, bitter thoughts of me; he will never understand the truth."

They passed into the shaded avenue. Ruth looked back as the old man from the lodge closed the gates after them.

"He is closing the gates, Aunt Jane," she said, softly; "closing the old life, and," with a wan smile, "beginning the new."

CHAPTER XI.

RUTH TAKES UP HER CROSS.

RUTH took up her cross. A very heavy cross it was, and weightily it rested upon the young shoulders which hitherto had borne but the light pressure of a happy existence.

She had known no sorrows in her sheltered, petted girlhood; no cruel winds of misfortune had been allowed to blow upon her tender frame. Had it been possible, had circumstances been different, the sad story she had been forced to hear would have been kept from her through life. Mrs. Lorrimer and Jane would have taken the tragic secret to their graves with them—the grief of their generation, not hers.

The irony of fate had decreed it otherwise. Twice had the bolt fallen in the same place; twice had it struck, and fatally.

Mrs. Lorrimer knew nothing of the elopement

escapade. Why should she know it? It would deeply grieve her, and she was hastening rapidly, with weakened feet, toward the swift-flowing river that guards that land of peace. If God willed, she should know all in that new life; so be it—but not here, not here; so argued Ruth and Jane.

Mrs. Lorrimer, as time weakened her faculties, appeared to view things in a different light—the light that belittles the affairs of man, that dwarfs the one-time mighty question of existence, that makes the longest life as but a single day, the greatest sorrow as a passing cloud.

Though she never repented the obstacles that had been placed in the way of Ruth's marriage, she was filled with deep sympathy for the sad, silent girl who went so noiselessly about the old house, never singing, or running up and down the wide staircase with Tetsy at her heels, or laughing in the old, merry, girlish way.

Not that Ruth was idle—oh no; she was constantly employed, feverishly seeking occupation.

People take sorrows so differently in this world. Temperaments, environments, inherited traits, must be taken into account when gauging the depths of grief and its possible effect.

With Ruth it ran a peculiar course: it made her reserved, sensitive, and melancholy. Unlike some young, impulsive natures, she did not seek solace in religion—quite the contrary; she fled from it; it could not help her, she said bitterly to herself. She and Jack had tried to do the best they could, yet God had no pity on them; He had parted them. Now she did not care what became of her. She grew hard, nursed and petted her trouble, mourning over it in secret, yet jealously guarding it, allowing no one to speak of it. It was her grief; she resented all interference.

Thus a year passed. Another fall, with the Michaelmas daisies and the golden-rod blooming thickly in the hedges, came to Lynnport. It was one bright morning in the early part of October—such a morning as comes with the lovely New England autumns. The blue haze was on the hills; a yellow mist hung above the harbor, the boats gleaming through its amber light as they rocked lazily on the quiet tide. Along the shore flew the wild ducks and plover, and the marshes were full of quail and woodcock.

Ruth was walking along the village street that pleasant October morning. She was alone, and the tears were in her eyes as she watched a full-rigged merchantman on the horizon, all sails set, her course toward the east. She stood a moment gazing seaward till it faded like a white mist in the distance.

An old wharf, on which a number of fishermen were sitting, their lines dangling in the water before them, lay just to the right of the street. Boxes and barrels were scattered upon the wharf, affording comfortable seats. She knew most of the men; she was tired, and went forward and seated herself upon one of the upturned boxes. A torn sail was drying near by, and some fish just caught were lying on the ground at her feet. The men turned around as she approached, and doffed their caps. She smiled and said "Good morning," then quietly watched the fishing.

From her position on the wharf she could see a great distance along the shore; in fact, almost to the harbor's mouth. Back of her lay the steep streets of the town, its church perched upon the jutting headland. She would not look that way—what had she to do with a church? She had never entered one since Jack went away, and did not think she ever would again. Presently, upon the sands at some distance, she detected a little figure advancing slowly along the water's edge. Ruth could not distinguish it clearly; it stooped constantly, and appeared to be gathering something from the stony beach.

"Jim Benton," she said, turning to one of the fishermen, "who is that?" pointing as she spoke to the slowly advancing figure.

The man looked in the direction she indicated, then burst into a loud laugh.

"That?" he said—"that's Timothy's Joe; and by thunder! if he isn't a-crabbin'."

"What! you don't mean little Joe?" she said. "Why, I didn't know he could walk."

"No more he can, Miss Lorrimer. He don't walk, he kinder creeps; sometimes for months he can't even do that. He's some better now. We fishermen told him, we says, 'Now, little Joe, when you're right smart you gather fiddler-crabs on the shore, and we'll give you a cent a dozen.' We likes them for bait—first-rate bait for blackfish and flounders."

Ruth did not speak; the sad story of poor little Joe's life was passing through her mind. Cursed with drinking, improvident parents, his very baby-hood had been a lesson in hardship, a constant seeking for refuge from blows and starvation. Then his mother died, and his father went to sea before the mast. The poor little mite embarked as scullion-boy in the cook's galley, and was nicknamed "Timothy's Joe." One night, in a drunken brawl on board ship, his father, maddened, crazed, struck the shrinking, cowering lad, felling him to the deck, then kicked him mercilessly. When Joe awoke to consciousness days after, in the ward of a hospital in a foreign land, he found one limb had been amputated and the other was twisted and distorted. His father died on the night that he maimed his boy—delirium tremens, the men said—and they buried him at sea.

By and by Joe was sent back to Lynnport. He had lived for the past two years with his grandmother, who did washing for a living. He was thirteen years old, but so small and misshapen that he appeared but eight.

Jim went back to his fishing, and Ruth, with deep sympathy in her eyes, watched the boy gradually approaching. She could distinguish perfectly his peculiar gait as he drew near. He had a crutch in one hand, and with the deformed foot pushed himself along with a sidewise, crablike motion. Around his waist, suspended by a cord, hung a tin kettle, in which every now and then he deposited a wriggling object, then a small layer of seaweed. Presently he came up the bank and stepped upon the wharf. He did not see Ruth; instead, went forward to the men.

"Say, fellers," he said, "I've got a lot of crabs —fine fat ones. Look at that!" and he held up a wriggling specimen. "I've got about four dozen; don't you want 'em?" he continued, wistfully. "It means four cents, and I've been workin' a good while. It's hard diggin' around them stones."

"Yes, we wants them, Joe," said Jim, "and we gives you an order for all you git, don't we, mates?"

"Aye, aye," said the men. "Joe's the big crab-merchant of Lynnport."

The boy laughed—such a ringing, hearty laugh that Ruth started. Could he be happy? What could make him happy? she wondered. Then he turned and saw her, and leaning on his crutch took off his ragged cap and blushed.

"Come here, Joe," said Ruth; "I want to talk to you." The boy came slowly forward and stood opposite her, his small pinched face close beside hers. "I wanted to ask you," she said, "why you laughed just now. Are you happy?"

He hesitated. "I ain't always happy," he said, shifting his cap from one hand to the other. Then, apologetically, "But I tries to be—oh! I tries to be."

"When are you unhappy?" she said, kindly.

"In the winters, when granny can't get much work, and granny and me is cold sometimes; and there ain't no crabbin' in winter, you know. Then when the pain is bad I ain't happy—the pain in my back. The doctors say when dad kicked me he hurt my spine."

"But you say you try to be happy?" she said.

"Oh yes, I tries hard. It is only sometimes I gives way—not often. It is right to try and be happy, you know."

Ruth did not speak immediately; she was thinking of Joe's reason for happiness—because it was right; then she said:

"Who first started you in the crabbing business?"

"Well, I'll tell you how that was. You see, I couldn't do nothin'. I wasn't any use to nobody; I could only set around on the wharf all day. One day some boys got a-fightin' on the wharf, and they pushed me and I fell overboard. Captain Jack Hathaway—did you know him? he was captain of his own ship, he was—he came along, and he threw off his coat—you see, I couldn't swim, 'cause I hadn't no good feet—and he just jumped right in, and he brought me to shore all right.   He is a fine man, and I tell you I was thankful to him.   After that he was good to me, and he told me to try the fiddler-crabbin'—he said they was fine bait—and he went around and asked the men to buy 'em."

When the boy finished speaking something happened that caused the row of old fishermen to look around in amazement, their lines dangling in mid-air. Ruth had drawn the boy to her and was sobbing.

"What has Joe been a-doin'?" said Jim Benton, coming forward.   "He ain't been troublin' you, Miss Lorrimer, has he?"

Ruth lifted her head.

"He has done me a great deal of good," she said; softly.   "Joe and I are going to be friends."   Joe looked down and blushed.   "He is going to show me how to be happy."   Then she rose.   "I am coming to see you and your grandmother very soon, Joe, and you must come to the manor and see me."

She gave the boy her hand.   He took it, and looked up into her face in such an adoring, reverential manner that she was greatly touched.   As she passed up the road he stood watching her.   He was twirling his cap and balancing himself upon his crutch; his face was flushed and smiling.   The men laughed at him.

"What do you see, Joe?" said Jim.   "Air you moonstruck?"

"I see," said Joe, in a whisper—"I see some one a'most as beautiful as a angel."

The men turned silently to their fishing; Joe's rhapsodies evidently were not understood.

Joe left them, and made his way to the tiniest house in the fishing-village, near the waterside.

In the latter part of October a sad calamity fell upon the quiet town: the old minister, who had faithfully served his people during a period of forty years, was called before the great Judge to give an account of his stewardship.   He had been sincerely beloved, and was deeply mourned by the entire community.   When all was over, and he was laid at rest in a quiet corner of the hillside graveyard, a serious and arduous duty devolved upon the committee selected to call the new incumbent.   After much delay and many meetings, where arguments filled the air of the parsonage parlor with a great and mighty clamor, their choice settled upon a young clergyman then filling the post of assistant in a Boston church. Letters passed and repassed. Finally the call was accepted, and the Rev. Arthur Clayton was duly installed as pastor of the Lynnport church.

It was late in December when he preached his first sermon to a crowded congregation, whose reverence and grave attention denoted their appreciation.

Arthur Clayton was not a handsome man—his face was far too rugged and strong. There was purpose and earnestness, however, in his keen eye, firm mouth, and well-formed chin. He was tall and well developed; in fact, was a good, common-sense, practical sort of man, with perhaps little sentiment or poetry in his composition, though his capacity for deep feeling was evinced by his tenderness to those in affliction.

He renounced his more lucrative position in Boston, with an encouraging future, having heard of the necessity among the fishermen of Lynnport for a man who understood them and their needs. He loved the sea and the sailors; so he came to dwell among them and be their friend.

The morning that he preached his first sermon in Lynnport, as his eye roved over the people before him, he noticed the two ladies in the Lorrimer pew —the square pew with the high, carved back and cushions. He conjectured they must be the quality of the place, the " old family."

Mrs. Lorrimer watched him earnestly as he spoke, simply, yet so effectively, no visionary ideas coupled with the good he hoped to do in his new work, asking earnestly for their friendship and aid. " If Ruth were only here," she thought, " she would not be so obdurate. Certainly a man like that could influence her."

Jane Weston had been deeply impressed. Here was a man after her own heart, who believed in praying and preaching, but who believed in working too. When she came out of church, and waited an instant on the high elevation of ground outside the edifice, she was joined rather abruptly by Mrs. Munn, who appeared to be in a state of subdued excitement.

" O Miss Weston," she cried, breathlessly, " wasn't that a fine sermon? Mr. Clayton is just the one we need. Not that I would say a word against the good old man that's gone; but don't you think it's just as well to go to heaven in some interestin' way? Dronin' sermons ain't very entertainin'. Ain't Miss Ruth goin' to come to hear him?"

"I don't know," said Jane, sadly. "She has become so interested in Timothy's Joe; perhaps he will bring her sometime."

"Don't it beat all," cried Mrs. Munn, "how she's taken to that boy? And he just adores her. I tell him he's doin' wrong: he's makin' a graven image of Miss Ruth, and fallin' down and worshipin' her. And he says—and his eyes a-shinin' like stars—'I love her better than anybody but God.' I couldn't say nothin' then. Poor creature! he ain't had any one to love before her. I'm so thankful, Miss Weston, I didn't have any children. Perhaps I wrong Munn, but in one of his tantrums he might 'a' done the same thing as Joe's father. But then I won't say anything against him—right on the church steps, too." She sighed—a long-drawn, contrite sigh. "Oh well, there's worse than Munn, there's worse than Munn; I always will contend that."

At that instant Mr. Clayton appeared at the church door, and, pausing a moment, stood there in the cold, wintry sunshine.

Mrs. Lorrimer was waiting in the church porch for

her carriage, which was rapidly approaching the foot of the steps that led to the level of the street, and she followed him as he stepped out into the light.

"Mr. Clayton," she said, her beautiful face suffused with a pleased, contented glow, "you have done me much good to-day. I am a great invalid, and made an extra effort to hear you, and have been more than rewarded." She smiled and held out her hand, which he took, bowing deeply. "Will you see me to my carriage?" she said. He offered his arm and guided her feeble steps down the steep incline, upon which, in places, a thin coating of ice was visible. Jane followed him.

When the two ladies were seated in the carriage Mrs. Lorrimer leaned from the window and said:

"We shall hope to see you soon at the homestead, Mr. Clayton. I have a granddaughter I wish you to meet."

"you to meet."

Mr. Clayton bowed; the carriage rolled away. He stood watching it a moment. "She has a granddaughter," he mused, as he made his way to the rectory, where he had taken his bachelor's quarters. "Since she was not at service she is probably an invalid. I will call very soon."

Joe had been in church, and sat in his accustomed

place by the side of his grandmother, in the very last seat by the door. It was drafty by the door, the seat was a hard one, but the old woman said she "didn't dress so well as her neighbors, she didn't want to take a top seat; she guessed the Lord would find her and Joe just as well there as He would in a square pew." So there they sat every Sunday, rain or shine, when Joe was able, always early, and always gave their little mite, both joining most vociferously in the singing of the old psalms, the grandmother's cracked treble mingling with Joe's sweet notes.

Joe had only one trouble at present; he grieved over it much in secret. Now that he had seen and heard the new minister he felt there was a possible solution of his overwhelming difficulty. It was about Miss Ruth: she never came to church. Once when he asked her—very timidly, it is true, for he felt he was taking a great liberty—she had grown white and turned away her head, saying:

"I once had a great trouble, Joe; you must not ask me about it. Since then I have never wished to go to church; but you must always go—it is right to go."

Joe was forced to be content with this answer,

but was not entirely satisfied. So he said to himself, as he watched Mr. Clayton that Sunday morning, that sometime, when he got better acquainted with the minister, he would tell him about Miss Ruth—tell him as a secret, of course. She was so good and kind to everybody, and had done so much for him and granny, and for lots of the poor folks in the fishing-town, that he wanted to see her come into church and walk up the aisle and sit in the beautifully carved high pew. He told his grandmother of his projects as he limped along beside her on his way home. Much to his surprise she silenced him peremptorily:

"Don't you go meddlin', Joe; it isn't your right to talk about Miss Ruth."

At this possible aspect of the affair his earnest face looked pained and drawn, his large, mournful eyes filled with tears.

"O granny, you ain't got no call to say that. I ain't got no legs to give, but I'd give both arms for Miss Ruth, and you know it. I'll ask Mr. Clayton, anyhow—he'll understand; he ain't goin' to get it all mixed up like that."

"Yer're a ridic'lous boy," said granny, peering at him over her glasses. "Come along; we'd better hurry home and get dinner—yer know Miss Ruth sent us a chicken fer dinner to-day."

"You hurted my feelin's," said Joe. "I don't want any dinner."

"I guess I'll bile the chicken, my teeth are so poor," was granny's answer.

"I don't want any dinner," mumbled Joe, wiping away a tear with his sleeve.

CHAPTER XII.

THE MINISTER'S WOOING.

SOME days after Mr. Clayton's instalment he made his first call at the manor-house. There had been a light fall of snow; the avenue was white with it. The great elms rustled their bare arms drearily above his head, as though protesting against the long, cold winter before them. The evergreens, heavy with an icy covering which had frozen on their green boughs, resembled white-draped ghosts. Across his path a few little shivering sparrows hopped at intervals, and a squirrel dropped a nut at his feet, then scampered away in terror. It was very quiet in the avenue; but a footstep could not be heard on account of the well-packed snow.

A turn in the road brought him in sight of the house, its white pillars gleaming in the vivid reflection of their snowy surroundings. On the pillars the brown, rustling branches of the vines glistened

as they swayed back and forth in the wind. On
the upper step of the piazza stood Ruth, clad in a
heavy cloak that fell to her feet, and her sweet face
peeped out from a fur hood.

She noticed Mr. Clayton approaching, and recognized him, as she had seen him more than once upon
the village streets. Once when he called on Kate
Hathaway, a few days previous, she had noticed his
approach through the shutters of the parlor, and fled
precipitately to the kitchen to ask Mrs. Munn if she
would give her a good recipe for making doughnuts.

Now she encountered him again. She had a
basket on her arm, and was on her way to the fishing-town on an errand of mercy. Impelled by a
feeling of perverseness she least of all could have
explained, she did not wish him to know of this
errand. She pushed the basket back of her. She
did not wish him to form a favorable opinion of her;
she wanted him to think her hard, cold, and bitter.
She tried to convince herself that she was so; that
she was changed in all things since Jack went away;
that she was no longer the Ruth Lorrimer of the old
days—only an indifferent woman, indifferent to all
kindly feeling; a mere mechanical being, who lived
and breathed without heart or soul.

She came down the steps and passed him in the snowy driveway, keeping her head averted and her slim figure erect.

He bowed and passed up the steps, wondering who she was.

After that Mr. Clayton came often to the homestead. Mrs. Lorrimer did not venture forth through that long, cold winter, and his frequent calls were a constant source of pleasure to her. She, in her laces and soft brocades, her jeweled hands folded in her lap, passed many happy hours drawn close to the fire, with Arthur Clayton beside her, his strong face and deep-toned voice lending a charm to the pleasant, sensible talks in which they indulged.

Ruth, like a spoiled, perverse child, refused to meet him. She did not want sympathy and advice expended on her, she said, bitterly. Mr. Clayton would deem it his duty to lecture her on her course, which she would not tolerate from any man.

When Mr. Clayton called again Mrs. Lorrimer told him that her granddaughter had had trouble; it had changed her, poor child!

"Was it a death?" said the minister.

"No, a disappointment."

"Oh!" said Mr. Clayton.

If Mrs. Lorrimer had looked closely she would have seen in his keen eye the ghost of a smile.

In a place like Lynnport it was not possible for two people to live within its limited borders and not know each other, at least by sight. That was the case with Ruth and Mr. Clayton. They passed each other many times on the steep, slippery streets and in the narrow alleys of the fishing-town. Mr. Clayton had become the idol of the fishermen. He formed clubs for them, talked with them, cheered them, and, greatest of all, won their confidence. They called him the " sailor parson," and a better sailor never pulled a dory or hauled a sail in the harbor of Lynnport.

Spring came late that year. The ice lasted long in the bay. It was May before the frozen earth appeared to wake up, and the bluebird's song was heard in the woods—a feeble song, as though the winds were still too sharp to give heart to the. melody.

Ruth had wandered one afternoon alone to the headland, the bold, pointed ledge of rocks upon which she had so often stood with Jack. She thought of him as she sat there watching the sea. Far below dashed the surf, booming and surging into the hollows of the rocks. The gulls were floating on the long billows, and the spotted back of a northern diver rose now and then upon the surface of the water.

" It will soon be two years since Jack went away," she thought—" two years next September." She leaned her chin in her hand, watching moodily the rolling waters before her. Presently the tears gathered and dropped into her lap. She brushed them hastily aside, and looking up saw Arthur Clayton observing her kindly and respectfully. She started hastily to her feet, and would have passed him without a word.

" Do not go," he said; " there is room enough for two on this great ledge "—he smiled—" and the view is for all."

If she ran away it would be childish; he would laugh at her; she would place herself in a ridiculous light. No, she would stay. She seated herself again. He turned from her and stood looking out to sea, drawing in long breaths of salt air. She watched him covertly—the well-cut profile, strong chin, dark, heavy hair, broad shoulders, and fine carriage.

Her past behavior appeared to assume whimsical

and childish proportions. What must he think of her?—that is, if he thought of her at all. She rose from her seat, and going to him, stood beside him and said:

"Mr. Clayton, I owe you an explanation." Her voice trembled a little as she spoke. "I am the only one of your parishioners who has never heard you preach. I have avoided you, I have refused to meet you." He turned and stood watching her gravely. "The only reason I can give for this is that I feared your persuasions to induce me to think differently. I should like to be friends with you, and I thank you for the many happy hours you have given grandmother."

"I am glad, Miss Lorrimer," he replied, kindly, "you have told me this. Suppose we become friends, and do not talk of church—just good friends."

"Oh, if you will, Mr. Clayton, I shall be so glad!"

"I give you my promise," he said. "I notice you go much among the fisher-folk; you must tell me about them—that is my chosen work."

She sat down upon the ledge. He seated himself by her side. She told him about Lynnport, her poor people, and little Joe, her comforter, as she called him.

"Why do you call him that?" said Mr. Clayton.

"He came to me," she said, softly, "when I was very unhappy, and he—he—helped me."

After that meeting on the cliffs they became good friends, and saw each other often: many times in the tiny, ill-smelling huts on the shore beside a sick-bed, or side by side stood and listened to the sad recital of some miserable story of want and loss.

The outcome of this can be readily foreseen—the effect at least upon one of the interested parties. Mr. Clayton awoke to the fact, slowly and gradually, it is true—he was not an impulsive man—that he was growing to care very much for Ruth Lorrimer. He watched for her, missed her when she was not near him, noticed the winning sweetness of her face, the silvery notes in her low voice.

When September came—it was two years since Jack had sailed—Mr. Clayton made up his mind that he loved Ruth Lorrimer, and if he could win her she should be his wife. The affection he gave was the kind one might expect in a man of strong, self-reliant character—deep, unchanging.   The river had found its true course, moving on through its channel, unswerving, to the sea.

Ruth did not for a moment suspect this state of affairs.   He did not mean she should.   A knowledge of it at present would ruin their pleasant friendship. He saw she cared nothing for him in that way. He suspected her story, though he knew nothing of its details.   He surmised that some one she loved had proved unworthy, and she was grieving her heart out over a shattered idol.

October was very lovely that year; the flowers bloomed late in the sheltered garden.   One sunny morning Ruth was walking with her grandmother slowly up and down the graveled path.

"Ruth, dear child," said Mrs. Lorrimer, as she leaned heavily upon her granddaughter's arm, " I have wanted to speak to you for some time.   You will not be angry with the old grandmother if she says what she thinks?"

"No," said Ruth, tenderly.   "What is it?"

Mrs. Lorrimer hesitated, leaning over a bed of scarlet dahlias as if to collect her thoughts.

"It is about yourself, Ruth, and—and—Mr. Clayton."

" Mr. Clayton!" said Ruth. '" What has he to do with me?"

" He has everything, Ruth; he loves you."

Ruth did not speak. She grew very white, then said, angrily :

" Did he tell you this?" She drew her arm away from Mrs. Lorrimer and stood watching her suspiciously.

" Jane and I have seen it for some time," faltered Mrs. Lorrimer. " Last evening, when Mr. Clayton was here and you were in Lynnport, we were looking over some old daguerreotypes. He saw one of you, taken when you were seventeen. You remember it, dear; you had it taken when I took you up to Boston, and you wore the new blue taffeta silk with the lace bertha. He took it in his hand and looked at it so long that Jane and I grew nervous; then he laid it down and said :

" ' This was before she had her great sorrow, was it not?'

" I said, ' Yes.' And perhaps something in my face may have made him say what he did. He looked earnestly at me and said :

" ' Mrs. Lorrimer, is there any hope for me?'

" I told him, Ruth, to wait."

"You had no right to tell him that." There was pain and anger in Ruth's voice. "I do not wish him to wait. What should he wait for?"

"You will marry some day, Ruth. Whom so worthy as Arthur Clayton? He is a good man, upright and honorable; he loves you. You could make me happy before I die." Mrs. Lorrimer hesitated, her voice trembled. "I cannot leave my little girl without a protector."

"Why need I marry; I cannot love any one enough for that; would any one want me for a wife without love?"

"You would grow to love Mr. Clayton. He would be patient, and all would come right in time."

"It is sacrilege," said Ruth. "What have I to give any man?"

Mrs. Lorrimer did not reply. Together in silence they left the garden.

This communication caused Ruth to visit her fisher-folk less often, much to little Joe's grief. As she took him for long walks with her upon the beach, however, where she helped him gather crabs, he was forced to be content.

Mr. Clayton suspected the reason for her avoidance of him, and did not harass her with his presence. He understood her and her sensitive nature.

The winter passed; it would soon be three years since Jack went away. Time had helped Ruth; things were outlined less distinctly. Her sorrow, when she thought of it, was as great, but she did not always think of it. She was shocked when, after some hours of diversion, she would find that she felt quite like the old Ruth who used to romp about the manor-house grounds. She would chide herself for this treason, as she called it, and conjure up partly faded visions of Jack's good-by and her wrecked hopes.

Arthur Clayton saw the change; so did Jane and Mrs. Lorrimer. One day in midsummer he asked Ruth, in a straightforward, manly speech, to marry him. He had found her in the garden, where she was standing amid her flowers, with a basket partly filled on the grass beside her, and a bunch of lilies in her hand. She listened to him gravely, her clear eyes searching his face; then she turned from him and looked through the opening in the pines to the ocean beyond. He saw her lips tremble when she said:

"I cannot answer you; I must first tell you a sad story. Will you hear it now?"

He bowed. "As you wish," he said.

She laid her lilies in the basket, and with one arm

resting on the well-sweep she told him the sad ending to her love for Jack.

"You will see, Mr. Clayton, why I could not love any one else.   One cannot feel the same twice; I gave Jack the best I had."

"I suspected much that you have told me," he said; "yet I risked all.   I hoped time would alter your feelings.   I think you will learn to care for me if you will give me the right to love and protect you.   Can you not, Ruth?   Give me the best love that is in you.   We will bury the past, and I shall be satisfied."

She stood looking meditatively upon the flowers in the basket at her feet, then said slowly, as though weighing carefully every word:

"I must have time to think of this.   I respect you, appreciate your worth, but I have no love to give any man.   I know it would please grandmother and make her very happy.   If I do as you wish I must marry in a different spirit.   I have not been softened by my trouble, and have renounced the forms of religion.   As your wife I must conform to the duties of my position."

"That would come in time," said Mr. Clayton.

"I cannot tell—perhaps.   I must be honest with

you; you must understand it all now," she cried, passionately, " then you cannot blame me."

" I understand," he said, kindly; " I am content. You shall have all the time you desire. If at the end you will come to me I shall thank God for the greatest blessing of my life. If He decrees other-wise I shall bow my head to His will; it will be a great blow—life will be never quite the same again."

She did not reply immediately. She stooped, took up the basket of flowers and the clipping-shears from the ground, and walked slowly by his side to the garden gate. When they reached the gate he held it open for her to pass through. She paused and said:

" Give me till winter, Mr. Clayton, to think about what you have told me."

" As you wish," he replied.

A few days after this conversation in the manor-house garden, Ruth sat in the parlor of the Hath-away cottage by Kate's side. A dainty tea-table stood near by, with the kettle singing pleasantly over the spirit-lamp, the Chinese tea-set and Can-ton-crape tea-cloth being a suitable accompaniment to the delicious aroma of the best imported tea. In those days the tea from China was undoubtedly of fine merit.   A dish of East India sweets stood by the side of the tea-caddy, and Mrs. Munn, in white apron and cap, sat near by, waiting to serve the ladies.

Ruth had been telling of her conversation with Mr. Clayton.   She had placed the tea-cup upon the table while she spoke, and was looking expectantly into Kate's face for her answer.

" I tell you this, Kate," she said, finally, when she received no reply, " and Mrs. Munn too, because you are my friends, and I want your advice."

Kate leaned forward.

" You have been honest with him, Ruth.   I think you would be a happier woman in your own home —your sphere for good would be enlarged.   You cannot live your life forever grieving for the past. I see in this a happy future.   Jack will never return—we have heard nothing from him, nor ever will."

Ruth winced at the sound of Jack's name.

" Let us not speak of him," she said.

Mrs. Munn folded her arms and set her mouth in a grim line.   She rose suddenly from her chair and handed a plate of buttered toast to Ruth, holding it out before her like a corporal presenting arms.

"What is *your* advice, Mrs. Munn?" said Ruth, refusing the toast with a wave of her hand.

"I am sorry you asked my advice, Miss Ruth," said Mrs. Munn, in a funereal tone. "I said once, and I say it again, that as long as my name is Sarah Munn—and there ain't any likelihood of my changin' it, as I know on—I'll never meddle in an affair of marriage again. I ain't got any advice to offer, Miss Ruth."

"Are you not interested in Ruth's welfare?" said Kate.

"You know all my interest is in you and Miss Ruth; but I dare not take it on me to offer advice after what has happened."

"Say what you think," said Ruth; "it need not be given as advice."

"Now, Miss Ruth, don't you badger me. Speakin' of badgerin' reminds me—let me tell you what happened over to Abigail Thomas's, on the shore road." The two ladies placed their tea-cups down and proceeded to listen. "It ain't so long ago, either," began Mrs. Munn, slowly, with a sigh, smoothing her apron down as she spoke. "Well, Abigail, she was a masterful woman, and her husband was a mite of a man. Ben Thomas was the weazeniest man I ever saw, and he give in to Abigail in everything. Well, the eldest girl was goin' to be married to a seafarin' man. Abigail didn't want her to get married; she wanted her to stay at home and work on the farm. Well, Ben, he didn't know what to do; he was pulled here and there by the women-folks. He was afraid of Abigail. He'd done always what she'd wanted, even to wearin' a high hat made to order, six inches taller than the regular height, till he looked ridiculous—"

"Oh, I remember Ben Thomas very well," interrupted Ruth.

"Well, they badgered him to death, poor man! They kept a-askin' his advice and then never takin' it, and goin' over and over the same thing day after day. He didn't have a minute's rest, and the end of it all was he drowned himself, or at least he tried to, in the cistern. They fished him out just in time; and on his vest they found these words printed on brown paper: 'Badgered to death.' After that Abigail left him alone, and the girl got married, and Ben wears the lowest-crowned hat I ever see to church —'tain't more'n an inch high." The ladies laughed. "And I've heard he never gives advice to anybody. Every time they get after him, botherin' him, he just kinder looks toward the cistern or sets his foot that way, and they all get just like lambs. No, Miss Ruth, I ain't goin' to be badgered, and I ain't goin' to give my advice." She rose from her seat, and, taking the plate of toast, moved majestically toward the door. " I'm goin' to make some fresh toast," she said. She paused on the threshold and looked back. " Whatever you do, Miss Ruth, do it in a God-fearin', pious manner. Make up your mind, then stick to it. That's the way I did with Munn. I didn't desert him—I ain't got that to reproach myself with." She disappeared down the narrow hall with the plate of toast, and the two ladies looked at each other and smiled.

CHAPTER XIII.

THE DEATH OF LITTLE JOE.

THE summer passed, and fall came again.

One day in October, after a heavy frost, Ruth and Joe went nutting in the woods. It was beautiful in the autumn-scented woods. The red and yellow leaves made a carpet beneath their feet more lovely than any woven by art, the brown, scarlet, and ocher shades blending with dull gray and purple tints.

The path led through a country road for some distance, a road overhanging the river-bank. Along the way Joe gathered late flowers, that struggled bravely beneath sheltered bits of stone wall and board fences, standing bright and strong, as though no biting frost had covered the land and opened the chestnut-burs. He made a garland of flowers for Ruth. She thanked him, hung the wreath upon her arm, and called him her true knight.

After walking for some time they reached the grove where the nut-trees grew thickest. They sat down to rest, placing the baskets beside them. It was intensely still in the retired spot; not a breeze rustled the nearly leafless trees, and the air was as soft and balmy as May.

Ruth sat resting against the side of a tree-trunk, looking dreamily before her. Joe watched her silently. He never interrupted her when she looked like that; he always waited for her to speak. Presently she turned to him.

"I am sorry company to-day," she said.

"No," said Joe; "I always like to be with you, even if you don't speak. Sometimes, when I feel tired, I sit all day and look and look before me just like that, and I don't say nothin' to nobody."

"What do you see, Joe, at those times?"

He blushed, hesitated, and turned his earnest little face aside.

"I see," he said, timidly, "a lovely place all bright; nobody is hungry or cold, and I am strong, and got new feet and a new back, and got lots o' work to do—much better work than crabbin'; and I says, I can't never have all those things here, so there is some other place where I will have them some day.   That's the place I thinks about when I sits and looks and don't speak."

"Does it look very beautiful to you, Joe?"

"I can't say as I knows just how it looks— whether there is houses and people—only I sees myself strong and well, and—and happy.   I don't want for anything—I has everything."

"That is heaven, Joe, that you are thinking about.   We all think of it at times."   Then drawing nearer to the boy she drew his head upon her shoulder and looked tenderly into his dark, expressive eyes—Joe's one claim to beauty.   "You must not leave me, Joe.   You have been my best solace for a great grief I once suffered.   You have opened my heart to the sufferings of others, and taught me there is more to live for than one's own happiness."

"I ain't a-goin' to leave you, Miss Ruth.   I don't think, even if I had good legs and everything, I'd be quite happy without you."

"Then we won't talk so sadly any more.   Let us gather the nuts; see, the ground is covered with them.   You sit still; it is hard walking over the rough twigs.   I'll bring you all I gather, and you can put them in the basket."

Ruth and Joe had a very pleasant day in those

sweet-scented woods. The wind blew gently through the dry leaves as the afternoon drew near. Now and then a covey of quail rustled the underbrush, or a saucy squirrel nibbled his dinner above their heads, dropping the empty shells at their feet. Once a fat partridge marched sedately across the path near them.

Joe was tired; the walk had been long, and he did not feel equal to much exertion. He rested, watching Ruth as she filled the baskets, a happy smile upon his face. When the rays of the sun slanted low, with shadows growing gigantic as they fell across the fields, he rose wearily, hobbling along by Ruth's side, making his way slowly from the woods to the open pastures bordering the highway.

Ruth had the baskets of nuts in her hands; over them she had laid a covering of crimson leaves.

When they reached the open field they stood side by side an instant, watching the sunset through an opening in the trees on the banks of the harbor. It was a glorious sight, that brilliant October sunset. The sky was lit into mountains of flame-colored clouds; the water beneath was crimson from the reflection. The sun hung above the dark trees, a gleaming meteor, and from its center radiated streaks of light that appeared to illuminate the earth.

Joe leaned against an old stone wall and clasped his hands.   In his limited vocabulary he could not express his feelings.

" Oh my, Miss Ruth, ain't it fine, ain't it bright!"

Ruth did not reply.   The intense beauty of the scene had entered her soul; she could not speak.

Presently Joe said, very timidly :

" Do you think heaven is like that "—he pointed toward the sky—" all bright like that? "

" It is more beautiful than that, Joe."

" Oh my!" said he, drawing in a long breath.

The walk home was slow, and for Joe very painful.   He had not been as well this fall; his grandmother said he was " kinder spindlin'," and had given him much herb-tea, to Joe's great disgust. He was a brave little fellow, seldom complaining, yet before they neared the village he sat down by the roadside, drops of sweat upon his forehead, and clenched his hands to keep back the tears.

Ruth was upon her knees beside him in an instant.

" What is it, Joe?" she said, anxiously.   " Are you in pain? "

"Oh, my back, Miss Ruth, my back! I'm all beat out. Don't worry"—he looked up into her face with a wan smile—"it isn't so bad. I guess I can walk pretty soon."

She waited and watched him for some moments, then said:

"Now, Joe, you have been my good knight for so long, it is time I returned some of my debts. I am going to carry you home. It is but a short distance, and you are not heavy."

"No, no, Miss Ruth, I never could. No, no—"

"I am going around by the cliff; it is a short way; nobody passes there," she said, coaxingly.

At this Joe tried to stand. He partially rose upon his crutch, steadied himself, then with a little moan fell back and lay still upon the ground—so still that Ruth's heart failed her as she leaned over him. He was partially conscious, though he did not speak.

She waited for nothing further, but lifting him in her arms she walked briskly forward. Ruth was strong, and the cripple was thin and light. She carried him down the steep hillside that ran near the cliffs, and skirting the banks she reached the fishing-hamlet, where the tiny house was situated.

His grandmother was at her day's work. The neighbors came in, and Joe was laid upon his cot in the corner of the one room the abode contained.

Ruth sat beside him, his hand in hers, and waited till the sun went down and the darkness of the short October day came upon them. Then she rose and closed the door, as the air that came in was crisp and cool, making a draft along the wooden floor. She put some wood upon the hearth; the flames rose and lighted the room, forming dancing shapes upon the ceiling.

Joe was free from pain now; the paroxysms had ceased. He was looking very peaceful, the firelight playing across his face.

"Miss Ruth," he said, "I didn't quite faint. I knew all the time when you was carryin' me down the hill, only I couldn't speak. You was so good to me, and I ain't a-goin' to forget. I can't do much, but granny says I'm a master hand at prayin'. I always prays for you reg'lar, Miss Ruth. Now I'll pray at other times too—odd times, you know."

"What do you ask for me, Joe, when you pray?"

The boy hesitated. "I ask that—that—sorrow you had will all go away; that sometime you'll go to church, and—and—sit in the big square pew. I ain't meanin' any offense, Miss Ruth, and—and—I did get one prayer answered about you. I asked that you and Mr. Clayton would be friends, and you are."

She turned away from the boy's clear gaze. "Here's granny," she said; and rising, opened the door for the old woman. Then she turned toward the cot. "I must go," she said.

The old woman bustled into the room and up to the cot.

"Wall, for the land's sake!" she said, bending her brown, wrinkled face over Joe. "Whatever hev yer been up to now? Yer ain't been a-tryin' to climb any nut-trees with a crutch, hev yer?" Joe laughed. Then she turned to Ruth:

"As I was a-comin' from Mrs. Burton's just now I see Sarah Munn. She said she see yer a-carryin' Joe. Yer was a-goin' down the cliff road at a pretty good pace. She screamed to yer—she was back in the woods a-gatherin' barberries—but yer didn't hear her. I didn't stop at the store for the tea or nothin'; I just hurried right home." Then she came close to Ruth and they walked to the door together. When she reached the door she stepped outside, then, pointing back into the room, said, " He ain't long for this world, poor creature!" She sighed. " I can't want to keep him, Miss Ruth. He's failin' fast. Dr. Goodyear says he won't last the winter out."

Ruth clutched the old woman's arm. " What!" she said, hoarsely. " Joe is not going to die ? "

" Yes," said granny, " he's a-goin'; he's a-goin' fast."

Ruth released her hold on the old woman's arm. Passing back into the room, she stood by the cot and looked down upon Joe.

" I came back, Joe," she said, " to say good night "—her voice trembled; the boy glanced up and smiled—" and to tell you that next Sunday I am going to church to sit in the square pew."

" O Miss Ruth!" said Joe. He partially raised himself. She stooped and kissed him, then went out into the night, closing the door softly behind her.

It was as granny had said—Joe was going fast. He never left his cot again, though the crutch was always kept close by its side, " in case," as he said, " it might be handy when I get better and feel like gettin' up."

It was just before Christmas that Mr. Clayton called one snowy afternoon for Ruth. Joe was worse and was asking for her. She had expected this summons many days; had waited for it with dread coupled with a bitter sense of pain and loss.

Why, she reasoned, should Joe be taken from her? He was the link between her rebellious sorrow and her present peace; for if not happy, she was at peace. His had been the hand that had pointed her the right course. Did God think she was strong enough to find her way alone? Perhaps; but she needed Joe, her little messenger of hope.

She walked along the snow-covered highway by Mr. Clayton's side, through the familiar streets of the town, down to the fishing-hamlet, where the winds blew fierce and cutting around the simple dwellings. It had been a gray afternoon; it was settling into a dark, starless night. Across the sky snow-clouds were hurrying; sleet and light rain filled the atmosphere at intervals with a dense mist.

On entering the house they encountered Dr. Goodyear, who had lifted Joe's head, propped him up with pillows, and had then gone forward and taken his position by the fire. Old granny sat at the foot of the bed, her head bent forward, resting against a counterpane thrown across the foot-board. On a table close to Joe's hand was a bunch of Christmas holly and evergreens. All pain had left the boy, and he looked happy and peaceful. His wistful eyes, which seemed to look out upon the world as though ever seeking a solution of his trouble, had a satisfied expression, as if the explanation was near at hand.

Ruth went quickly to him. She knew he was going to leave her—going very soon; she recognized it in that new expression upon his face.

" Joe," she said, " are you better? "

" Much better," he said. " I have no pain now. I've been thinkin' I might have them take my crutch away—I sha'n't want it any more. I'm glad I sha'n't need it. It was hard, Miss Ruth, always walkin' with a crutch."

" Yes, Joe," she said, " it was very hard."

" I wanted to see you come up the aisle once in church—that's what I was keepin' the crutch here for. But I don't mind that now. Mr. Clayton says I shall not mind anything soon; I'll be well and happy."

Ruth put her arms about him. "Yes, dear little Joe," she said, "you will be well and happy."

Joe did not speak for some time after that. He rested his head wearily against Ruth's shoulder and lay still. It was growing dark. Granny lighted the candles upon the chimney-shelf and drew the curtain across the window near the door. She would have drawn it over the one at the foot of the bed that faced the sea, but Joe said, "No, granny, I want to see the water and the lighthouse;" so they left the curtain drawn aside.

When the night came on and the lingering glow of the short winter twilight faded from the sky, Joe became restless. Ruth moved her arm from beneath his head and laid him back upon his pillow. He looked up at her with his sweet, trustful smile.

"You are so good to me," he said. "I kinder wish, sometimes, that I could get well. I'd like to go crabbin' with you again; I know lots of places where they're fat as can be. I guess it's all right, though; Mr. Clayton says 'tis. I couldn't never be well, you know."

"You will soon be well—quite well, dear little boy," said Ruth, with a tremor in her voice.

"Yes, quite well and strong, like the other boys.

Oh, I guess it's all right. I wonder if I'll feel any better to-morrow? I don't think I feel as well to-night."

He did not speak again for some time; then, opening his eyes, he looked around the room and said:

"O Mr. Clayton, I can't see the light or nothin'."

Mr. Clayton put his strong arm around the little deformed shoulders, and turning his face toward Ruth, he said:

"You see Miss Ruth, don't you, Joe?"

"Yes, I sees her, but not with my eyes; I sees her with my heart." He gave a little sigh and closed his eyes forever.

Ruth fell upon her knees by the bedside, and threw her arms across the quiet little figure, and bowed her head. She did not weep—she could not; her grief and sense of loss were too great for that.

Dr. Goodyear stood silently by the fireplace, looking gravely into the flickering flames that rose sparkling from the hickory logs.

Old granny rocked herself back and forth upon her low seat, her apron over her head.

"If it hadn't 'a' been for his dad," she moaned, "he might 'a' been a strong boy to-day, and pulled an oar with the best of 'em. Ah! he was a hard, bad man, and to his own, too."

Ruth did not heed her. She rose slowly from her knees, and walking totteringly to the door, threw it open, and stood a moment in the cold, icy air. She was faint, and leaned tremblingly against the door, looking up at the dark, storm-driven clouds. She tried to think of Joe as well and happy, straight and strong and occupied; not wishing for aught he left here; understanding the mystery of death; he the sage, she the ignorant one ; he gone forward into the light, she groping in the darkness.

Arthur Clayton followed her to the door and stood silently by her side. Suddenly she turned to him as to a refuge of strength, and laid her hand upon his arm.

"My little comforter has gone," she said. "Help me to bear it. I come to you."

He took her hand in his, and together they went in and stood by Joe, where he lay so still upon his cot. His face was peaceful, as though death had come as his best-loved friend.

Ruth placed the bunch of Christmas holly in one small hand.

"We could not have given him such a happy

Christmas as he will have with the angels," she said, tearfully. "He was my good angel. God sent him to me. I shall be a better woman because little Joe has lived."

Arthur took her home. On the way they talked of many things; talked in a calm, sincere strain of the future. They were not the impulsive, impassioned words that had passed between Jack and her in that past springtime of her first love, when, all unmindful of the world, her home, her better judgment, she would have gone with her lover, forgetting duty, to the ends of the earth. No, they were the words of a calm, sincere woman who has bid the past keep its secrets, nor parade them forth in the garish light; who has taken up the broken links and joined them by the power of a quiet affection—that affection, on the man's side at least, as strong in its depth and endurance as the turbulent passions of early youth.

"I cannot tell you, Arthur," she said, as she leaned upon his arm, looking up at him, "why it was, when I stood outside granny's door and knew Joe had left me, it seemed I must turn to you. Some influence compelled me, forced me to feel you would help me, comfort me. Perhaps Joe stood near on his way to God, counseled me, and I felt his presence."

Mr. Clayton removed his hat reverently, and said :

" All praises to Him, Ruth. Through the hand of a little child He has opened to me a great happiness."

Ruth felt calm, at rest, even happy; not, of course, the wild, impetuous happiness that was hers during that past summer, when the birds seemed to sing sweeter and the flowers bloom fairer than ever before; instead, a restful feeling, as though she had steered her bark from a stormy sea into a safe haven, and was rocking lazily on the tide, a stronger hand than hers at the helm.

Little Joe was buried Christmas day, in a new plot that Ruth had purchased. She was the last to leave him to his quiet sleep. She lingered some time beside the mound of frozen earth, then turned reluctantly away.

" Dear little Joe," she murmured, " I shall try to be a good woman, and shall always remember the fisher-folk for your sake; you would have liked me to, Joe." She stood and waited, as if he could answer her, then looking into the sky she said, " He cannot answer me, yet I know his influence has helped shape my life, and always will." When she reached the gate of the hillside graveyard she looked back tearfully. The wind blew icy cold. She clasped her cloak tightly at her throat. " Good-by, Joe," she said. " You have given me strength to take up my new life and help me to forget the old. Good-by."

She went slowly down the steep incline and passed the church.   Mr. Clayton came out and joined her. He saw the tear-stains upon her face.

" I stayed by his grave till the others had gone," she said, softly. " I needed him to-day. I have been haunted by thoughts of—of—Jack." She looked up tearfully. " They were only thoughts; I shall soon be calm. You will not blame me ? "

He looked tenderly upon her. " I understand, Ruth," he said, " I understand. You have been truthful with me; I shall not expect too much."

Suddenly she turned passionately from him. " I am not a good woman; I rebel," she said. " You will bear with me, and—and—help me ? "

" I will, God helping me," he said, earnestly.

CHAPTER XIV.

MRS. LORRIMER'S ILLNESS.

WHEN it became known in Lynnport that Mr. Clayton and Miss Lorrimer were to be married, nothing but commendation and the highest praises in favor of the alliance were heard on every side. "So suitable in every way," said the busy ones who generally settled the affairs of the town. "Proper ages, proper positions, and Miss Lorrimer will inherit her grandmother's wealth. What an instrument for good she will become under the guidance of such a man as Arthur Clayton!"

It was some days after little Joe's death when Ruth told her grandmother of her plans. The old lady was sitting in her favorite high-backed chair in the drawing-room. She rarely moved from it now, except to be carried to her apartment. She was very feeble, her tenure of life short and uncertain.

Ruth was sitting that afternoon by the spinet, singing an old Scotch love-song that had been a favorite of Joe's. The refrain,

"He loved me ay well in spite of a',"

had pleased Joe, who had said that was what he believed in; "in spite of a'"—that was how he wanted to love people.

Ruth was thinking of Arthur Clayton as she sang. He loved her "in spite of a'." She had been truthful, had told him she had given Jack her best love; yet he loved her just the same, believed in her, and was patient with her. Her hands fell with a crash upon the keys; she leaned her head upon them.

"What is it, child?" called Mrs. Lorrimer's soft voice, anxiously.

Ruth went to her, and sat down on a low footrest at her feet, just as she used to when she was a little girl.

"Grandmother," she said, "I am going to marry Arthur Clayton. I have told him all about Jack, and he is satisfied. But oh! it is so different, so different from what I—I—had always thought—" Her voice trembled; she did not finish the sentence.

"My dear child, I am glad; you have made me

very happy.   I have wished for this a long while.
Now I can die in peace."   She placed her hands
on Ruth's head as though in benediction.

Presently Jane came in, carrying Tetsy, who in
the last few years had grown too stout and asthmatic
for much locomotion.

"Jane," said her sister, "come here.   I want to
tell you that all is as we hoped: Ruth is going to
marry Mr. Clayton."

"I am glad," said Jane, heartily; "he is a good
man."

Ruth rose slowly from her low position.   A reac-
tion had set in.   The present joy became contrasted
in her mind with that time, only a few short years
ago, when Jack had been forbidden the house and
she had been forced to meet him clandestinely.
She brushed her hair nervously from her forehead.
She must not think of that time; it was not right.

Jane watched her sharply; then, placing Tetsy
upon the sofa—who was deeply angered by the
action, evincing his displeasure in low mutterings—
she went to Ruth and said:

"Ruth, your heart is in this marriage, is it not?
If not, give it up while there is time."   Jane spoke
almost peremptorily.

"I wish it, Aunt Jane," said Ruth, with gentle dignity. "No one has coerced me. Arthur knows I do not love him as I loved Jack, but I love him with all the heart I have left. I am looking forward, as his wife, to leading a useful life and doing my duty."

"If," said Jane, slowly, "Jack should come back?"

Ruth started, drawing her breath hard.

"He will never come back, and if—he should, were I Arthur Clayton's wife I should still do my duty."

"Ruth," she said, "you will be a happy woman some day; the river will find its true course."

It was February when Mrs. Lorrimer came downstairs for the last time. The stately chatelaine of the manor would no longer sit in her rustling brocades among the portraits of her ancestors, no longer dispense the old-time courteous hospitality of the mansion. She had looked her last, from her seat in the north drawing-room, upon the rolling waters of the harbor. She sat now in her sunny window near her bed, watching the lengthening February days and the snow slowly melting from the hillside.

Hers was a tranquil old age. The dark shadows of her early youth had become tempered through the lapse of years. Much of the bitterness that had lain dormant, only to be aroused to life once more through Ruth's luckless love-affair, had passed away; the vague terrors that had assumed giant proportions faded forever. Ruth was safe in the sheltered care of a good man; she felt no further anxiety for her. So the old lady sat and dreamed and dozed in the pale sunshine of those early spring days. The delicate outline of her chiseled features grew sharper and her faded eyes dimmer. She sat patiently waiting. Her thoughts were peaceful— thoughts such as a child might have—as she watched the busy little winter wrens disputing with the early bluebirds and robins for the crumbs thrown upon the cold earth for them by Ruth; she smiled when they pecked at one another with shrill clamor over some tempting morsel.

Ruth came in one day with a cluster of pale crocuses in her hand; she had found them in a sheltered place under the garden hedge, where the sun shone earliest in the morning.

Her grandmother took them with a smile, and held them against Ruth's face.

"They seem like yourself, Ruth," she said, "so pale and fair; you have no red cheeks, dear, any more."

"No," said Ruth. "I am growing old, you know, grandmother; I cannot look like a chubby child always."

Mrs. Lorrimer sighed, then drawing Ruth to her she kissed her on her brow.

"My child," she said, "you have been a good granddaughter; you have made much of the happiness of my life. I have something I wish to say to you." She paused and scanned the earnest face watching her. "Arthur is patient," she said, "and would not urge you; I, dear, wish to see you married before I leave you. I should like to see you safe; it would make me content."

Ruth folded her hands and gazed from the window over the woods and hills of the distant farming country. She could not see the ocean from where she stood, yet in her ears it seemed to surge and throb and moan. In fancy she beheld great ships, and—and—Jack, where was he? Was he dead or living? Had he forgotten her? She drew herself together with an effort, and said:

"As you wish, grandmother; I have given my

promise." Then, more hurriedly: "Let there be no parade and show; that is not necessary."

"You are Miss Lorrimer, of the manor," said the old lady, with gentle dignity; "does not your position have its obligations?"

"I could not stand it," said Ruth, quickly. "No, let us be married quietly here in this room by your side. I am going to be a clergyman's wife; I do not wish to commence with pomp and display. Do you not understand, grandmother, that I am going to give up my life to duty?"

"Do not say that, Ruth," exclaimed her grandmother, quickly, "or I shall feel remorse. You will be happy. It is not all duty, dear; is there no love in it?"

"Oh, do not ask me, do not ask me!" She walked to the window and stood looking out for a long time. She did not see the sloping hillside, or the pale green peeping here and there from the brown earth, or the shivering robins. Her vision was hidden by a thick mist of unshed tears, and her fancy saw the wharves of Lynnport, the "Bonny Kate," and Jack. Presently she came back and stood by Mrs. Lorrimer's chair.

"I am better now," she said, sadly. "I get thinking sometimes, that is all. Oh," she concluded, passionately, "if one could only stop thinking!"

It all came about as Ruth wished. Some weeks after, when spring had really come to the land, not coyly, bashfully, but in all its great beauty of green fields, flowers, and sunshine, with singing birds and hurrying brooks, Ruth was married. She stood in Mrs. Lorrimer's room, in her wedding-dress of glistening satin and priceless lace. Mrs. Lorrimer had insisted upon this; no simple muslin gown for the last of the Lorrimers, for the heiress of the manor —no, Ruth must uphold her position. When she came to the old lady before the ceremony, with the hereditary lace veil of the Lorrimers upon her soft brown hair, her grandmother clasped about her throat the family pearls that had graced many a young bride in the days gone by.

"The Lorrimer pearls, dear," she whispered; "may they take a blessing with them."

Ruth felt their cold clasp upon her neck, and shivered.

They were married and gone; gone to Boston, to Mr. Clayton's old home, for the honeymoon. The mansion settled down to its wonted quiet, with its stately owner sitting and dreaming in her sunny window.

Lynnport considered itself defrauded of a wedding-feast. Many remarks of disapprobation were leveled at the heads of the " old family."

" Just as though she was ashamed of him," said Mrs. Burton. " I never did understand Ruth Lorrimer; she has changed in the last few years. I sometimes think she had a disappointment."

This remark had been addressed to Dr. Goodyear, one morning, as he stood clipping his rose-vines, cutting them back for budding later in the season. Mrs. Burton was leaning over the gate watching him.

" There you ladies go," he said, loudly; " it is always a disappointment with you. Look at me, Mrs. Burton, if you want to see a victim of disappointment." He came toward the gate, holding a thorny rose-vine in one hand and the great clipping-shears in the other. " I have waited to get married for thirty years, yet you ladies never settled upon me as a possible victim of blighted hopes. You are not discriminating, Mrs. Burton; you take Ruth Lorrimer and weave a romance about her because she is young and fair; you leave me out of your reckoning because I am—ahem!—old—and fat."

Mrs. Burton laughed. "Perhaps you are right, doctor," she said. "We women are romantic; we do love a wedding and a bride. Ruth has changed; you certainly have noticed that?"

"I haven't noticed anything," said the doctor, innocently. "Keep on hoping; perhaps I'll have a wedding some day and gratify you," the doctor concluded, with a gloomy smile that sat ill upon his jolly face.

Mrs. Burton shook her head and passed down the hill.

The doctor stood looking after her, ruminating. "I hope the women will not gossip about Ruth, poor child! The talkers of Lynnport have good tongues when they set them going. Ruth's a lucky girl if she only knew it; Arthur Clayton is a man in a thousand."

The doctor became so absorbed in his thoughts that he did not see Mrs. Munn dart rapidly around the side of the house to the rear door; in fact, he was partially hidden by the low-falling branches of the elm that grew in the street in front of his house.

He became conscious presently of loud voices, and cries from his old housekeeper of " Doctor, doctor, where are you?" He hurried into the house, to see Mrs. Munn with tears streaming down her face, and her hands beating the air as she walked up and down his tiny kitchen.

" Be calm, Mrs. Munn," he said, sternly. " What is the matter?"

" Oh deary, deary! she's gone, she's gone!"

" Who's gone?" he said, walking after her; and taking her arm, he forced her to stand still.

" The old lady—Mrs. Lorrimer. They just went upstairs, Miss Jane and her maid, and they found her in her chair by the window, where she always sits. She was so still they thought she was asleep; when they went closer they found she was gone. O doctor, she looked beautiful; she was smiling like a child, and the sunshine was so bright on her white hair."

" When did this happen?" said the doctor.

" Not an hour ago; the whole house is upset. I was up there with a message from Miss Kate, and I told Miss Jane that I'd run all the way to town and tell you. Miss Jane wanted you, though what good you can do, for the life of me I can't see; when death comes you have got to stand, like the rest of us, with folded hands."

"That will do, Mrs. Munn," said the doctor, gravely; "I shall go immediately. Did they say when they expected Mrs. Clayton home?"

"The day after to-morrow, Miss Jane said. Ah, poor Miss Ruth! she'll begin her wedded life with a sorrow."

The doctor did not wait to hear anything more; presently the sound of his wagon-wheels was heard as he drove out of the yard.

"He's a masterful man," said Mrs. Munn, looking after him as he drove past the kitchen window; then, turning to the old housekeeper, added, " How long have you been here, Martha?"

" A good many years, Sarah Munn, a good many years."

" Did the doctor never think of gettin' married, think you?" queried Mrs. Munn.

" Gettin' married!" screamed Martha. " Good land! not as I knows on. Why, what'd become of me if he got married?"

" I ain't deaf, Martha, if you are," said Mrs. Munn, with asperity. " Do you want the neighbors to hear us talkin' about the doctor's gettin' married?"

" No, but you are so scareful."

" Scareful or not scareful, I shouldn't be surprised if he'd get married some day."

" He's pretty old," said Martha, hopefully.

" He's none too old; why, look at Dan Monson,
down at the cove; wasn't he nigh onto eighty?
Didn't he marry after swearin' he never would?—
no women should step across his threshold and
spend his money; he called them all instruments
of Satan."

" I remember," said Martha, mournfully. " Old
Dan got punished; Mrs. Monson was a fearful character."

" Good enough for him, crabbed, unreasonable
creature!" said Mrs. Munn.

" Have you heard of any likely person for the
doctor, Sarah?" said Martha, dolefully.

" No, I ain't; I just have an idea of my own;
perhaps I am mistaken. I sha'n't say nothin' about
it, and don't you; the doctor wouldn't like it."

" I sha'n't say nothin', Sarah; only I wish you
hadn't told me. Of course it'll be a young thing
that'll pull everything to pieces in the house, tear
up the garden, and then break his heart by runnin'
away with some good-for-nothin'."

Mrs. Munn had risen to go; she stood on the stone door-step of the kitchen, her hand upon the knob, and turned and eyed Martha in amazement at the conclusion of this speech.

"Well, for the land's sake, Martha, how you do run on! Have you been readin' any of those foolish love-stories at your time of life? I don't think he's such a fool as you want to make him out."

Stepping briskly over the step, she passed around the side path to the gate; she held her skirts very high, her large gaitered feet making deep impressions in the soft earth. Martha stood watching her. When she reached the gate she called back:

"Don't you go and get discouraged; no one's goin' to tear up this garden, I can tell you that."

Then, squaring her shoulders, she marched down the hill to the lower street, the consciousness of being the first to convey the important news of the death at the manor-house lending an added stiffness to her erect carriage.

Ruth came home from her wedding-journey in time to see her grandmother laid in the grim Lorrimer vault in the little graveyard. She shed many tears as she clung to her husband's arm that lovely June day, and heard the click of the gates of the vault, and knew that the beautiful face which had never held aught for her but a smile of love was hidden from her forever. She sat for some time on the soft grass of the terrace, waiting till the grave-yard was quiet and the great concourse of people and the long line of carriages had disappeared down the hill, when she said:

"Arthur, I shall never live at the manor again; it cannot be the same without grandmother. We will begin our life in the rectory."

So they began life in the rectory, a fine old roomy house, square, with gambrel-roof and dormer-windows, a relic of Puritan days. It had been bought and presented to the church by Mrs. Lorrimer for the aged rector, Mr. Clayton's predecessor.

When Jane remonstrated with Ruth upon her decision, she said, sadly:

"Do not urge me, Aunt Jane. The old house is full of ghosts—ghosts in the hall, on the stairs, and in the garret; I see them everywhere, and hear their footsteps. I shall be happier in the rectory."

"I shall stay; I am not afraid of any ghost," said Jane, decidedly. "Ghosts! what nonsense!"

Jane stayed in the old house, though she seldom entered the garret or the north drawing-room. She wished Ruth had not spoken of ghosts; not that she believed in such arrant foolishness—oh no; still, one sometimes thought of strange things when one was alone in such a large house. She grew to dread the sight of the paintings on the wainscoted walls of the drawing-room, and kept the door closed, placing a great carved seat before it. People asked her why she did so, and she said there was a draft from the room; she would not have confessed to seeing ghosts, though they were beginning to lurk for her also in the shadowy room, where the portrait of her father looked down upon the high, carved chair, now, alas! empty by the fireless hearth.

Sometimes Jane, with Tetsy in her arms, accompanied by a housemaid, would make a tour of the stately apartment and superintend the readjusting of furniture, while the maid dusted, and opened the windows to let in the air and the sunlight. She would gaze sadly at the silent spinet before which her beautiful sister sat so often in the days long ago, and where baby Ruth loved to beat her dimpled hands on the keys. At these recollections Jane would stand motionless in the center of the great high-ceilinged room, and, much to the maid's surprise, look before her into vacancy; then with a long-drawn sigh would start and give her orders briskly. The dusting and sweeping finished, she would order the shutters closed, the curtains drawn, and leave the room to the spectral visions her fancy had conjured, from the realities that had gone forever.

Looking back into the dim apartment from the cheerful hall, she appeared to see a shadowy form in the dress of other days, with powdered hair and stiff brocade, standing in all her exquisite beauty before the fire, and by her side the dark, sinister face of the black-browed captain.

" Close the door!" she would say, sharply, to the maid; " I feel the draft about my feet; the wind is blowing from the north."

Poor Jane was very lonely, and to her unspeakable disgust she was beginning to appreciate that in her rugged organization lurked a set of sensitive nerves.

" Yes," she said to herself, " I am lonely; I miss Mary, I miss Ruth." Many a tear dropped upon Tetsy's back as she held him in her arms. " It is hard to be old and alone, and no one to tell it to but Tetsy."

CHAPTER XV.

DR. GOODYEAR TRIUMPHANT.

RUTH had been married over a year. Very peacefully and quietly had life passed in the rectory. The young wife had become accustomed to her new career; the unending round of parish duties incumbent upon her position interested her, giving her little time for other things.

Ruth could not say she was happy or unhappy— she did not analyze her feelings on the subject; by force of will and constant occupation she silenced repinings and regrets. Life was pleasant, and her husband was kind. and devoted. Each day revealed to her the noble traits in his character: the unselfishness and gentleness combined with strength, which made him stand a man among men. No smallness, no petty meanness, had room in a being formed in such a mold.

Ruth had deemed her heart and entire being had

gone through a period of transition after Jack left her; the capabilities of love had been destroyed at that great, overpowering crisis, never to live again. She was startled and overwhelmed when, at the birth of her child, the flood came rushing back upon her soul. She gazed with passionate eagerness into the tiny face, a wealth of love in her eyes. This little helpless creature aroused her from the indifference she had supposed her natural state; made her know new hopes, new desires. She would live again and be happy; she had an object in view, a destiny, a life-work.

Her husband watched her sadly; she had never revealed that smile for him. He turned away his head, his firm lips trembled; he did not speak, only leaned over her where she lay with that ecstatic joy lighting her features, the child upon her arm, and kissed her silently.

Sweet, submissive, gentle, a model wife she was, but not a loving one. The barrier that had been between them the day they were married was there still; an invisible barrier, yet recognized by both.

Ruth's joy was short-lived; the child was delicate; the little one soon left her with empty arms. Like a dark curtain the old apathy settled upon her; she knew the truth now—that love had not died within her, but her husband did not share it; she could not give it to him. "O Father," she murmured, the day her child was buried, "have pity on me! make me a good woman, and more worthy of my husband's love."

Jane came often to the rectory, so often that the Lynnport people thought she was growing weary of her lonely life in the partly closed manor. What the gossips surmised was strictly true: Jane was lonely and depressed; if it had not been for Tetsy she could not have endured the silence and dreariness of the empty house.

Tetsy proved himself a friend in need. Perhaps his dog nature understood more than mortals surmise; at any rate, he never left his mistress, and was cordiality and devotion combined. He was growing quite genteel in size, owing to constantly pattering after her, upstairs and down, wherever her nervous steps led her. Though old, he was apparently renewing the days of his youth, and at times indulged in mild capers when his mistress was saddest, at which superannuated antics Jane would smile, then become alarmed for her favorite's health. He would offer her his paw at odd, inconceivable moments, and when this would not arouse her from a reverie would jump into her lap, whining softly to himself, and gaze into her face with his large intelligent eyes.

In the early fall, some fifteen months after Mrs. Lorrimer's death, a dire calamity fell upon the inmates of the homestead: Tetsy was lost or stolen; he had not been seen for nearly a whole day. Jane was distracted; with head-dress disheveled and shawl flying from her shoulders, she ran up and down stairs and out into the garden, calling his name wildly. The stable-man, with broom and pitchfork, ransacked every conceivable part of his department, Tetsy at times having a predilection for certain musty corners of the stable, where rats were supposed to flee before him; but no Tetsy responded. The cook and maid searched garret and cellar without success. At last, when all efforts had failed, Jane sat down in the hall, and, unmindful of the stares of the maid and the open-mouthed stable-man, burst into tears.

"He was all I had," she said, brokenly; "he was a great comfort to me. I suppose some dreadful boys have stolen him and will abuse him."

"No," said the man, "they won't abuse him;

they'll only keep him till yer offers a reward—a good big reward—then they'll bring him back; that's all the mean critters want."

This motive for action roused Jane, and she started up. " Go to the village," she cried; " offer them anything they ask. I will give any price," she continued, recklessly.

The man departed with all possible speed upon his errand.

The morning of that day a scene had been enacted between Dr. Goodyear and two vicious urchins from the fishing-town. He had been driving slowly along a sequestered road on his way home from a professional call at a distant farm. Seeing two boys quarreling in a field, with a little fluffy terrier tied to a tree near by, he stopped and watched them curiously; not that fighting boys were an unusual sight to the doctor, but this dog had a strangely familiar look. Where had he seen him before, with the blue ribbon on his neck? Very few dogs in Lynnport wore blue ribbons. Suddenly it dawned upon him that it was Tetsy. It did not take him very long to leap from his gig, jump the stone wall, and cross the field.

" Boys," he said, sternly, drawing them apart,

tearing the jackets of each as he did so, " what
are you fighting about? Where did you get that
dog?"

" He's our dog," said one, sullenly.

" Don't lie to me," said the doctor; " I know that
dog—you have stolen him. If you don't get out of
this pretty quick I'll have you both in the lockup;
march, double quick—do you hear?"

" He did it," said one, beginning to cry; " he
stole him out of Miss Weston's garden. He said
we'd make money out of him. I didn't want to do
it; he made me."

" Get out of here," said the doctor, waving his
hand and glaring fiercely upon them.

The boys slunk away. The doctor lifted poor,
trembling, frightened Tetsy in his arms, and strode,
muttering, across the meadows to his gig. Just as
he was about to place his foot upon the step of his
carriage the greatest temptation of his life assailed
him, and to which, after a brief, tempestuous mental
struggle, he yielded. Then began the process of
deception : he stuffed Tetsy under his coat and kept
him there by violent pressure; he skirted the lonely
back roads like a hunted criminal, finally arriving
after dark at his own house; he passed his aston-

ished housekeeper upon the door-step without a word, and hastened to his laboratory, where no one was ever permitted to enter.

In relating this incident later in the evening to Mrs. Munn, Martha had said the doctor bulged out so on one side that she thought he had some horrid thing to dissect.

After closing the laboratory door carefully, and trying the lock twice to see if it was secure, he intimated to Martha, while she waited on him at supper, that some ghostly relic held possession of his private apartment. "It would be better," he advised, gravely, "not to go anywhere near the place if you feel nervous."

"Never fear, doctor," said Martha, anxiously; "I wouldn't go near that room for anything."

After supper the mare was again put into the shafts, and the doctor sped hastily to the homestead.

"It's only a chance," he muttered, as he drove along. "All's fair in love and war; at least the poets say so, and I suppose the poets are authority on such matters. I'm ashamed of the thing, but I'm going to see it through."

He found the old house in darkness, with the exception of a light in the square hall, where Jane was sitting, her gray head bent over her hands, bowed in grief for the loss of her pet.

The doctor stepped up to her. " Don't fret, Jane," he said, kindly. " I am sorry for you; I saw by the posters in the village that Tetsy was lost; but don't give up like that; we'll find him yet."

" No, he's gone," she replied, mournfully; " some bad boys have drowned him. I have sent all over the country to-day; if he were alive some one would know it. I was so fond of the poor little dog; I know people laughed at me, but I haven't had so many to love in my life that they need have envied me Tetsy."

" Jane," said the doctor, cheerfully, " something tells me—I cannot tell what it is, perhaps an intui-tion—that Tetsy is alive. Why should any one harm a pretty little dog like that ? "

Jane looked up; the doctor had never called him " a pretty little dog " before.

" I think some bad boy, or—man, is keeping him concealed for the reward," he continued, reflectively.

" Do you really, doctor ? "

" I most certainly do," he replied, with convic-tion. " I shall make it my most urgent business to unearth the miscreant and restore your dog. You know, Jane, I can accomplish much if I set about it, and we most assuredly cannot allow this highway robbery in Lynnport." The doctor assumed a warlike air, which was consoling to Jane, bringing hopes of his ultimate success.

"O doctor, if you can do this, if you can find Tetsy, I shall be forever grateful; I shall—" She paused. Her tear-stained face and tottering head-dress looked pathetic in the dim candle-light; her loneliness touched the doctor deeply—the great silent house, the woman growing old amid its dreariness.

"Will you give me yourself, Jane, if I find Tetsy?" The doctor's deep voice took on a lower tone.

Jane drew a long breath; gazed about the shadowy hall and to the closed door of the drawing-room, thence to the staircase with its wide balustrades, where no more the footsteps she had loved would pass.

"I am very lonely, doctor," she said, in a low voice; "I will do as you wish if you find Tetsy; I cannot stand my life here any longer."

This rather peculiar consent did not dismay the doctor in the least; he was satisfied; he had won;

he was a conqueror.   But his triumph was not all unmixed joy; his conscience began to prick fiercely, but he silenced it by mental reminders of ideas promulgated by the poets, and said:

"I shall find him if he is above-ground; I have hopes of restoring him to you soon.   I shall work all night.   Jane, you have made me a happy man; you have—"

"You have not found him yet, doctor," reminded Jane, with a touch of her old sharpness.

"True," he remarked, slightly crestfallen.

The doctor went his way.   In order to divert suspicion if questions were asked in the future, he drove the greater part of the n'ght, knocking up sleeping households, much to their disgust, in his zeal for his cause.   Then, going as far as the four corners, which he reached in the gray light of the early morning, he put up his horse, and slept the sleep—hardly of the just, as his conscience, being a tender one, insisted upon retaliating in sundry smarts and pricks.

After the doctor left his house the evening before, Mrs. Munn called to have a chat with Martha. The two women sat in the pleasant kitchen before the bright fire, and talked.   The tea-pot was on the stove, two steaming cups stood on the table, and a

little plate of caraway-seed cookies was near at
hand.

"Have you heard anything more about the doctor's marryin'?" asked Martha, anxiously.

"No, I ain't; perhaps I was mistaken, though I
think yet he'll marry sometime. Why shouldn't
he? He's got money, a good home, and, land
knows, he's old enough. Where is he to-night?"

"Out on calls, I suppose; there's a deal of sickness
this fall in Lynnport. Goodness me! what's that?"

A low, muffled howl was heard coming from the
interior of the house, the kitchen being in the extension. The two women started to their feet; Mrs.
Munn stepped toward the door that opened into the
main part of the house.

"Oh, don't go, don't go!" said Martha. "It's
something in the doctor's private room; it's something he's goin' to cut up."

"I shall go," said Mrs. Munn. "It sounds like
something human—I mean it's not an animal or
anything like that. I'm a-goin'."

Martha caught Mrs. Munn's gown as another
more prolonged wail came echoing along the hall.

"I'm afeard to go; I wouldn't go for anything
on earth."

" I'm a-goin'," reiterated Mrs. Munn. She stalked fearlessly down the long passageway to the doctor's room.   As she neared the door the noise became louder, finally terminating in a shrill scream, finishing off in a low muttering and grumbling.

Mrs. Munn knelt down on her knees and applied her eye to the keyhole; she did not speak for a moment.   Martha was calling from the end of the hall to know what she saw.   Finally she rose, after gazing a moment upon poor imprisoned Tetsy, who sat in the arm-chair by the fire, his head raised in the air, emitting howl after howl of exceeding mournfulness.   At the foot of the chair was a pan of water and a plate of dinner.   Mrs. Munn did not say anything, though she thought a good deal as she walked back to Martha.

" That'll fetch her ; whoever would have supposed the doctor was as smart as that ?   I do declare, I admire that man.   I wouldn't say a word about this, not if they wanted to burn me at the stake the way they did all the other Christian martyrs.   Just to think of it ! —the whole place aroused about that dog, and he here all the time, and the doctor takin' him back in the mornin', and Miss Jane all smiles, and—"

At this juncture she spoke:

"Martha, it's only a little dog as I think has had his leg set, and he's lonely."

They sat down by the fire again; no more howls were heard—Tetsy had gone to sleep. When Mrs. Munn left, as she was putting on her shawl she said, solemnly:

"I ain't changed my mind one mite about the doctor's marryin'; the feelin' has come over me awful strong just lately, since I've been here to-night." Martha sighed. "Don't get downhearted about it; I think she's old; he ain't, at his time o' life, goin' to bring a silly young thing here. Good night, Martha."

"Good night, Mrs. Munn."

When Tetsy was placed in Jane's arms by the doctor she was too overcome even to listen coherently to his rambling account of midnight wanderings and hair-breadth escapes in his search for the lost one. Finally, after patting Tetsy's curly head for the twentieth time, she turned peremptorily to the doctor.

"Well, where did you find him? I'm sure I don't understand a word you are saying."

"I found him tied to a tree in a field; some boys

must have stolen him and left him there, no doubt frightened away by some one."

"Poor little dog, how cruel! Well, doctor, you have my word; I am not the woman to go back on a promise. You have fulfilled your part of the compact; I shall fulfil mine."

"Jane, you are a fine woman; I am the happiest of men."

He would have been happier if it had not been for the twinges of his rebellious conscience, which refused to be quieted.

The following winter Jane Weston became Mrs. Ezekiel Goodyear, and went to live in the doctor's cozy house on the aristocratic upper street of the town.

The manor was closed—left solitary and deserted in its fields of snow. Like the lonely monarch of a fallen kingdom, it was neglected in its age, its past glories were forgotten. The ghosts had it all to themselves; silently at midnight they might wander unmolested up and down the stately rooms, and patter on the staircase, or join in ghostly revels in the wide hall. No one hindered them; they were the owners now, the sole possessors, where once was life and joy.

The old caretaker in the cottage by the gate made entry at stated intervals into the silent house, to see that all was safe. He did not stay long at such times; he felt the cold and dreariness, and sighed as he walked from room to room.

"Ah well! the 'old family' is all gone; they were a fine stock." Then back to his cozy fireside he would go.

The night the bride and groom returned, Mrs. Munn went over to help Martha in her arrangements for the supper she intended preparing for them. The two women were in the kitchen busy at their task. Martha was feeling dispirited; she felt her stay at the doctor's uncertain, and grieved accordingly.

"Don't you fret," consoled Mrs. Munn; "don't cross streams till you come to them. I never did have patience with people that was always up to their necks in a stream, when they ain't within a hundred miles of water. You just wait."

After supper Mrs. Goodyear came out to the kitchen and shook hands with Mrs. Munn, then said cheerfully to Martha:

"You will stay with us—we could not get along without you."

Martha burst into tears. "O Mrs. Goodyear," she sobbed, " I'll stay as long as you want me."

After she went back to the parlor Mrs. Munn whispered mysteriously to Martha, as she was washing up the supper dishes:

" Ain't I got foresight?   Didn't I predict this? "

" Yes, you have, Sarah Munn," said Martha, eying her admiringly, as she polished a delicate china tea-cup, one of the new set the doctor had bought. " I never could quite understand why you was so positive about his marryin' that time after you peeped into his private room through the keyhole."

" Well, I'm kinder gifted that way; things come to me sudden.   I guess I inherited it from father's side of the house; he had an uncle that was a born soothsayer.   People came to him from all round the country; he was a wonderful man."

" You don't say so, Mrs. Munn!" cried Martha, drying her hands on the towel that hung on the kitchen door.   " Did he predict for you? "

" Yes, he did," said Mrs. Munn, gloomily, looking into the fire.   " I didn't heed him.   He said Munn wa'n't no account; was a cantankerous creature.   I just rushed out of his house, and never spoke to him again but once; that was at Munn's funeral.   He come all the way from the islands, and what do you think he come for?—just to spite me. He stood in the door of the house, and after the service was over, when I was comin' out, he looked at me sharp, and says, ' Didn't I tell you so, Sarah?' Then he puts on his hat and off he walks. I was taken aback for a minute, but I just walks after him, and I says, ' You were mistaken for once; Munn was a good man, and I am his sorrowin' widow.' "

After this the two women did not speak for some moments; nothing was heard in the kitchen but the crackling of the fire and the clatter of dishes. Then Mrs. Munn said:

" Well, I'm glad for you, Martha; and now I must be goin'. Miss Kate will want me. And mind you are good to Tetsy; he's cross-grained at times, but Mrs. Goodyear thinks a sight of him, and I guess "—this more slowly—" the doctor does too."

CHAPTER XVI.

LIFE IN THE RECTORY.

THE years passed peacefully for Ruth; summers and winters glided by with little change in her quiet existence.   She became the good angel of the fishermen and their families, as her husband was their friend and support in times of want and trouble. Ruth was a rich woman, and her hands were always held out to the needy, more especially the children, whom, in memory of her own dear one and Joe, she never refused.

No more little ones came to the rectory, and the great passion which filled Ruth's heart when her arms first held her child, rebounded back upon herself with a force that almost stunned her, when she realized it had no natural outlet.

Arthur Clayton had hoped things would be different in time: she would grow to care for him; his great love would compel hers in return.   He would not acknowledge even to himself that he was mistaken; that the years had brought no answer, to his prayer, no recompense to his patience. He suffered the pangs of a great grief, making no outcry. As months drifted into years, and her calm, serene face met his daily without the love-light for which he waited, a grieved expression settled upon his strong features, marking deep lines about his mouth, and a few threads of gray appeared in his dark hair. He hid his sorrow from his wife, who did not suspect the grief that was changing him, making him an old man before his time.

One afternoon, after they had been married some years, a hasty summons came to the rectory: a sick man wished to see the minister out at the light. Mr. Clayton had just returned from a round of visits in the farming district, and looked pale and tired.

"Who is it?" he asked.

"It's old Pete Morrell," said the messenger; "you know him. He was out fishing in that blow the other day; he lost his sail, he was run up on the rocks on the reef, got hurt, and they took him in at the light."

"Very well," said Mr. Clayton, "I will come."

Some moments later he was out on the water, rowing rapidly toward the reef upon which the lighthouse had been built. It was a gray day, and the wind was blowing; whitecaps bounded about his boat, the oars splashed spray into his face, the gulls flew screaming above his head. He was a powerful man, and pulled hard at the oars; he was used to the exercise, and loved the wildness of the water on a day like this. The salt breeze instilled new life into him, and he inhaled long breaths as his muscular arms propelled the oars.

Upon reaching the reef he found the lighthouse-keeper had gone to the town for oil and supplies, and his old rheumatic wife could not leave her chair. The wounded man had been made as comfortable as possible under the circumstances. When Mr. Clayton entered he found him lying on the cot in the small spare room off the living-room, looking lonely and dispirited.

"I've been a-thinkin', Mr. Clayton," he said, after the minister had seated himself, "that I ain't been a very good man; I've been intemperate and swearin'. Since I've lain here, and had nothin' to do but think and groan and look out at the water, and hear it roarin' round the rocks all day and all night, I've thought I ain't had my anchor out; I've been a-driftin'—a-driftin' out to sea."

"Well, Pete," said Mr. Clayton, "you're on the right course now. It has come to you, my man, late, but it has come; thank God, your shipwreck has been the means of grace."

Pete raised himself on his cot, and leaning toward the minister grasped his hand.

"You ain't full o' talk about what I have been —you spares me that; you takes me from now on. I'm thankful to you, Mr. Clayton, and I hope when I get on my legs again I'll be a better man; perhaps I can be a friend to you sometime."

"I hope you will always be my friend," said Mr. Clayton, heartily.

If he had known when Pete would have redeemed that wish to be his friend, would he have sat there so calmly, looking out upon the waters that rolled by the windows of the lighthouse?

When the keeper came home Mr. Clayton took his departure. It was growing dark; a storm was gathering, and the heavens were full of threatening clouds. The keeper came down to the edge of the rocks to see Mr. Clayton off. His boat had been fastened to an iron staple embedded in the rock, and was pulling and straining heavily at its bounds, as the rough action of the waves beat against it.

"There's a storm comin' up," said the keeper, scanning the clouds; "it'll be a big blow they'll have off the reef to-night. It's a hard pull up to town, wind and tide against you, Mr. Clayton."

Mr. Clayton stepped into the boat. "I've pulled through a rougher sea than this," he said, smiling. "Take care of Pete, poor fellow! I'll be down at the light soon again."

He pulled into the deep water and was soon out on the tide, a small speck in the waste of white-capped waves. He found it a heavy task pulling the boat through the fierce current that beat back his strongest efforts, and made small headway. He was half-way to the town when a blinding rainstorm came upon him, a drenching, penetrating rain, that soaked through his clothing. In the teeth of the cutting gale that accompanied it, he shivered and trembled with a chill that entered into his being with an icy intensity. When he reached the wharf it was dark; the lights were twinkling in the windows of the houses. An old fisherman who was tying up his boat to the pier hurried forward to assist the minister, who could scarcely rise from his seat in the boat; he felt cramped and cold, his teeth were chattering, and his limbs refused to support him.

"Hey, Mr. Clayton, you're wet through; it's a bad night, and no mistake. Been down to see Pete at the light?"

"Yes," answered Mr. Clayton. He then hurried away to the rectory, the old man calling after him: "Take something hot, Mr. Clayton, take something hot; you're chilled through."·

When once ensconced in the light and warmth of his pleasant home, the motive for action removed, he gave way to the weariness that assailed him, sinking into a chair before the fire, remaining silent, pale, and motionless.

"You are not well, Arthur," said Ruth, as she sat opposite him sewing, the candle-light falling upon her calm face.

"I am tired," he said; "I shall be better to-morrow."

To-morrow, however, brought a sad visitant to the rectory. The stalwart rector, who had not known in his hitherto healthy existence what ill-ness meant, now succumbed to a fever—a serious fever, that ran its course of weeks, and sapped the life and strength from the giant frame. It left but a semblance of its former greatness in the pale, emaciated man who lay back languidly upon his pillow, hardly knowing what time of year it was, and too weak to question.

Ruth had been a faithful nurse, snatching hours of rest whenever it was possible, leaving little to the care of the hired attendant or of Jane, who had proffered her services.

"I shall watch by my husband," she had replied, firmly, when remonstrated with by her aunt; "it is my duty; I am happier when I am at work."

During the periods of wild delirium Ruth sat by the bed, listening to strange words and sentences that fell from his lips; words that, at first disjointed and unintelligible, gradually assumed a meaning that seemed to scourge her like a whip of many thongs, and pierced her heart with bitter pangs of remorse. She knew now the silent grief he had endured during the years of their married life; never murmuring, never reproaching, going on in the even tenor of his way, hoping, trusting, loving her with a deep and lasting affection, and leaving the result to his Maker.

At times, when he would look at her intently, not

knowing her, his eyes roving and restless, she would clasp his hand, and holding it tightly the tears would drop upon it.

"You know me, Arthur," she would say, softly; "I am your wife, I am Ruth."

"No, you are not Ruth," he would cry; "I do not know you. Ruth never looked like that; she would not care, she would not cry. Why should she? She told me she never loved me. Ruth is always calm and quiet; Ruth has no heart; long ago she told me that, and I, fool that I was, did not believe her."

"O Arthur!" moaned poor Ruth, well-nigh crushed. She turned her head aside; she could no longer look into that bewildered, entreating face.

When he returned to consciousness, and to the prospect of health, it was spring again; a beautiful May was smiling on the quiet little town, the fishermen had gone out for flounders and blackfish, and the waters of the harbor sparkled in the sunlight. Lilac-bushes were in full blossom in the front yard of the rectory; the apple-trees on the south side of the house looked as though pink clouds had descended from the sky, and were resting on their green boughs.

Arthur, in peaceful convalescence, with Ruth by his side, was seated under the shade of the lilacs, looking out to sea; now and then he would glance longingly toward the little church on the headland. He held in his hand a bunch of arbutus, a gift from one of the village children. The couple had not spoken for some time; Ruth was sewing on a dainty piece of linen for the house, and Arthur was watching her slim fingers and fair hair, upon which the sunshine fell, turning the brown to gold. Suddenly she looked up from her work, conscious of his scrutiny.

"What are you thinking of, Arthur?" she said.

" I was thinking how different it might have been, Ruth, if God had called me to Himself. You would have been free, and a happier woman; now you must take up your yoke again and struggle on."

She dropped her work with a sharp, stifled cry; the tears came into her eyes; rising, she came and stood before her husband, and looked into his face. " "Arthur," she said, " do not reproach me; I have suffered enough. I have done wrong; give me one more trial. I made no effort, simply drifted with the tide, and made no struggle against it—let it lead me where it would. Since baby died I have been as one dead also. I shall be a different woman, I know I shall; only trust me."

He looked sadly upon her sweet, beseeching face.

"You cannot change, Ruth; I do not blame you. I took the risk; it was not your fault, it was my blindness. We have both made a mistake—the common lot of mortals; we must now put forth our noblest efforts to make the best of life. God, in His own good time, will make right our mistakes; if not here, surely in that better world."

It was very still in the rectory garden; there were no passers in the street beyond. The apple-blossoms were softly fluttering to the ground; now and then a bird rustled to its nest in the lilac-bushes.

Ruth did not reply; she was looking up into the sky, to the banks of drifting clouds that were moving lazily onward.

"Arthur," she said, turning toward him suddenly, "you do not understand. I have not tried to love you as I promised when we were married; I blame myself sorely for that, more sorely than you will ever know. When you were ill, and it seemed as though you were going from me, I felt how lonely and empty my life would be without you; I saw then

what I had been doing through all these years.
You will forgive me?"

She held out her trembling hands toward him.

"I have nothing to forgive, Ruth," he said, with
a tender, loving smile.   "Let us not talk about it
any more; let us begin all over again, as the children say."

She put her hand upon his shoulder and, bending
over him, kissed him.   It was the first time she had
ever kissed him voluntarily; his pale face flushed
and the bunch of arbutus dropped from his hand.

One afternoon, some days after this conversation,
Ruth and her husband were walking slowly along
the grassy street that led to Dr. Goodyear's cottage.   Arthur could take short walks now, and was
rejoicing in his renewed strength.   Dandelions were
blooming thickly along the paths, and tiny blue
grass-flowers blew in the wind at their feet as they
passed on.   When nearing the cottage they saw
Jane and the doctor standing side by side in a corner of the garden; at the'r feet was a wooden box.
The doctor had a spade in his hand, his coat was
hanging over the limb of a tree near by, and a pile
of newly turned earth stood near a hole he was digging in the ground.   On the kitchen door-step, watch-

ing them solemnly, were Mrs. Munn and Martha. As Arthur and Ruth entered the gate the doctor dropped his spade, and he and Jane came forward to meet them.

Ruth saw tear-stains on Jane's face.

"Tetsy is dead," she said; "he died last night." Then she turned to the doctor. "You have not dug the hole nearly deep enough."

"The box is too large—I told you so this morning," he replied, wiping the perspiration from his brow.

"I will not have a cramped little box," she said, shortly; "Tetsy always liked plenty of room. Don't you remember how he liked a whole chair to himself?"

"I am sorry for you, Aunt Jane," said Ruth. "Poor little Tetsy! he was very old, though."

"Well, what if he was? I did not want to lose him."

The doctor looked up with a comical expression at Arthur, who turned his face aside and smiled; then, returning to his task, plodded stolidly at the hole he was digging. The box was buried and the earth returned to its place, then patted down smoothly by the doctor's spade.

"Now, Ezekiel," said Jane, "I want this spot marked." He looked inquiringly at her. "I want," she continued, "one of your rose-bushes placed here—one of your ' Cloth of Gold.'"

"What!" he gasped, "one of my ' Cloth of Gold ' bushes, the finest I have? Jane, do not be unreasonable."

"I want it," she said.

"Would not some annuals do? I have plenty of seeds"—this with alacrity. " How about bachelor's-buttons or—or—widow's-tears?" He paused.

Jane looked sharply at him. Could he be laughing at her? No, his expression was too solemn for amusement.

"I do not wish annuals; I wish one of your ' Cloth of Gold ' bushes. Don't you suppose I value Tetsy more than one of your rose-bushes?"

The doctor sighed, then started perceptibly; remorse had taken possession of him. If it had not been for Tetsy he would never have called Jane Weston his wife; here he was begrudging her a rose-bush on his grave, miserable man that he was! If Jane knew of his deception what would she say? Would she leave him and go back to the manor? She looked capable of anything, standing there watching him determinedly. Yes, she would leave him; he deserved to be forsaken; he was a coward and a deceiver. He started on a run for his rose-garden.

"Would you not like two bushes, Jane?" he called, as he hurried away; "I can spare any number you like."

Jane glanced at him in surprise. "One will do," she said.

Presently the doctor returned and planted the bush, the finest one he had in his collection of fine roses. He patted the earth, feeling a pleasure in doing the best he could for the lowly instrument of his present happiness.

"He was a fine dog," he said, with a burst of eloquence, forgetting the numerous times Tetsy had clung to his trousers in days past and pursued him at breakneck speed down the avenue of elms at the manor. "A fine dog, a most intelligent animal; perhaps a little excitable at times, but that was no doubt due to his sagacity."

"I was very fond of him," said Jane, brokenly, turning away; "I shall miss him greatly." Whatever Tetsy's faults of temper, his mistress was sincere in her devotion.

Mrs. Munn and Martha came strolling across the grass to see the grave, and the rest waited for them.

"It looks nice, doctor," said Mrs. Munn. "You thought a sight of Tetsy, didn't you?" She looked sharply at the doctor, who was putting on his coat and did not notice her glance. "I mind so well the night he was lost," she continued. "I was here, and me and Martha was alone in the kitchen; we thought there was a spirit in the house, such a fearful and blood-curdlin' noise as came from your office; but it wasn't nothin' after all; only it gave us such a fright."

The doctor glanced at Mrs. Munn. What did the woman suspect? he wondered. Something, he was sure; he never had liked Mrs. Munn's sharpness.

Jane had moved toward the house; Ruth and Arthur followed; they did not catch the conclusion of the conversation.

"What kind of a noise was it?" said the doctor, innocently.

"It was a howlin' and kind of low grumblin'."

"Oh, that was probably some acids that I have in my laboratory. They explode at times—in fact, quite frequently; you must never be alarmed at anything like that in a doctor's house."

" I wasn't alarmed," said Mrs. Munn, quietly; " I was only thinkin' it happened the night Tetsy was lost." She stooped and picked up a grass-flower from the ground. " These grass-flowers is real pretty, doctor," she said, looking him squarely in the face.

The doctor buttoned his coat with an alacrity unusual to him, and did not reply; then he walked quickly toward the house. When he reached the porch he paused and looked back toward the two women, who still stood by the newly transplanted rose-bush.

" Mrs. Munn is a suspicious, meddling creature," he muttered; " that woman knows a little too much —for a woman." Then he went into the house and shut the door with a bang.

CHAPTER XVII.

A BETTER condition of feeling had arisen between Arthur and Ruth, a confidence and faith in each other that changed·much of the weary endurance practised on either side to a peaceful acquiescence. They understood each other as they never had before; understood the struggles, the heartaches, the useless repinings and vain regrets.

Many a time at the dusk of evening, when the shadows were creeping stealthily about the pleasant rectory parlor, the minister and his wife sat beside each other, hand in hand, talking about what had once been a sealed book between them, an impassable gulf across which their feet dared not pass. They would speak of their doubts and fears, and would start refreshed from this peaceful converse. It was as though the winds from distant fields of rest were sweeping across their souls, opening up the dark places, lifting the curtains that hung straight and impenetrable before Ruth's bruised spirit. Bruised nerves are difficult of treatment— far better annihilation; it takes years and patience to effect a cure.

A strange and unexpected event took place about this time. Arthur was well and strong once more —at least as strong as he would ever be again after such a severe strain on the system as his recent illness.

He was paying pastoral calls on his scattered parishioners in the farming district, and had been absent three days. Ruth was alone in the rectory. It was midsummer, and the corn was high in the fields; a great heat had settled upon the town. In the harbor the water looked motionless and oily; no breeze stirred the limp sails or rustled the reeds near the water's edge. The song of the birds was stilled, only feeble pipings coming from the distant woods; the dust lay thick upon the country roads, rising in clouds when the horses, with steaming sides, plodded wearily over them.

Ruth had been sitting with old granny, who was bedridden from rheumatism and had become Ruth's charge. She was a patient old creature, lying all day on her neat bed, happy and contented, thankful to God for having sent her such a good friend as Mrs. Clayton, who kept her from becoming a public care. Ruth was sitting beside her this warm afternoon; she had been reading aloud, when suddenly, looking up from her book, she noticed the room had become darkened, and that a rustling, as of increasing wind, was heard in the branches of the pines near the house. She went to the door and looked out: the waters of the bay were rising and beating against the wooden piers of the wharf; beyond the harbor, outside the bar, long lines of white breakers were rolling in toward the reef; the sky was obscured by masses of dull, black-hued clouds with crimson-tinted edges. She shaded her eyes with her hand a moment, looking seaward; then, coming back into the room, she said:

"Granny, there is a storm coming; I must hurry home; I think there is time to reach the rectory before the rain falls."

She hastened away, and had almost reached the end of the narrow lane where the fishing-town joined the business street of Lynnport, when she was accosted by a rough, unkempt-looking man, who stepped suddenly from a sailors' boardinghouse in the vicinity, and barred her further progress.

"Pardon, ma'am," he said, removing his battered cap; "are you Mrs. Clayton, the minister's wife?"

Ruth started; she was taken by surprise for an instant, but she was not naturally a timid woman, and had become familiar with the sailors and their characteristics.

"Yes," she said; "what do you want?"

The man hesitated, fumbling nervously with his hat. He had a sick, hopeless look, as though the world had dealt hardly with him, and he had been worsted in the struggle.

"I am sick and poor," he said, doggedly; "I thought perhaps—" He hesitated. "I heard you was kind to us sailor men. It's hard for me to ask; I've always worked, but I got the fever out in China, and I ain't been any good since, or likely to be."

"Have you been long in Lynnport?" said Ruth, studying him carefully.

"No, not in some years; I came back after I got out o' hospital—worked my way back when I could hardly crawl."

"What captain did you sail under?" said Ruth.

At that instant a distant but menacing peal of thunder rumbled across the sky.

"I went out with Captain Jack Hathaway, master of the 'Bonny Kate,'" he said, looking away from her.

Ruth did not reply instantly; then she said, a tremor in her voice:

"I knew of him; I will help you." Taking out her purse she poured its contents into his hand. "I have an interest in all the seamen that sail from Lynnport; I shall not forget you."

He thanked her, and she hurried away from him up the steep hill.

The storm was drawing nearer slowly, the wind having partially died away. She stood upon the hill an instant, looking back at the man, who was leaning wearily against the side of the lodging-house in an attitude of hopeless dejection.

"Where have I seen him?" she mused. "Ah yes, I remember: it was the day Jack took me to see the ship; this man was in the cabin cleaning the glass. It seems so long ago—like another life." She stood some moments thinking intently. "It was so bright and sunny that day; Jack showed me all about the ship, and looked so proud and happy, and—there—" She clenched her hands, and bit her lips till the blood started. "I will not think of those days," she said, fiercely; "I dare not." She spoke aloud; her voice sounded strange and harsh.

She went into the rectory and sat down by the window of the cozy study that faced the sea, to watch the oncoming of the storm. It was late in the afternoon, and the darkness of the coming evening, coupled with the threatening heavens, lent an aspect of gloom to all objects. Ruth sat very still, her hands clasped in her lap; the house was quiet—the ticking of the clock on the landing of the stairs could be distinctly heard. Though surrounded with the familiar objects of her husband's work—his desk, papers, opened sermon-case, and his coat across a chair—the sense of his presence did not come to her. She was thinking of her sailor lover; of the time when she was a girl and used to meet him in the fields around Lynnport, when he gathered flowers for her. Once he secured an oriole's nest; she had it still among the treasures she had not looked at for many years, yet jealously guarded from destruction.

The storm increased, the room darkened; she sat quietly, unheeding the outward gloom, bidding the specters come forth, setting the pieces on the board before her, and commanding them to go through their allotted parts. Presently the maid came in with the candles.

"Take them away," said Ruth; "I wish to watch the storm."

It was now quite late; the storm, which had been slow in gathering, was a giant in its accumulated force, and the peals rumbled with reverberating crashes across the sky, followed almost immediately by flashes of blinding lightning. She drew back from the window, the light blinded her; the power and might of the works of the Creator manifest before her alarmed her, and she put her hands before her face. When she removed them she saw, pressed against the window, the features of a haggard countenance peering into the room, with eyes fixed upon her, its unkempt shock of hair flying in wild gusts of wind.

She darted from the room and down the hall to the kitchen.

"Quick, quick!" she called, as she opened the kitchen door and stood on the threshold of the lighted interior; "some one is hiding about the house; I saw him at the window of the study. Come with me."

The two maids followed her tremblingly; upon opening the front door they found the drenched figure of a man huddled upon the stone steps. Ruth leaned over him; the wind blew her hair wildly about her face, and the rain dashed in driving gusts into the hall, causing the candle held by one of the women to flutter tremulously in the draft.

The man lifted his face; it was the sailor she had helped that afternoon in the lane of the fishing-town. He staggered to his feet, and she bade him enter; the water dropped from his tattered garments upon the hall floor; he looked white and hopeless.

"Take him to the kitchen," she said to the women; "let him dry his garments, then send him to me in the study."

An hour later the man stood before her in the study; the candles were lighted. The crash of the storm had lessened; the peals were less vibrant, coming at longer intervals, though the lightning still played bewildering pranks upon the window-curtains.

"Tell me what brought you here," said Ruth, severely; "what motive had you in following and spying upon me?"

"I'll tell you, ma'am; I tried to this afternoon,

but I couldn't; you was kind to me, and I couldn't talk of it." He paused.

"Go on," said Ruth, calmly.

"Well, I was sent back from hospital to Lynnport by Captain Hathaway, who was a good friend to me after I got the fever. I told you this afternoon I caught the fever in China. In the bed next to mine was a young feller from Lynnport who had broke his leg a-fallin' from a mast, and he talked about the old place a'most all the time. He was only a boy, and it was his first trip; he was homesick for his mother. This happened about eight months ago. One day Captain Jack he come in to see me, and the sick boy was a-goin' on, and he got a-talkin' about folks, and he spoke about the Lorrimers, and about Miss Ruth bein' so good to the sailors and all the seafarin' folks. (He didn't call you Mrs. Clayton, and the Captain thought you was still Miss Lorrimer. I didn't know, either; I hadn't been in Lynnport in many years.) The Captain he just sat there with his hand over his eyes, and listened while that sick boy rattled on. When he got up and went out o' the ward he was white, and he staggered some. The next day he come to me, and he says: 'I made a mistake once, my man; I'm sorry for it. I want you to do somethin' for me; I want you, when you are better, to go to Lynnport, find Miss Ruth Lorrimer, and give her this letter.'" As the man finished speaking he took from his pocket a letter and held it in his hand. "When I got here," he continued ("I came aboard a coaster; I was nearly spent—all gone like)—that was some days ago—when I could, I found out about you; I found out you—was—was married. I didn't know whether to see you then or not, as the—the—letter was directed to Miss Ruth Lorrimer, not Mrs. Arthur Clayton. The Captain said it was for Miss Ruth Lorrimer."

Ruth trembled and swayed slightly toward the man, the candle-light shining upon her face, which looked pale as snow in its uncertain gleam; then she held out her hand for the letter.

"Captain Hathaway," she said, as her fingers closed upon the letter—"is he well?"

"He is well," the man answered, looking closely at her.

"Has he been long in China?"

"He has returned to Boston but twice since he left Lynnport. He hasn't sailed his own ship for some years, though he still owns the brig; he is captain now of the company's wharves at Hong-Kong."

"Did—did—he send me any message besides this letter?" Ruth tried to look calmly upon the man; her blue eyes, gleaming almost black in intensity in her white face, belied her outward composure.

"He said," answered the man, slowly, "that the letter would explain everything, and that you would understand. I was to return on the first outward-bound vessel with the answer; I was to tell him how you looked, and all about the old place, and about the garden at the homestead."

Ruth did not appear to hear him; she glanced absently past him. She held the letter an instant in her hand, so tightly the paper was crushed in her grasp, then raised it close to her face, reading the inscription carefully and earnestly, word for word, letter for letter: "Miss Ruth Lorrimer, Lynnport Harbor." There was no Ruth Lorrimer now; there had been living once a girl of that name; now she was dead—dead long ago. This letter was not for her; she had no right to read its contents; she was a wife, and belonged to her husband; an old lover had no rights.

The man waited respectfully; he understood it all,

feeling a keen sympathy for the sad-faced woman before him. A vision rose before his face of the eager, hopeful look of the man who gave him the letter to deliver, saying, " I made a mistake once, my man ; I'm sorry for it." He could see it all: the wharf at Hong-Kong, the trading-ships, the stalwart man bending earnestly toward him with the bronzed, bearded face and the dash of gray in his hair. He waited; the roll of thunder had grown into a sullen, retreating murmur, the clock on the stairs ticked loudly.

Ruth held the letter toward the flickering candle ; her hand trembled, its form throwing a wavering shadow upon the low ceiling of the study.

The man made a hasty movement, then drew back; he had no right to interfere, he was only an onlooker.

She placed the letter in the flame, watched it slowly burn to ashes, its charred remains fluttering down among her husband's papers upon his writing-table.

" When you return to Hong-Kong," she said, " tell Captain Hathaway there is no Ruth Lorrimer ; you could not deliver your letter. Tell him that Mrs. Arthur Clayton hopes he is well and happy, as she is well and—and—happy." Her last words came with a short gasp, and she stepped outside the light thrown from the candle.

The man bowed and walked toward the door; then he hesitated.

"Why do you wait?" she said.

"Is there no further message?" He looked wistful and undecided.

"There is no further message," she replied.

He went out, closing the door softly behind him.

Ruth stood where he had left her, looking straight before her to where the little heap of brown ashes rested on her husband's papers on the table. When the outer door closed, and she heard the retreating steps of the man on the walk leading down the hillside, she went upstairs and returned with a box in her hand, a box of sandalwood inlaid with pearl, a possession bequeathed by her young mother.

The night had grown chilly after the storm; a strong breeze blew in from the sea, rustled the curtains at the windows, and sent sweet odors into the room from the vines and flowers without.

She ordered a wood-fire upon the hearth, and sat down before it with the box upon her lap, then opened it, looking sadly at its contents. There was

very little in it; to a casual observer what it contained would have appeared worthless. She sat
very still for some time, the tears standing thick in
her eyes.

"It is right," she said; "I must not keep them
any longer. I am glad Jack has not thrown his life
away; I shall not grieve further for that." Suddenly she closed the box with a quick motion, and
stood up, holding it in her hand, then, placing it
upon the table, looked expectantly toward the door;
she had heard her husband's step upon the walk.
He entered the house and stood in the hall without.
She rose, opened the study door, and with a smile
met him upon the threshold.

"You escaped the storm, did you not?" she said,
quietly, observing his dry garments.

"Yes, I took shelter in a farm-house." He went
to the blaze and stood before it, then caught sight
of the box upon the table.

She took it in her hand and went to him.

"Arthur," she said, "something strange has happened to-day; I·wish to tell you about it." Then,
in a gentle, quiet way, and without great emotion,
she told him all. "This box contains a few treasures; I do not know why I have kept them—they

have no value in price, and no right to any value in sentiment. I have brought them here to-night to destroy them." She opened the box, and held up a bunch of dry, withered daisies, the crumbling petals dropping upon her dress, thence to the floor. An oriole's nest lay beneath the daisies, and a packet of letters, not many and not long ones. One by one she took her treasures and laid them upon the blaze, and watched them vanish into ashes; then she gazed sadly into the empty box.

"I could not have done this a year ago, Arthur," she said; "I should have deemed it sacrilege; now I have strength to feel it is right and best; I am glad I have heard from him and know that he is well."

Arthur drew her to him and kissed her. "My wife," he said, "my Ruth!"

After this news Ruth went forth refreshed to her daily cares, for cares she had many. The Lady Bountiful of the parish, the good angel of the fishermen, her time was fully occupied and her fortune was used to much practical good among her poor friends. In the cold of the bitter winter nights no cottage was left without its fire, no sufferer without comfort; she was idolized by the people, as her husband was respected and revered. The knowledge of Jack's condition was like a beacon-light in the darkness; he was well, he was occupied; he was not the wreck she had sometimes thought he might become: she was grateful for that.

Mrs. Munn met her one afternoon returning from the death-bed of a crippled child. As she climbed the hilly street toward the rectory she was thinking of little Joe; thinking tender, loving thoughts of her "comforter," her first friend after her trouble.

"For the land's sake!" cried Mrs. Munn, barring her progress by stepping directly in front of her in the narrow way; "you look beat out; you're as pale as a sheet. Why do you have to be doctor and undertaker, friend and supporter, and goodness knows what, all at once? They say the back is fitted for the burden; I never did nor won't believe that. You can overburden a good-natured back; I'll always contend that. You need rest, Mrs. Clayton."

"I am a little tired to-day, Mrs. Munn, though I would not be contented to be idle; I have much work to do, work that has been given me to do."

"Well, I suppose work has been given us all, but I believe in shuttin' your eyes once in a while when the work comes pilin' on—kind of lookin' off the other way, innocent like; I used to do that with Munn when he come in with fifty things to do all at once. Try it, Mrs. Clayton; try shuttin' your eyes to some things; you can't be takin' care of the whole fishin'-town."

Ruth laughed and passed on.

Mrs. Munn stood looking after her. " Talk about angels," she muttered; " I don't want to see any better angel than Miss Ruth when I get to heaven, if—if—I ever do," she finished, slowly. " She's one of the best women that ever lived, and I believe it's all on account of her trouble. They say trouble is the makin' of some people, but it's a mighty hard teacher." She went her way, solemnly shaking her head, her gaunt, angular figure held as straight as a mast.

CHAPTER XVIII.

THE DONATION PARTY.

A VAST idea had been promulgated in Lynnport by the united efforts of the ladies of Mr. Clayton's parish. This important movement was none other than to tender a great entertainment to the rector and his wife—an entertainment worthy of the ladies and the recipients. It was late in the fall when this idea was first advanced, so necessarily the affair must bear somewhat the guise of a Thanksgiving festivity. Meeting after meeting was held at Dr. Goodyear's cottage, at which Mrs. Burton presided, as possessing the most executive ability. It was finally decided that the entire congregation should unite in presenting a costly present of silver to Mrs. Clayton, and that the parish, rich and poor, old and young, should meet at the rectory on the evening of the 2d of December, for a jollification, when the gift would be tendered. This latter conclusion reached, it was necessary to acquaint Ruth with the decision, all except the presentation.

She entered heartily into the preparations. The large parlors of the rectory were thrown open, and the kitchen, a rambling extension, had the floor sanded for any games in which the younger members might desire to indulge. Garlands of greens were brought from the woods to festoon the walls, and were draped above the doors and windows.

The only member of the parish who held somewhat aloof from the mighty event which was causing a ferment in quiet Lynnport was Dr. Goodyear. He listened when consulted in regard to details, and made mighty efforts to suggest novel features for the success of the enterprise; but a close observer could have detected his labored interest, and in this case that close observer was his wife. She suspected something was amiss, and watched him closely, her keen eyes on the alert for any suspicious movements on his part.

It was the last day of November, a gray, cold day, and the clouds were hanging low over the water. The ridge of hills toward the north was covered with a thick mist; flocks of ducks and wild geese screamed harshly as they flew toward the south, their discordant notes echoing through the still atmosphere; a few dead leaves that still remained upon the ground whirled in fitful gusts of wind.

There had been a ring around the moon the night before. Jim Benton had told his cronies as they lounged upon the wharf, their jackets buttoned up to their necks, that "there was goin' to be a storm; and I tell yer, mates, a big one this time. I see a sun-dog in the sky night afore last, and I ain't one not to take a reef in my sail and make all things shipshape when there's a sun-dog around."

"You're always a-prophesyin', Jim," said one of the men, shaking the ashes out of his pipe; "I ain't seen no sun-dog."

"I have," said Jim, kicking an old lobster-crate out of his way, "and I predicts a hurricane."

The rest of the men stood looking solemnly over the gray, turbulent waters, and said nothing.

At this instant Dr. Goodyear joined the men; he glanced searchingly around an instant, as though some one were following him, then said:

"Have any of you a dog to sell—a terrier, not large, yellow coat, curly, pretty stout, and moderately good disposition?"

The men turned all in a row and stood facing him

in surprise; Jim scratched his head meditatingly; the man with the pipe had taken it from his mouth, and was holding it upside down, the fire and ashes dropping unheeded upon the wharf.

"You want a dog, doctor?" finally said Jim.

"That's what I have been asking for," said the doctor, calmly.

"Well," said Jim, slowly, "I knows of a dog—a nice little feller too—down in the fishin'-town at the house next to granny's, only he's a pup and tears things; he tore all the clothes off the line and chewed some on 'em. He'll get over that, though; he's good breed and yellow color and curly, just the way you want him."

The doctor's face fell at the description of the tearing propensities of the pup, but suddenly brightened, as though strengthened by some inner resolution.

"Go down to the town, Jim; I'll wait here. Get the dog, bring him to me; if I like him I'll pay what they ask."

"Aye," said Jim, as he rolled away in true sailor fashion. As he stepped off the wharf to the level of the street he called back: "You'll have to make allowances for his bein' a pup."

After he had gone the doctor sat down on an

overturned bait-barrel and waited; the men turned to their silent scrutiny of the water.

The pup proved to be satisfactory, though possessed of rather too much animal spirits, evincing such in wild dashes at the doctor's coat-tails, which failing to dislodge he fell over on his back, legs in the air.

" He'll do," said the doctor, catching him up. He held his handkerchief over the dog's head, and buttoning his coat over the struggling body prepared to depart with his possession, the men watching him gravely.

" Is it for yourself, doctor? " said Jim.

" No, it's for Mrs. Goodyear," answered the doctor, shortly, pushing the puppy's head down, as, covered with the handkerchief, he was endeavoring to peer forth from the collar of the doctor's greatcoat.   He went slowly up the hill; when he neared the top the men had the satisfaction of seeing the dog suddenly drop from the 'doctor's grasp, and begin a wild career, with much shrill barking, down the steep incline, the doctor in hot pursuit.   The dog was caught midway on the descent, and presently the doctor entered his garden gate with his yelping companion.

His wife saw him from her bedroom window; saw, too, what he had in his arms. She met him at the front door.

"I won't have him," she said; "take him right back."

"O Jane," said the doctor, appealingly, as he held the puppy out to her, "I've had such a run; I want to tell you something."

"I should think you had; I saw you; at your time of life making such a spectacle of yourself, . chasing dogs all round town."

"I didn't chase him all round town," said the doctor, meekly; "I only chased him on the hill a short distance."

"Well, it's all the same; I won't have him."

"Jane, come into the study; I want to tell you something; after that, if you like, we'll send the puppy back; I bought him because I thought you missed Tetsy and would like him." The doctor looked grave. Jane silently followed him; something in his voice made her quiet. After entering his office he pulled forward an easy-chair, bidding her be seated; then, seating himself opposite her, holding the puppy in his lap, he told the story of his deception, the means he had used to win her, and his ultimate condition of tortured conscience. He dared not look at her as he proceeded, keeping his eyes averted, surreptitiously wiping his perspiring forehead at intervals. How would she take it? Would she go back to the manor, and leave him alone in his old age? These were the thoughts that darted through his mind.

After he concluded, silence reigned for a few moments in the small room. Jane looked at the doctor, whose head was bowed over the puppy, that had fallen asleep; then her gaze wandered to the window and the gray autumnal landscape without.

"Doctor," she said—her voice sounded low and gentle—"I cannot say but this might have made a difference had I known it before we were married; now—" She paused. "Ezekiel, we are very happy in our old age; we were both lonely; perhaps, after all, Tetsy was a blessing in disguise." She laid her hand on the doctor's gray head. "I'll keep the puppy; we'll call him Tetsy No. 2."

Tetsy No. 2 looked up at this announcement with a most idiotic puppy-grin upon his face; Jane smiled, took him in her arms, and peace was restored in the cottage. The doctor, with beaming countenance, hummed at intervals, during the rest of the day, strains of old melodies heard in his boyhood. Jane listened from her room above, and watched Tetsy No. 2 demolish a crocheted tidy without interference. She was quiet and pensive; her usually high-pitched voice was subdued; there were tears in her eyes as she stood a long while watching the sea from the dormer-window of her room.

"Ezekiel is a good man," she murmured once—"a very good man."

It was the night of the great party to be given at the rectory. The weather had grown cold; the air was full of fine snow, that, hardly perceptible, cut the pedestrians' faces like tiny needles, and the wind blew fiercely from the northeast. All day long great breakers on the outer reef boomed sullenly, dashing white spray into the air as they rushed swirling toward the rocks. The tide was high in the harbor, reaching the tops of the wharves; the fishing-fleet lay at anchor, no vessel venturing forth. The gulls screamed as they swooped above the waves, their light flight carried forward on the wind.

As night drew near the windows in the spacious rectory shone with the brilliant gleam thrown from many candles.

Jim Benton looked into the dark sky as he waited outside the door a moment before entering, and said to himself:

"There's goin' to be a fearful storm—I see the sun-dog again last night."

Mr. and Mrs. Clayton stood in the large parlor to receive their guests. Ruth wore a white dress and some flowers in her hair, that soft brown hair that showed now many a thread of silver; she looked bright and smiling as the candle-light fell upon her. She felt happy to-night, happier than she had felt for ten years, for it was ten years since her lover had sailed away and left her desolate.

The collation was spread in the kitchen; after that came the presentation of the silver pitcher. Then the games commenced—old-fashioned, romping games, taken part in by nearly all the guests. Even Mrs. Munn was persuaded to take a hand in a game of forfeits; when she was obliged to kiss Jim Benton much amusement was manifested by the company. To every one's amazement she marched up to Jim where he sat blushing in a corner. "I guess I ain't goin' to spoil sport if I know it," she said; "I've done many a hard thing in my life—I guess I can do this," and she imprinted a loud kiss on his cheek.

He rose as though he had been struck, and, putting his hand to his cheek, looked at her; then, thinking he must also do his part, he stepped close to her and kissed her in return.

"That ain't the game, Jim," she said, marching off; "we're playin' forfeits."

"Oh," he said, sitting down, "I didn't know how you played the game."

Later in the evening, when the games were beginning to flag, and some of the older members had taken their departure, a strange, unaccountable depression seized Ruth. It fell upon her as a cloud falls upon a sunny landscape, shutting out all color and light, the heavy folds of its dark curtain obscuring life and cheer. Perhaps, like many sensitive organizations, she was unconsciously influenced by the rising storm, that evinced itself in heavy gusts of wind that rattled the casements, and in driving sleet that dashed at intervals against the window-panes. She went to the window and, parting the curtain, pressed her face against the glass and looked into the night. A mantle of snow lay upon the ground and was rapidly piling in drifts against the north side of the house. Arthur joined her at the window and looked over her shoulder.

"It is a wild night," he said, peering out into the darkness.

"Yes," she replied, in a low voice; "God pity those at sea!"

He looked at her earnestly. "You look tired, Ruth," he said; "the evening has been a wearing one; yet it has also been a great pleasure to us both to feel that we possess the good-will of our people."

"Yes, it has been pleasant; I do not know why I feel this depression stealing over me. Look which way I will I see nothing but blackness, storms, and shipwreck, one face looking up at me from the waves; and it—is white, and—it—it—is Jack's face, and he is dead." She looked wistfully before her, holding her hand outstretched, then dropped it wearily by her side. "Can it be, Arthur," she said, looking into his face earnestly, "that some strong influence exists between two who in this world have been much to each other, that by some mysterious power one feels the other's danger?"

"I cannot tell," he said—"perhaps; the workings of a mind are incomprehensible."

She turned to the room again; her guests were . departing; one by one they passed out into the storm of the winter's night.

As Jim wound his woolen muffler about his throat he said to Mr. Clayton:

"I predicted this storm, Mr. Clayton; I ain't often mistaken; it's goin' to be the worst this 'ere coast has seen in many a year."

"I hope not, Jim, I hope not," said Mr. Clayton, as he held the door with his hand, forcibly preventing it from shutting in his visitor's face, or the wind tearing it from its fastenings.

"It's a tearer," replied Jim; "reminds me of when I was mate o'—"

"Come on, Jim Benton," called Mrs. Munn, from the gate; "do you want to freeze out the whole house? I can't wait all night; ain't you goin' to see me home?"

Jim did not stay to recount reminiscences; he hurried after the tall muffled figure that waited near the gate.

After all had gone, and the house was quiet, Ruth and her husband sat down before the fire in his cozy study. He had put on his slippers and was resting in his easy-chair, his head leaning against its cushioned back. She sat facing him, watching the crackling logs, seeing in the ruddy flame pictures of other days; pictures of the garden at the manor, of her girlhood's stately home, the avenue of elms, and the garret with its wealth of discarded treasures.

"Arthur," she said, "I love the sea; its salt breath is life and rest; yet on such a night as this I tremble with fear; there is awful power in its might. Think of the poor men on the ocean to-night." She paused and turned her gaze from the glowing fire. At this instant a terrific gust tore the shutter from its hold, the sleet and snow dashed against the glass, and the wind in the chimney blew the ashes and sparks out into the room. She covered her face with her hands, then, dropping them in her lap, said softly:

"Arthur, let us pray for those at sea; let us pray for one who, no doubt, as we all do, needs many prayers; he is on the deep to-night." She spoke solemnly, with strong conviction.

They knelt down before the fire and prayed for those in peril on the deep; then Ruth rose, and in a trembling voice sang the hymn for the sailors—the hymn that little Joe had loved; that she sang to him so often during those weary months of suffering before he died:

> "Oh, save the sailor man,
> As, on the ocean wide,
> With God beside him at the helm,
> He braves the fiercest tide.

> " He brings the wanderer home
> Beneath the sheltered hill,
> Who trusteth in His might to save;
> He bids the wave be still."

She sighed after she finished the last line, and walked restlessly to the window.

" The storm is increasing," she said, looking back into the room. " I can scarcely see the light, the snow is blinding; listen to the surf, is it not fearful?" Suddenly she paused, holding her finger raised; then darting back into the room, her head inclined forward, she grasped her husband's arm.

" Arthur," she cried, " listen! do you not hear the guns, the guns from the outer reef?—a wreck off Lynnport light!"

He rose from his chair and listened intently an instant. " It is a wreck," he said, hoarsely—" a wreck on the outer reef."

CHAPTER XIX.

THE GREAT STORM.

MR. CLAYTON hurried to the window and threw it open. A terrific gust of cold air rushed into the room, a whirling mass of snow and sleet accompanying it, and the draft caused a dull rumbling in the chimney. He leaned out into the night.

"I am right," he cried; "it is a wreck—a wreck on the outer reef. God have mercy on their souls!"

Ruth clasped her hands; her face had grown very white.

"What shall we do?" she said, brokenly.

"Do?" he replied, throwing off his house-coat. "Bring me my storm-coat, quick; I must go to the beach and work while there is time."

She brought him his heavy winter coat, helped him put it on, then stood before him and said:

"Arthur, I am going with you; do not attempt to persuade me to remain here—it would be useless. I am going, I am determined."

"Come," he said; "perhaps it would be better so."

At that instant, above the deep booming of the surf and the howling of the gale, was heard the muffled sound of guns. Ruth placed her hands over her ears and shuddered.

"Hurry, hurry!" she said; "let us go to the beach."

The wildest confusion reigned throughout the little town. Against the black background of the dark, tempestuous night, hurrying figures bearing aloft burning fagots were hastening to the beach. Women in groups, with shawls pinned over their heads, were calling and weeping, as they struggled against the wind on the steep road down the hillside that led to the lower street, thence a mile along the shore road, past the Lorrimer manor, to the sea.

The scene on the sands was bewildering and pathetic—pathetic in the sight of puny strength against tremendous power. Men ran hither and thither with hoarse shouts, scarcely hearing one another's voices above the mighty roar of the waters. The life-boats had been dragged by the hardy fishermen along the beach, from the sheltered cove near the harbor's mouth. They were now upon the shore, just outside the range of foaming breakers that dashed far up the sands, a solid wall of glistening water.

The ship was hard and fast on the outer reef. The gleam from the lighthouse revealed occasional hazy glimpses of her masts, as they careened backward and forward from the pounding she was receiving on the sharp-edged rocks. The seas were breaking over the stranded vessel, throwing spray and foam to the topmast, which loomed heavenward, like a mighty ghost of the sea rising from the dark surface of the waves.

When Ruth and her husband reached the shore they were nearly breathless battling with the icy gale. They stood a moment together on the sands, beyond the reach of the heaving breakers. Mr. Clayton's keen eyes wandered from the life-boats to the wreck.

" Jim Benton," he called, as he saw Jim hurrying by with a lighted fagot, " bring the light here."

" Aye, aye," said Jim, as he came up to them. " She's lost, Mr. Clayton; it's no use; the sea has washed them off the riggin' before this; there ain't a man aboard that 'ere craft."

Mr. Clayton did not reply immediately; the light thrown from the glowing fagot fell across his strong, resolute face. He glanced over the waste of heaving, surging waters, then said:

"Never give up, Jim. There are men aboard that vessel—who are firing the guns? There may be one man, there may be more; we must make an effort for their lives."

"It ain't no use," muttered Jim, turning away.

Mr. Clayton left Ruth, and, joining a group of 'fishermen who stood near by in tarpaulins and oilskin caps, said:

"My men, let us make a trial for their lives. Those poor fellows should not drown before our eyes without a stroke from us."

"It's no use, Mr. Clayton," said the spokesman of the group; "yer couldn't launch the boats—they'd swamp. Me and my mates has talked it over; we think the best way is just to wait right here. When the vessel goes to pieces perhaps some o' the crew will come in on the spars; yer see the tide sets this way."

"It is a shame," said Mr. Clayton, "it is cruel, it is unmanly, to stand with folded hands. I will go to the rescue; who will join me? I say the boats can be launched."

Silence followed this speech; nothing answered

him but the wild shrieking of the wind, the crashing and booming of the surf.

"Am I to go alone?" he said, sadly, looking around upon the weather-beaten faces.

"I ain't a-goin' to certain death," said the spokesman. "If there was a chance I'd go—I'd risk it; but I've got Lizzie and the children to think on."

The group of fisherwomen now joined the men.

"Don't you leave us!" they wailed. Their cold, toil-worn hands were holding their. shawls about their heads; their garments were flying wildly in the gale. Each one stepped beside her husband. "Remember the children!" they cried.

"We can't go, Mr. Clayton," they said, respectfully.

"Will no one go with me?" he repeated, loudly; "no one?" He waited.

Suddenly a hoarse voice answered:

"I'll go, Mr. Clayton, and my three boys; it sha'n't never be said that old Pete Morrell and his boys was skeered o' death, or wouldn't lend a helpin' hand to a feller-sufferer."

At these words Ruth joined her husband and laid her hand upon his arm.

"Arthur," she said, "Arthur, think of me."

He turned and caught her in his arms.

"Ruth," he said, hoarsely, "God is calling me. I hear His voice in the wind and the waves; I dare not refuse to listen; I must go; I must obey His will."

She released herself from his grasp (the fishermen had turned away), and looked into her husband's face. What was this light upon it, this light she had never seen, had been too blind, too obstinate to see; this gleam of the spiritual endeavoring to break through the trammels of the mortal, this triumph of soul over body? At once the curtain parted and she saw within her own heart: she loved her husband; had loved him for a long while, and had not known it. That other image had faded, faded, until its misty outline looked spectral and unreal. Yes, she loved him, and God would punish her by taking him from her (she stretched out her arms to him). All through these years she had lived a mistake, and cheated herself by a vain delusion; in the terrors of the storm came her punishment.

"Arthur, do not leave me!" she said; "I cannot live without you; I know myself at last—do not leave me!"

He turned to her a happy face. "Ruth," he

murmured, " my Ruth!" His voice shook. " If it is His will, I shall return to you; if not, then, my own wife, I have found you—I am content." He turned from her quickly. " Launch the boats," he cried. " Come, Pete, to the oars; I shall take the helm."

Amid the wild roaring of that fearful winter's storm the life-boat was launched; twice they ventured, twice were driven back. As the men waited to recover strength for another effort, a man came running across the beach from the headland; he was from the lighthouse. The bridge between the reef and the mainland had been carried away by the force of the rising waters; he had rowed across the narrow inlet, at the risk of his life, to tell the news. The vessel was the " Bonny Kate," from Hong-Kong, bound east—the light-keeper knew her well. Owing to the force of the hurricane the ship had been driven from her course. Some men were in the rigging, but many had been washed overboard; the sea was going clear over the ship, carrying everything before it. In the cross-trees was one man. The sails were gone, and the creaking of the timbers could be heard in the lighthouse tower above the gale.

"Who commands her?" asked the minister.

"The keeper didn't know," the man said; "guessed it must be Captain Hathaway—least-ways he'd heard he had been running her the last few trips."

Ruth sprang forward; the water crept about her feet; she did not heed it, did not know she stood ankle-deep in the foaming surf. "You shall not go, Arthur," she screamed; "you shall not; you are mine." She clung to him, her small hands holding him like a vise; her hood had blown back, her hair was waving in the wind.

"Be silent, Ruth; I shall do my duty."

"Not for him, not for him; I cannot bear it; your life shall not be given for his. Spare me this, my Heavenly Father, spare me this!" Ruth fell upon her knees; the waters curled about her; she did not heed their treacherous lapping nor feel their cold embrace—in fact, was semi-conscious till the kindly hands of the fisherwomen dragged her farther up the beach. There she crouched, a small, trembling heap, her head bowed upon her knees, the sleet falling upon her brown hair, and the wind howling about her. The fisherwomen fell upon their knees around her; they were praying. She could hear their voices rising and falling; she could not join them, could not pray; her lips were parched, her mind was clouded.

"The boat has gone!" the women said, as they rose from their knees. One brawny matron, pointing seaward, cried: "They have safely passed the outer line of breakers; they are nearing the ship."

Ruth raised her head, yet could distinguish nothing save impenetrable darkness outside the line of red light cast from the fagots.

"Gone," she murmured, "gone!" She held her hands tightly clasped. "Gone, and I have just found him! My eyes have only opened to the happiness that has hovered by my side all these years, that I have forcibly held back with determined hands." She realized that she had been clinging to, loving a shadow, a phantom of her brain, an image clothed in the trappings of her imagination; the real substance had been refused for a dream. The dream had vanished; the reality, with its threatened aspect of impending doom, was all that was left her. In the storm the Creator made plain her blind mistake; in the storm the true love of her life had come to her.

"They are returning, they are returning!"

Hoarse shouts were heard from the groups of men as they hurried back and forth upon the shore with their flickering lights. The women rushed forward; they could scarcely stand upon their feet. The wind had risen in its fury; the white tops of the waves appeared to rise to meet the blackness of the sky. Suddenly upon the crest of the waves rose the life-boat, like a feather at the mercy of the storm.

The fishermen congregated in one group, to throw as much light as possible from their united torches upon the surf. The boat struggled bravely; she held three men besides the life-savers who had gone to the rescue. At the helm sat Arthur Clayton, his strong hand guiding the boat, his lips moving in prayer to the God of storms. What was that following them, that white-crested mass which advanced, moving solidly with the swiftly running tide? On, on it came, seized the life-boat in its strength, twisted it, turned it as a straw in its giant force, played with it as though in sport, then with a swirl and a roar rushed on, and the boat was seen no more. Eight human souls were battling for life in the roaring surf.

There was a groan from the men and a shrill scream from the women. Ruth stood up among them; she could not speak, was as one dead; she possessed no sense of feeling; her eyes were wide and staring at the boiling surf. On, on, came that wall of water, rolling in with a roar like thunder; on, on, nearer advanced the mighty wave—the "death-wave," they called it afterward. It came to Ruth's feet and laid down two silent figures, the . sleet and snow frozen upon their faces and garments; two figures that lay rigid and still, the arm of one thrown about the other's neck, and the eyes closed in the white faces. Ruth drew near to them; the fisherwomen clustered about her, the men closed in upon her. She waved them back.

"Don't touch them," she said; "they are mine."

She leaned over them; down upon her knees she fell, and with the hem of her cloak wiped the frozen spray from their faces. "Jack," she whispered, "Jack; Arthur." That was all she said.

A merciful God shut out those white faces and the wild, stormy night from her vision. The outline of the staggering wreck, the blazing fagots, and the thunder of the frenzied sea faded into oblivion; she dropped quietly beside the silent forms upon the sand. When she came to herself and recognized the kindly faces that clustered ministering about her bed, the night had passed, the gray light of the somber morning was stealing furtively through closed shutters about her room, chasing the gloom before it.

The storm had worn itself out; the wind had lessened, blowing at intervals long sobbing breaths, as if in grief for the death of the sailors who had found a resting-place beneath the waters.

Jane and Mrs. Munn stood near the side of the bed watching her anxiously. Ruth raised herself in bed and stared at them.

"Where have they laid them," she whispered—"my dead that the sea gave back to me?"

Jane put her arms about her. "Ruth," she said, "God has not taken both; He has been good and merciful. One has recovered, and is in granny's house in the fishing-town; they carried him there; he has spoken, but is very weak; the other is dead."

"Which one is living?" said Ruth, hoarsely.

"Your husband, Arthur, is living; he has spoken once; it was only one word—it was 'Ruth.'"

Ruth threw her arms wildly above her head, then lay back upon her pillow white and still. They arranged her pillow, pulled the shutters closer, and without a word stepped softly from the room. A peaceful light was on Jane's face. The tears were running down Mrs. Munn's cheeks; in the hall outside she threw her apron over her head and rocked herself to and fro.

"Poor Miss Ruth!" she said; "poor Mr. Jack! It is all right now, though; he is at peace and she has found her right place. Oh, it is a mysterious Providence who orders all things for the best, if we would only be patient; yet it's hard to be.patient, it's hard."

"Yes," said Jane, softly, "it's hard."

She could say no more; the experience through which she had passed during the last hours awed her, making her bow her head in resignation before the wonderful workings of that great Power which holds and dispenses the affairs of man.

Suddenly Mrs. Munn plucked her sleeve. Jane had forgotten her surroundings; the rectory hall faded from her vision; she saw instead the wide garret at the homestead, a passionate face looking into hers, a passionate voice crying out, in the intensity of its sorrow, "I will not give him up for his father's sin;" and now—here Jane brushed away two tears—the storm was over, Ruth safe in the harbor, her life's sorrow passed. She turned to Mrs.

Munn, who stood watching her earnestly, wondering at the tears in the stern eyes.

"What is it, Sarah?" she said.

"I was thinkin' after all that Miss Kate is the only sincere mourner poor Mr. Jack will have in this world."

Over Jane's plain face shone the light of a prophetess. "The sins of the fathers," she said, solemnly, then paused and grasped Mrs. Munn's hand. "We will mourn, Sarah; poor boy, poor boy!"

Jack was laid to rest in the hillside graveyard, in the old Hathaway plot, where the four cedars stood, one at each corner of the narrow space. Many mourned the sad fate of the handsome, gallant Captain, so well loved throughout the village before he sailed away for foreign ports. He looked peaceful as he lay in the majesty of his last sleep; his hair, prematurely gray, hid the cruel scar upon his forehead, where the life-boat struck him when the wave overturned them. In one hand was a bunch of grasses and daisies gathered from Ruth's small hothouse off the rectory parlor. Jane had placed them there— Ruth had told her to; she had asked no questions, had simply done as Ruth wished her.

Ruth came forth from the great shock a changed

woman; the clouds had dispersed. Through a great crisis her feet had found the true way. When Arthur returned to her she placed her arms about his neck and laid her head upon his breast.

"My husband," she murmured, "Jack has given his life for you and me."

"Yes," he said, then told her all—told her in the quiet of the rectory study, with the storm lulled without and within, with thankfulness and a great peace in their hearts.

"When we reached the ship," he said, "there were few to save, many of the crew having been washed overboard some hours before. At the main-top were three men, holding on with partly frozen hands, huddling close together, the waves almost reaching them when the vessel careened. The brig was fast going to pieces; the bulwarks were torn from their fastenings, the iron bolts were twisted, and masses of timber were swept into the sea. We approached as near as we dared; the men dropped when the vessel careened almost to the water's edge; we threw ropes to them and dragged them, more dead than alive, into the boat. Captain Hathaway thanked me; he spoke solemnly, as though he had committed himself to his Maker and was resigned."

Arthur paused a moment, looking sadly into the cheerful fire on the hearth. "I told him who I was; he said, 'Did you know I was aboard my ship?' 'I thought you might be,' I replied; 'I did not know.' The Captain did not speak for a moment, then said, as if to himself, 'It was a noble deed to risk his life for mine.' He spoke no further till we reached the breakers just beyond the outer bar, then said, in a trembling tone, 'I did not know there were such men in the world as you have proved yourself, Mr. Clayton; Ruth must be a happy woman.' He hesitated. 'My messenger from Lynnport gave me her message,' he concluded."

Arthur's voice ceased. Ruth did not reply; she saw pictures in the fire: that long-ago summer, the Michaelmas daisies and golden-rod blooming on the roadside on that sad fall day when she went back to the manor a broken-hearted girl.

"When the boat overturned," resumed Arthur, "the Captain could have saved himself; he thought only of me. He received the death-blow upon his head by dragging me, with almost superhuman force, from my position at the helm. The blow stunned him, but he rallied, and seizing me struggled through the surf; he seemed to be possessed of the strength of a giant. You know the rest, Ruth; I can say no more." His voice trembled. The fire shone red through a mist of tears in his eyes.

They sat together silently for a while, then Ruth rose, went to the window, drew aside the curtains, and looked out.

"Come, Arthur," she said, looking back into the room. He rose, crossed the room, and stood beside her. "See how beautiful the night is!" she said; "how bright the stars shine!"

The snow lay upon the ground; the night was clear and brilliant. From the headland upon which the rectory stood there was a wide view of the sea and the quiet, sleeping village at their feet, with its lights in the cottage windows. In the distance, near the shore, a clump of pines stood, dark and mysterious, the surroundings of the empty manor with its wandering ghosts. The gleam from the lighthouse lay a long yellow streak upon the smooth waters flowing over the graves of the brave men who lost their lives for humanity: stanch old Pete Morrell, his three boys, and the crew of the "Bonny Kate."

"The storm is over," said Ruth, with tears in her eyes, "and Jack in God's hands."

"Yes," said Arthur, "the storm is over; yet graves strew the shore-line."

His arm was about her; together they stood looking into the starlit sky.

"Jack understands it all now," she said, wistfully.

"Yes," said Arthur, earnestly, "he understands it all. I believe firmly, Ruth, the tangled, uncertain beginnings here will be perfected there; in that new existence will be found the completion of our feeble efforts."

They let the curtain down, shutting out the sea and the stars.

"He gave himself for me, his life for mine," he said—"the noblest deed of man."

He stood a moment looking sadly into the fire. There was a shadow on his face, a shadow that had come to stay as long as life should last: the consciousness that another had gone down to death in his place. Ruth divined this with the quickened perception of her awakened love. She did not speak, however; what could she say? No happiness is unalloyed, yet now they could bear their crosses together, the weight lightened, barriers leveled, all mystery solved.

CHAPTER XX.

PEACE.

THE story of the great storm had been discussed, had its day, and, though not forgotten, was lulled by time into but occasional reminders of that night of horror.

Many summers have the grasses grown upon the grave in the Hathaway plot, bringing peace, through the soothing influence of years and reflection, to the loving, grieving sister, who in her deformity and weakness remains under the sheltering care of the lynx-eyed Mrs. Munn.

Mrs. Munn is as sharp-tongued, as shrewd, as of yore. Jim Benton asked her to share his home, also half of the proceeds of his fishing, which agreement she refused with decision.

"No, no, Jim," she said; "we will always be good friends, I hope, but nothing more. A caged bird ain't as good as a free one; I've been caged, now I'm free—I know all about it. I wouldn't leave Miss Kate for a king; I've got a nice bit of money in the bank for my old days. I thank you, but I say no."

Jim went away, scratching his head reflectively as he returned to his bachelor quarters. His mates found him taciturn for a few days, but this unusual mood passed away, leaving him the same good-natured fellow, spinning his yarns as he baits his hooks or throws his line for a troll.

It was a charming day in June; fleecy banks of clouds were drifting across the sky, piling up in white, spiritlike shapes in the west. The birds were singing triumphantly as they flew from tree to tree, sweet-tuned warblers, the crimson-throated finch, the oriole, the robin, and the bluebird joining in a hymn of praise to the beauty of the day.

Dr. Goodyear was standing among his roses, the shears in his hands; Jane was looking on as he clipped his beloved blossoms. Tetsy No. 2 waited sedately by his mistress's side. He had improved much since his puppy days of boisterous hilarity. No longer does he demolish the clothes drying upon the line, or chase the boys wildly through the village street, startled elderly ladies fleeing before him;

nor does he return to his scandalized mistress with his mouth full of feathers plucked from the neighbors' chickens. He has become a well-behaved, dignified member of the dog family; even staid Tetsy No. 1 would not have blushed for his usurper, or have felt the honor of the family in peril. He watched his mistress with an adoring glance as she stood tall and straight by the side of the doctor, receiving into a basket each exquisite blossom as he clipped it from the vine. Tetsy cast an occasional glance of suspicion—sagacious creature that he was—upon his portly master; he had never succeeded in convincing himself that the doctor's demonstrative attempts at affection were genuine. A certain distrust of his master was instilled into him in puppy days, an intuition that his presence was only tolerated. However, being somewhat of a philosopher, he accepts the good that lies before him in the love of his kindly mistress, and enjoys a very happy dog existence.

"It does not seem possible," said Jane, as she plucked some superfluous leaves from a rose-branch in her hand and scattered them on the ground, "that little Jack can be four years old to-day. Dear, dear, how the years do fly! I think these will look very well on the table. Ruth told me she had invited a dozen children for the birthday party; how the boy will romp, to be sure!"

"He's a fine boy," said the doctor, reaching up so high for a brilliant rose above his head that his suspender tore partly across the back. "Drat those suspenders!" he said; "what did you want that rose for, Jane? You knew I couldn't reach it."

"Ezekiel, how nonsensically you talk! I never wanted that rose. Come now, we have plenty; Ruth will be waiting."

A little later the old couple passed slowly through the grass-grown lane of the upper street in the direction of the rectory, the basket of roses held between them. Dignified Tetsy walked behind, scorning the friendly overtures of others of his kind with a true instinct of superiority.

The harbor glistened in the sunshine; Jane thought, as they paused a moment upon the heights above the lower street, that never had Lynnport looked so lovely. True, she had seen no other parts of the world, the great universe, for her, being compassed within the narrow confines of the tiny settlement.

She gazed a moment, perhaps a trifle wistfully,

out to sea, to the distant border where the water seemed to meet the sky.

"I have often thought," she said, looking tenderly upon the bowed figure at her side, "that I should like to have gone beyond that line on the horizon and seen something of life." She paused, then continued, in a low voice, placing her hand over her husband's on the handle of the basket, the two pair of faded eyes looking into each other's with a tearful, satisfied smile: "Perhaps it is better as it is; I don't complain."

"I guess," said the doctor, "everything comes to Lynnport. It isn't the place, Jane; it's the human nature in it that makes life."

The fishing-fleet had rounded the lighthouse reef and was drifting on swiftly before the tide, the sails glistening in the sun. Far off, like a shadow against the horizon, rode a foreign brig, all sails set, floating on the air like the wings of a wild sea-bird.

Jane took up the basket of roses she had placed on the grass an instant, and they walked on.

"It always makes me sad to see a foreign ship," she said, as they moved along; "poor Jack Hathaway!"

A narrow lane leading from the upper street led toward the graveyard. A sudden impulse seized Jane to put a few roses on Captain Hathaway's grave.

"You know," she said, "little Jack is his namesake."

On nearing the gates of the inclosure they noticed two figures coming toward them; they were the minister and his wife. As they approached Jane detected the traces of tears on Ruth's face.

Ruth had not changed much; the girlish sweetness of youth had naturally altered somewhat with the passing years—only in coloring and outline, however, not in expression. She looked the gentle, loving woman, an ideal minister's wife.

Arthur had aged more than she; his gray hair had turned to white, and he was slower in step. Since the wreck of the "Bonny Kate" he had never been quite the same.

"I was going to put some roses on Captain Hathaway's grave," said Jane. "I told Ezekiel on our boy's birthday I thought it would be a proper thing to do."

"Never mind, Aunt Jane," said Ruth, in a low voice; "I have done that, on his grave and little

Joe's. Let me be the only one; let me have that privilege to-day."

So the four walked on to the rectory, through the soft sunshine of that lovely June day.

Little Jack was in the rectory garden as the party approached, surrounded by his friends. He was in sailor dress, and his sturdy legs, at sight of his mother, flew out in a wild gallop to the gate.

" O mother!" he said, " see—see what Jim has given me!" He held up a little boat neatly and perfectly fitted with masts and sails.

Jim was leaning upon the fence, watching the boy's delight with a good-natured smile upon his face.

" He's a born sailor," he said; " the very breath of the sea is in him, Mr. Clayton; he'll run a fast clipper by the time he's twenty-one, I warrant you."

Ruth did not speak; she entered the gate and stood upon the lower step of the porch, watching her boy with a proud, tender glance as he rejoined his playmates. Presently he came up to her again, his handsome face aglow with health and freshness.

" O mother!" he said, " everybody is telling what they are going to be when they get big; I haven't said what I'd be yet. Shall I ? "

"Yes, Jack," said his mother, "tell us what you will be."

Arthur had joined his wife; the doctor and Jane stood a few paces from them on the graveled walk; Jim leaned earnestly over the fence.

"I'll be," said the boy, throwing back his head, "a sailor, just like that brave man father tells me about, who saved him in that storm and brought him safe home to mother."

Ruth clasped her boy and held him against her heart.

"My boy," she said, "my own! may you, with God's help, grow to be like that good man who gave your mother the happiness of her life!"

Then she placed Jack upon his feet, went into the house, and sat down at the study window to watch the happy scene in the rectory garden, where the children had their tea-table spread under the shade of the lilac-bushes.

NOTE.

SOME years before the writing of this story a party
of pleasure-seekers were cruising in a sailing-yacht
at the head of the Sound, not far from where its
waters join the ocean.   One of the number noticed a
rambling, dilapidated mansion situated upon a rather
bold headland.   Drawing the rest of the party's attention to it, he inquired of the captain if he knew
its history.

"That," said the captain, "is the Lorrimer manor-
house.   The family has become extinct; they were
a great family, I believe, once, and owned most of
the village.   That's the village back there a little
way from the coast."   He pointed, as he spoke, to
a tiny town, its weather-beaten, unpainted houses
huddled on the steep hillside.

" What is its name? " asked the inquisitive pas-
senger.

" It's name," said the captain, " is Lynnport;
queer old place, more dead than alive."

They sailed away, watching the grim, silent mansion till it faded from their sight.

www.ingramcontent.com/pod-product-compliance
Lightning Source LLC
Chambersburg PA
CBHW021757110726
47902CB00006B/1547